Nothing Can Make Me Do This

Nothing Can Make Me Do This

DAVID HUDDLE

TUPELO PRESS

North Adams, Massachusetts

Library of Congress Cataloging-in-Publication Data

Huddle, David, 1942-
Nothing can make me do this / David Huddle.
    p. cm.
A novel in a short story type sequence that enters the minds of Horace House-
man and his closest relatives through fifty years.
ISBN 978-1-936797-11-0 (pbk. : alk. paper) -- ISBN 978-1-936797-12-7 (hardcover
: alk. paper)
1. Families--Fiction. 2. Life change events--Fiction. 3. Love-hate relationships--
Fiction. 4. Family secrets--Fiction. 5. Psychological fiction. 6. Domestic fiction.
I. Title.
PS3558.U287N65 2012
813'.54--dc22
                    2011032208

Cover and text designed by Ann Aspell.
Cover art: "Looking Down Main" by Meryl Lebowitz (www.meryllebowitz.
com/), and "Lying Down" by Luciana Frigerio (www.lucianafrigerio.com/).
Used with permission of the artists.

First edition: October 2011.

Tupelo Press
P.O. Box 1767
243 Union Street, Eclipse Mill, Loft 305
North Adams, Massachusetts 01247
Telephone: (413) 664–9611 / Fax: (413) 664–9711
editor@tupelopress.org / www.tupelopress.org

Tupelo Press is an award-winning independent literary press that publishes fine
fiction, non-fiction, and poetry in books that are a joy to hold as well as read.
Tupelo Press is a registered 501(c)3 non-profit organization, and we rely on public
support to carry out our mission of publishing extraordinary work that may be
outside the realm of large commercial publishers. Financial donations are welcome and are tax deductible.

 Supported in part by an award from the National Endowment for the Arts

For Hollins

with thanks for helping me find my first writing life
in 1968–1969

and my second in 2009–2012.

Contents

Nothing Can Make Me Do This

The Way of the Blue-Winged Wangdoodle

I'M EVE COLLINS. When I was a girl trying to navigate the stormy seas of puberty, my grandmother, Clara Houseman, discovered four pornographic videos in the bottom of the wooden crate my grandfather used as a shoeshine kit. If she had thought it over for a day or so, my grandmother would not have spoken of it to anyone other than him. Shocked as she was in the moment, she called my mother before she even talked with her husband. My grandfather, whose name was Horace, recently retired after ten years as Provost of the University of Vermont, was in his late sixties, but entirely alert. He'd recently taken up walking down to the lake and back twice a day. Clara and Horace are both dead now, but I've lately found myself mulling over those days of family upheaval and disgrace. I picture Clara standing in the sunlight of Horace's study, holding in her hands the stack of video cases with their lurid pictures and titles, studying them one at a time. Horace's filth, as she famously came to call what she'd found. I'm still not certain how I came to know that the shoeshine kit was where Horace had stashed his filth.

My mother counseled my grandmother not to make a big deal about it but to try to get my grandfather to talk with her about what she'd found. "Ask him what he thinks he's doing," my mother said on the phone in my presence, which, in spite of her calm tone, raised my level of interest. I was twelve and bored by my mother's frequent telephone conversations with her mother. In my mind, the very word "mother" had taken on the definition "totally uninteresting human being." But this sentence my mother had just uttered was something I might have overheard in gym class or out by the block of lockers where eighth-graders clustered between classes. I quickly turned my head to see what her face looked like, which was the wrong move to make if I wanted to keep eavesdropping. "I gotta go," she said. "Eve needs something. Talk to you later, Mom." Then she and I were there in the kitchen eye to eye with each other. I suddenly got a clue that I was starting a new chapter in the brief but compelling story of my life.

In that moment — approximately four o'clock of a Wednesday afternoon in April — my mother must have decided that this episode of our family's antics was an occasion to bring me into what she might have termed *a mature discussion of appropriate and inappropriate behavior.* I can't help thinking I saw something in her expression that had nothing to do with me and everything to do with her, something frantic and uncertain. She was lost, she was in pain, she didn't know what to do or to whom she should look for advice — I realize what I understand now, but at the time, I did my best to shut out any thought that my mother was anything other than the predictable authority who'd brought me into this world. She was an institution, not a person,

NOTHING CAN MAKE ME DO THIS

and thus evidence of any human flaw was disturbing to me. Spiritual hysteria certainly wasn't what I wanted to see in my mother's face.

My mother adored her father. That, too, was a fact I'd never questioned — I adored him, too. He was big, handsome, and articulate, confident in that way that a man can be that both infuriates and comforts a woman. Horace Houseman was legendary in the family, in the town, and in the university for his competence, his common sense, his careful way of speaking. He'd worn coat and tie from his days at Washington & Lee. There were very few occasions when he put on casual clothes. Even at the beach, when he wasn't actually out on the sand by the water, he wore seersucker jackets, white duck pants, and pastel ties. He was the only man of my acquaintance who lived that way, and I confess that I still admire him for it. If my positive view of my grandfather remains unshaken in spite of my acquaintance with "his filth," that is probably because I am removed from him by two generations rather than one. My mother was too close to him to accept the contradiction that had just been revealed to her — an admirable and beloved man with an interest in, to put it delicately, inappropriate sex.

"Your grandfather," she began. And cleared her throat. "Your grandfather has done something very wrong," she said. The look she gave me seemed to imply that I was the one who had done the bad thing. I said nothing, which was unusual for me — I was a mouthy kid. And I returned her gaze, which was also unusual. I didn't like looking her in the eyes. I'd noticed that Midnight, our cocker spaniel, whom I considered my half-brother, didn't like meeting the gaze of anyone, and I understood why he was like that. You have to protect that part of your mind that might become visible if you let someone get a good look in there. Beast though he was, Midnight was the closest thing I had to a spiritual teacher. I suspect it's that way for a lot of the children who grow up around cats or dogs. Midnight was a creature who took his orders straight from divine headquarters. He had taught me a primitive and valuable principle of life — don't let anybody look into your brain. More and more in the past year I'd had thoughts that made me ashamed of myself; yet at the same time I couldn't wait for an occasion to try to bring them up again to see what was going to come of them.

My mother's eyes were tearing up, and so I thought I'd try to rescue her. "What was Granddad doing?" I asked. I meant to be helpful. It seemed to me that she just needed a little encouragement to say what she knew she had to tell me. I wanted her to know that I was a big kid, entirely ready to take in the awful news. My question riled her up enough to make her stick out her chin and use the tone of voice with me that usually meant I'd better watch my mouth.

"Eve, do you know what pornography is?"

"Yes," I said, though the instant I said it, I realized that I knew only vaguely what it was.

"Well, you shouldn't, but I thought you probably did. Your grandfather was looking at pornography." Her face blazed up as pink as the hollyhocks beside our garage.

"A book?" I asked.

She hesitated, apparently trying to measure my acquaintance with pornography. "Pictures," she said. "Movies, actually."

I had nothing to say to that. I'd seen things on TV that I figured I shouldn't be seeing, but there they were. It embarrassed me to imagine my grandfather deliberately looking at women with their shirts off lying on top of men with their shirts off. It had always seemed accidental when I saw those scenes on TV — they'd been sort of sprung on me, like a surprise birthday party or something. And I'd even turned off the TV a couple of times when the shirtless men and women started kissing really hot and heavy. "Hot and heavy" was a phrase my grandfather sometimes used, and now I knew where he'd gotten it.

My mother and I froze in our positions there in our utterly familiar kitchen, she leaning against the counter by the phone and I sitting at the table theoretically getting cracking on my homework while I ate the three Oreos I was allowed after school. My mother continued to look at me, but her face had lost its urgency. She was thinking about something, and I wasn't uncomfortable being in there with her in that long passage of silence. I almost felt as if just by being there, I was helping her figure out how to help my grandfather. The odd thing is that I never even considered that my grandmother was probably the one who needed help. Somehow I understood that a man the age of my grandfather looking at dirty pictures had to be desperate. My mother, on the other hand, was — to use a phrase of my father's that I've come to value — "living on Planet Pain."

•

Probably because she so adored her father, my mother's care for my father always seemed to me to be located in the B range of her emotional life. Which is not to say that she didn't love him. But it is to say that she took him for granted.

It is also to say that they were steadfast companions. She trusted him as she trusted no one else. She didn't mind listing his weaknesses to his face, or aloud in my presence, and he didn't object to or try to amend her list: He was lazy but lucky. He was a contractor and a landlord, and he drove around Burlington in a truck looking after his various projects and properties. Essentially he made his living — our living — with his mouth. He talked to people: plumbers, electricians, carpenters, real estate agents, tenants, building inspectors, prospective buyers and sellers, even the occasional architect. He had an office in our basement, but he spent very little time in it. "Your father can't tell you what he owns or what he's working on," she liked to say, "but in any given day he can drive around town and show you at least twenty-five or thirty houses and buildings that he's buying or selling or renting or fixing up or tearing down. In any given week, he'll talk to maybe a hundred people he's doing business with, but he'd have a hard time naming ten of them at dinner tonight. He's a nightmare when it comes to taxes, and it's a miracle we all haven't been put in jail by the IRS. He's disorganized, has no sense of style, doesn't pay any attention to what clothes he wears, can't sit through a movie or a concert, will behave erratically at any social occasion and will most likely do or say something inappropriate when I take him out in public." She made these pronouncements during dinner, made them in a cheerful tone of voice. Rather than objecting, my father grinned and chuckled while she went on, pointing her fork at him as she escalated her rhetoric. He had a moustache, and in his case it enhanced his laugh, his smile, his general good humor. He had the look of a young fellow who has in mind three or four mildly bad actions he's planning to take. I think my mother married him because he was not even the same species of creature as Horace Houseman. My mother treated my father as if he were a brother — sometimes an older brother, sometimes a younger, but always with a tone of affection and mild-to-medium disapproval in her voice.

A few more facts about my father: He carried three cell phones with him in his truck and often was in conversation on at least two of them at a time. His name was Bill. When I was ten, he had invited me to call him Bill, and I'd taken him up on it. I, too, thought of Bill as a kind of sibling, like maybe a much older step-brother. We got along "famously," I learned to say of him after I'd gone away to college. Bill was a chaotic individual, but I can safely say that the idea of looking at pornographic videos probably never occurred to him, and if it had, he'd have merely snorted and shook his head. "No time for that," he'd say. "Dirty Picture City — you go there, they might not let you out for a month or two." Anybody who knew Bill knew he wouldn't have been able to sit still long enough to look at any video, pornographic or otherwise. The last and most notable thing about my father is that he often had an extravagant way of saying things. "A wild tongue," my mother would say in her listing of his flaws. For example, of my mother, when she shook her fork at him like that, he liked to cut his eyes toward me and say, "Wedding cake on fire." Or "Knock a redwood down with her toes." Or "Look out, Evey, here comes the lady tornado." Or of the political ads we'd see on TV, he'd hoot and laugh and say, "That man's trying to sell me a rain forest out here in the desert." And of me, whenever he wanted to make me laugh, he'd find a name for me, like "Little Miss Eyebrows," or "Here comes Queen Scabby Knees," or "Hide your horses, Nelly, here comes Evey Golden Ears." Where he got these phrases I never knew, but I loved them, and I was always at least slightly flattered by the things he'd say about me. Rarely the same thing twice. My favorite was "Sweet Splendor," though he called me that only twice and both times I was dressed up to go to church with my mother. I hold Bill responsible for the reckless things that sometimes come out of my own mouth. Nothing I ever said sounded as good as the lamest of his verbal inventions; even so, I do appreciate a fresh phrase when I hear it.

As for my mother, whenever she listed off her version of Bill's less than admirable way of life — and while she still had her fork waggling at him — she'd grin and say, "But you know what? If I need him, he's there. The man is there before I even have to ask him."

•

The idea first appeared in my brain as a silly thought: *I'm the one who can fix this. I can have a talk with him.* My grandfather and I had this lovingly distant relationship. "The battleship and the sailboat," Bill once said of us when he saw us sitting on the porch one afternoon. Which is to say that our conversations were usually fragmented, oblique, and inconclusive. He liked to drive me downtown to get ice cream cones or to shop for birthday presents or to meet so-and-so who was maybe going to give a sack full of money to the university. He liked to show me off to friends and shop people and rich old geezers. And I confess that I liked being shown off. I didn't fancy I was the prettiest girl my age, but I did think I might be one of the cleverest. I was a precocious child, articulate, mannerly, and even knowledgeable about a few things. And only a little bit peculiar and only slightly aware of that aspect of myself. When I was being shown off—and therefore making an effort to be interesting — remarks burbled up from inside me that were surprising, both to the people to whom I said them and to myself. "I've taken an interest in giraffes lately," I once said to a banker my grandfather had just introduced me to. "Have you read *The Rainbow Goblins*?" I asked the British lady who ran the Everyday Bookshop when I was seven. It made her eyebrows lift an inch or so and stay that way while she studied me carefully. People took note of me when I wanted them to. My grandfather Horace almost always chuckled when it happened. I saw no reason to change my ways. Even as a grown-up, I don't stifle myself in this regard.

So when I knew I could do it without being overheard, I called over there and asked my grandmother if I could speak to him. That wasn't unusual — from when I was little, I'd called him to tell him notable events in my life, finding a robin's egg in the back yard, reading *Chicken Soup with Rice* all by myself. But this time I surprised him when I asked if could talk to him that Saturday afternoon. There was a silence, during which I could imagine what my grandfather thought: *Something's up here.* Or maybe he just heard a difference in my voice. He wouldn't have been wrong about that. I count that phone call as one of my first grown-up actions. Even if I didn't know what I was doing.

·

My mother's name was Hannah. Hannah has been dead a couple of years now. Though considerably slowed down, Bill's alive, still driving a truck, and still the dearest man I know. But Hannah and Clara and Horace and Midnight have all gone the way of the blue-winged wangdoodle, a phrase of Bill's — for when he couldn't find one of his tools or something in the truck — that was a favorite from my childhood. Each of those deaths was startlingly painful to me, like getting shot or beaten up by someone I loved, and Bill's phrase, by making me grin every time I thought of it, helped me put myself back together again. You could say that I got through my mourning by the way of the blue-winged wangdoodle. Bill is still grieving hard about Hannah's death. "Easier to get along with no bones in my body," I heard him say to the kitchen sink one morning not long ago. "Ain't no love in the daylight today," he muttered a moment later.

You see, for suffering, I needed Bill to give me the words. In the time when my marriage was disintegrating — when I was discovering what a despicable man my husband was — I could speak of it directly to no one, and yet I needed to put words to it or to get it out of myself. My mind wouldn't work in any way that was a help to me, but some part of it must have been trying to move me along, because one Sunday afternoon when the two of us were in the house alone, I asked Bill what had happened to those old dirty movies of my grandfather Horace.

"Deep in the archives, baby," he told me. "Never could figure out what to do with 'em. So I kept 'em." He tapped his foot and looked uncomfortable

"Can you show them to me?" I asked him.

Bill studied me long and hard. I must have looked like I

was about to cry, and he knew my request was irrational and destructive. He rubbed his moustache, which I'd never seen him do. He tried to grin at me, but he was unsuccessful, and his expression, before he gave up the effort, was a grimace.

So he went downstairs to his office — "WILLIAM COLLINS / CONTRACTOR" was the sign on the door that no one outside the family had ever seen — and fetched up the video cases, brought them back to where I sat on the sofa, and stood in front of me with the sack of them in his hands. "You're sure about this?" he asked me.

I nodded.

He spread them out on the coffee table in front me, laid them out to face me in a row like cards he was dealing: *Suck It Up!*, *Hot Boxes*, *The Jism Chronicles*, and *Barely Legal, Part 3*. The covers displayed men and women wearing what I was pretty sure were wigs, but what those pictures showed was evidently what I needed to see: penises and vaginas, anuses, buttocks, and breasts. The latter were so inflated that they hardly resembled breasts as I was acquainted with them. The urge to weep flew right out of me then, which was fine, because I'd hated all those days of feeling like I needed to cry. There was a woman's mouth opened very wide to receive a monstrous penis, an image that held my attention for some moments. Somehow seeing the pictures on those boxes told me what I needed to know about the true nature of my husband — he was utterly without spirit. A gifted poet, he often went days without saying a word, and I'd come to understand that he enjoyed inflicting his silences on me. The woman's open mouth waiting for that absurd penis instructed me: my husband was a hurtful man, and I'd been a fool not see it before I married him. I never for a moment took those pictures as telling me anything about my grandfather.

Bill himself didn't know what was troubling me at that time. So what he said applied to Horace, because he thought it was Horace that was on my mind. "Your poor old grandfather," Bill said. "I guess he couldn't keep his feet out of the swamp. Feel some sorrow for him, Sweetie. He'd have never wanted your eyes to take in these sights."

Then I asked Bill to take me to dinner down at the Daily Planet where we'd always gone on Thursdays when my mother had played tennis with her ladies' group.

"Planet's been closed for a while, Sweetie, but we can go to Smokejacks. They got martinis down there to kill the boogie man."

◆

Horace's study was a large room over the garage — a room that was attached to the house but that always seemed to me separate. Appropriately separate. I'd been in it only a few times before, and two of those occasions had been sneak visits. You know how it is when you're a child — if there's a chance to explore a forbidden room in your grandparents' house, you do it the first chance you get. The year I turned twelve, I'd had two chances, and in both cases I'd had plenty of time to walk around in there and take it in. I'd say "poke around," but that wouldn't be accurate. There was such a high level of tidiness in that space that I hardly dared to touch any surface or open any drawers. Large windows were on three sides, and the whole room fairly blazed with light. The odd thing was, there weren't any dust motes floating in my grandfather's sunlight.

There was his completely bare desk, his enormous chair — high-backed with thick black pads for his arms and elbows — and there was another big chair on the other side of the desk. Even before I went in, I knew he'd invite me to sit in that visitor's chair. It was a nice chair — very expensive, I guessed — but I didn't relish the idea. I hadn't even tried it out in my secret visits.

"Please sit down, Eve," my grandfather told me after I'd knocked and stepped through the already-open door. He'd left it that way for me. It was toward the end of April, and it was a day of uncommon deliciousness outside. But I knew I was in for a profoundly indoor experience. I was, as they say in the old-fashioned children's books, *vexed* by the obligation I'd taken on to have this conversation. Which is not to say that I wasn't also curious about what would transpire between the two of us.

Horace — and that's what I have to call him here because that's what he became to me in the course of our conversation, though in my life until that day, I had never called him that even to myself — Horace seemed different in some way. My first impression was that he had dressed as if he were receiving a foreign diplomat. But then I revised that idea, because his clothes weren't dark and formal. He'd chosen a well-tailored tweed sport coat, a pink shirt, and a boldly striped tie. They were the kind of clothes you saw in the windows of Michael Kehoe's before it closed. I appreciated that my grandfather had dressed up for me. He wanted to charm me. To me that afternoon, that was an even bolder and more novel idea than a visit from a foreign diplomat. A man like him aiming to charm a kid like me!

"So," he said, leaning forward, smiling, and steepling

his fingers. "Eve," he said. Then he leaned back in his chair, pushed it back a notch or two further than I'd have thought he would. But I understood that he wanted me to think he was relaxed. "I want you to tell me about growing up, Eve. You're right in the middle of it. And I'm so old I've forgotten what it feels like. I'd like to hear what you think about it."

His sentences had the sound of words he'd thought about and rehearsed in his mind. Even so, I wasn't ready for such an invitation. I paused a moment before opening my mouth. Then I began to speak of school. It was a logical choice, because school was most of my life then — I was in eighth grade, and most of my classmates were really twitchy. They were changing from the kids they'd been last year and the year before, and our teachers were like characters in books or movies. I had a lot to say about school, but I recognized my tactic as evasion. I was making what Bill might have called "Eve noise" so that I could gather my thoughts to figure out what Horace wanted to hear from me and what I could say that would please him. My grandfather must have understood that I was just "pushing the breeze over my tongue," as Bill would have put it, because I saw my grandfather's eyelids sink slightly and saw a little feathering of the skin around his mouth and nose that told me he was stifling a yawn. It was then that I realized — as I was telling him about my project for geography — that I was struggling with a situation that grown-ups had created and that only grown-ups would be able to fix. But so far as I knew, my mother and grandmother had not communicated with my grandfather about his videos. I knew that for my sake, my grandfather wanted to make this a conversation of some importance, but he had no idea how to proceed. And I knew that Bill very likely didn't know that anybody in the family needed any kind of help and was probably right at that moment riding around in his truck talking on two cell phones at once or grinning and saying amusing things to the electricians who were working on his new apartment complex. It was when my mind picked up on the track of Bill with one careless hand on the steering wheel that it occurred to me to wake my grandfather up. With his extravagant way of talking, Bill sometimes did that — maybe on purpose — to people. Startled them. So I had a weapon or two of my own that I could use to defend myself in this torture chamber they'd put me in.

"Horace" — and in my mind, I could hardly believe I had addressed him by his first name — "what's it like to be an adult? Nobody's ever told me what adults do when they're not around other people. Besides work and make money, I mean. What's your secret? What do you do when you're by yourself?"

As if someone had slipped up behind him and poked him on either side of his ribcage, my grandfather shot up in his big chair. His face blazed up red, and his mouth twisted like he'd taken a swig of dishwater. This was frightening to me, because in all the hours I'd been in my grandfather's presence, I'd known him only as the graceful and decorous man of whom Bill liked to say, "Horace's feathers are slicked down so tight it'd take a lightning bolt up his butt to make him stop waltzing."

Nervous as I was, I was nevertheless thrilled with myself for getting a rise out of my grandfather. It'd never happened before — even the time I accidentally pushed his plate of waffles in his lap at the IHOP, he'd acted like I'd just done something cute. This time I felt a crackling in the air, and the only way I know how to describe it is to say that this was empowering.

He didn't take long to regain his poise, and I admired him for that. I didn't want my grandfather to turn into a raving monster right before my eyes. He sat back in his chair and seemed to will himself back to a state of relaxation. He even steepled his fingers again, this time bracing his elbows against the chair arms. He kept his eyes on me the whole time, but he didn't speak for some very long moments. "I don't mind if you call me Horace," he finally said. "After all, I've been calling you 'Eve' ever since you were born. I don't mind it. Eve. Horace. Fine. But let me think about your question a moment before I answer you, my dear."

Once again I found myself locked in an eye-to-eye prison of silence with a grown-up. With my mother in the kitchen, that had seemed sort of normal. With my grandfather here in his study, it seemed abnormal and risky. The longer we sat there the more anxious I became. I didn't dare break the stare that had frozen in the space between us. If anxiety can escalate up to a point of pain, that's what happened to me. I'd landed on Planet Pain. The real source of my fear was that he would lean over and pull out the shoeshine box that he kept beside his desk, open it up, and spread the cases of his dirty videos in front of me. Some kids I knew said they got freaked out by movies that showed cities being wiped out by global-warming tsunamis, or monsters taking over Los Angeles, or pretty girls getting kidnapped and raped and tortured to death by some pervert. Those thoughts were disturbing to me, but what I realized in that moment was that the one thing in all of life that I didn't want to happen to me was for my grandfather to show me his pornography. The fear of that happening grew in me until it felt like I had something in my chest trying to burst out like those monster babies in *Alien*. When my grandfather moved and actually leaned over in the direction of his shoebox, my mouth seemed to open of its own accord. I began talking without the slightest idea of what I was going to say.

"Okay, Granddad, I'll tell you my secret. You have to keep it to yourself. I don't want Grandmama or Bill or my mom finding it out, and if one of them says a word to me about this, I'll know that you told them. I sometimes come home from school because I have to see Midnight. I can get out of study hall because Mrs. Caples likes me and lets me go home to get my asthma medication. Okay, so I lie to her about my asthma medication. She probably knows that, but she writes me an excuse and lets me do it. When I get home and come in the door, you should see how happy Midnight is. I like that part of it, how he wiggles his butt and gets one of his toys in his mouth and brings it to me. But what I really like is when he settles down, there on the rug by the front door, I get down there with him and scratch his back and his ears and his belly. I smell the pads of his front paws, both of them. That's really what does it for me, the way his feet smell. I talk to him even though he can't talk back. I tell him if there's anything bothering me, but even if I don't have anything bad to tell him, I always feel better for having paid him a visit like that. Down on the floor. When I leave I tell him I'm sorry I can't take him back to school with me. But I don't really want him at school with me — he'd be a mess. I take his paw smell back with me, and I can remember it at least until school's out."

Horace watched me the whole time, and we both knew my talking like that was a new experience for both of us. I knew it was dumb, what I'd just told him about Midnight. If it'd been Bill I told this secret to, he'd have said something like "A dog may be a coyote and a wolf, kid, but it ain't a human being. Just a bag of funky old smells is all you've got there." But Horace wasn't going to dismiss what I'd told him. He wasn't going to kid me about it. I could see that he'd listened to me, and he'd liked it that I'd told him about getting down on the rug with Midnight. Maybe he'd even liked the part about the paw smell. A split-second sliver of a smile came to his face. Then he leaned over toward the shoe box.

I sat forward in my chair. Dread like a lightning bolt shot up my butt.

What Horace set before me, on the desk, what he turned to face me was an old black and white picture blown up to about the size of a notebook page. No frame or cover, just the picture itself. It was of a young man facing a young woman out in the surf of some place like Fort Lauderdale or the Outer Banks. She was wearing an old-fashioned one-piece suit that didn't look at all funny on her. The young man's face was turned away from me, and even though his back looked strong, his shoulders were broad, and the proud way he stood was sort of familiar, I didn't recognize him. It took me nearly a minute to grasp that the woman was my grandmother — and I don't really know how I understood it. Her hair was long enough that there were wet strands of it along her shoulders. She was so thin it seemed impossible that my grandmother had ever been shaped like that. The closer I looked at her, the prettier she was, and pretty was not a

NOTHING CAN MAKE ME DO THIS

word I'd ever associated with my grandmother. When I got my nose right up to the picture, I could see that she was looking straight at the young man — *Horace!,* I thought — maybe that was the word she was saying right that second. I wished I could have heard all the words she was saying, but that was a crazy thought. At the moment, though, I understood that the young man was my grandfather, and that the picture must have been taken around the time they'd gotten married. It might even have been on their honeymoon.

"You know who that is, don't you?" His voice was very low.

I nodded and hoped I wouldn't have to say anything. I felt like we were so connected right then that he could read my mind.

"I think something like that might be ahead of you," Horace said in the quietest and most intimate tone of voice he'd ever used with me. Then neither of us had any more words for a while. Which was fine.

·

In the years that came after our "little talk," as we referred to it, though my grandfather and I never again came quite that close to each other we nevertheless developed an easiness with each other. An understanding seemed to underlie our exchanges. So far as I know, no one required him to speak openly of his pornography. When he died, my mother and grandmother dispatched Bill into the light-soaked study with the mission of capturing Horace's smut, bringing it out, and getting rid of it. The three of us stood outside the study door, waiting for him, and after a while he came out, grinning and carrying a black plastic bag. He was full of himself with amusement — I expect he'd forgotten all about Horace's secret until the women had dispatched him in there to purge it from the household. "Got the goods," said Bill, lifting the black sack. "Got the old stinky treasure. Got the compost."

I felt myself smile at him and glancing at my mother and grandmother, I realized that our smiles were probably identical — bemused, restrained, relieved, but maybe in the slightest contortion of our lips, there was some guilt. Maybe we all felt that we'd somehow failed Horace.

The last thing to be said, however, is that I visited Horace in the hospice house where he went to stay for the last weeks of his life. He was eighty and strong enough to sit for most of the day in an easy chair beside his bed. Though he couldn't do it by himself, he persuaded the hospice staff to help him shave every morning and to help him put on a clean shirt and tie a respectable knot in his tie. When I first stepped into his room that last day, he looked as if he might live several more years. But when I pulled the chair up to face him — as he liked for me to do — I saw that the glint in his eyes and the radiance of his skin had its source in the mild fever he'd taken to running.

"Eve," he said. "I want you to know I'm grateful to you for coming here to visit me. You've been such an enlivening force that I'm tempted to overstay my welcome here."

I could tell that he'd rehearsed his words. I couldn't say anything to him, but I knew I didn't have to. I put my hand on his.

"You know, I think you understood me better than anyone in the family," he said.

I was surprised at that, and I felt an unwholesome pride in his having that thought. Over both my grandmother and my mother, he favored me. I was wrong to savor that news, but I did.

"It wasn't anybody's fault, really," he went on. "I was just made this way." He stopped and caught his breath. "I wanted to be close to people. Especially in the family. I really did. But I couldn't manage it."

Horace was quiet for a long while, and of course I was, too. I'd gotten used to those long periods of sitting with him in the pleasant calmness of the hospice house. I heard soft noises out in the hallway that meant his nurse would be coming in soon. I stood up. His eyes followed me, and so I bent down to kiss his forehead.

"Eve," he said. Then there was a little hitch in his voice. "You know, loneliness is not such a bad companion."

All right, I cried then. At that moment I thought he'd just released the one spontaneous sentence he'd ever spoken in his life. But I think I had that wrong — he'd probably been thinking for a few days about his distance from all of us, and maybe the words had just then come together for him. A few months later — after Horace had gone the way of the blue-winged wangdoodle — I told Bill what he'd said. We were in his truck, driving through town, and Bill gave me a quick blast of his bad-boy smile before he turned back to the street ahead of us. He didn't say anything, and though that was unusual for him, it was fine with me.

Doubt Administration

HORACE WANTS TO BE GOOD, but now he's kissed Louise Cannizaro, the Dean of the Honors College. On the mouth. He's pretty certain the kiss was tenderly received. So now he's constructed and entertained some lascivious scenarios in which he and Louise cavort in motel beds and take showers together. There is soaping of the back. Soaping of the front.

Not good, the little saint in Horace's brain whispers to him throughout his day. *You are not good*, the saint says.

I want to be, Horace replies. *I have been*, he argues on his behalf. *For most of my life*, he says.

Louise Cannizaro is new to the university, says his little saint. *You hired her, you're her immediate supervisor, and now you are thinking about soaping her nether parts.*

•

"I want to raise the level of doubt," Mrs. Sydney Graham tells Horace. She holds a huge chunk of the Kroft fortune, most of which she's eager to donate to the University of Vermont.

Mrs. Graham has summoned him here to her bedroom. Now she wants Horace to assure her that her bequest will not underwrite scientific research. "I'm sick and tired of these people who think they know everything," she says. "The confident ones!" she snorts, giving Horace a squinting of her eyes that clearly conveys her opinion of him.

Horace is aware of his appearance. Though born to a small-town, middle-class family, his whole adult life he's cultivated the appearance of blue-blood poise. He's about as buttoned up and correct as anyone who's likely to enter this room during the days Mrs. Sydney Graham has left to inhabit it. And he isn't about to fake a loss of self-assurance for an old lady trying to bully him with her money and the fact that she's on her deathbed. Even so, he has his duties and his obligations. Horace believes that he serves the university honorably. "The Departments of Religion and Philosophy are sorely in need of new classrooms and office space," he says. "They will be sympathetic to your values," he murmurs. "I'll have the chair persons of those departments come here to tell you about the courses they teach and what they hope their students take away from their classes," he tells her.

Mrs. Graham eyes him long enough to make a lesser man fidget. At the moment her face looks like a topographic map of the Alps. He'd like to look away, but he doesn't. "Ancient" is the word that comes to Horace's mind. "Doubt," she enunciates. Clearly it's a syllable she savors. "Dr. Houseman, can I trust you to see that the money I leave to the university will enhance the place of doubt in our country?"

Horace looks her straight in the eye and wishes he had the ability to lie to her with a straight face. "Yes," he says, raising his voice to signal conviction. How the dickens is he supposed to channel her money away from those pigs in the science departments? They'll be in his office with their plans for the Kroft money before the old lady even signs the check. The ninnies in religion and philosophy won't have a clue about what do with funding of this magnitude. It will embarrass them to be put in charge of it.

"Here's my attorney's card." She extends it to him but not so far that he doesn't have to stand up to reach for it. "Tell Mr. Brady that we've talked. He's well aware of my requirements. You'll find that he's very sharp with language."

Horace hadn't expected Mrs. Graham to be so easy. "Thank you," he says. She doesn't reply. When he turns to the door, he thinks he hears her say it again. "Doubt."

"Certainly," he whispers, pleased with himself to have made it out of that stifling room without breaking a sweat.

•

Why he's been so good so long is something of a mystery to Horace. Discipline. Upbringing. And yes, well, all right, luck. But good wasn't ever a goal, was it?

The luck is that in just about every instance when he's seen the opportunity to behave unscrupulously, he's also seen compelling reasons not to do so. In sexual matters this has been consistently the case. He's imagined — or thought with incomplete certainty — that several desirable women of his acquaintance have desired him back. He thinks he's seen it in their faces. Or even sensed it from their bodies, the way, for example, they've come up beside him and pressed themselves against the back of his arm. He's felt their breasts with his triceps. But such occasions have been cocktail parties and receptions and such. The women have had drinks. Which he knows stimulates them. Even Clara, he's observed, takes on a subtly randy air when she's had more than a single glass of wine. He's also certain that he's the only one who's taken note of that aspect of Clara's behavior and speech. But if the other women have desired him — and he customarily entertains doubt that they actually have — then he's also forgiven them. He thinks most women are less disciplined about desire than he is.

But Horace knows that it's not really discipline. Within minutes of considering an erotic invitation, his imagination transports him into the aftermath of the sexual encounter — dreadful soap operas of post-orgasmic remorse.

What leads Horace into temptation leads him right back out of it. There's the luck of it. A moralistic imagination.

·

In their poker group, Sonny Carson christened Horace "The Eagle Scout." It was because Horace couldn't keep himself from watching how the players divided the money of each pot — and from policing any errors in the division. There weren't many of those errors, and they were never off more than a quarter or fifty cents either way. But Horace seemed to catch the errors whenever they occurred. He tried to be unobtrusive in his corrections. But the players noticed. Especially his friend Sonny, who generally drank so much that he often spilled his money on the floor and put too much or too little in the pot when it was his turn to bet and whose poker playing was sometimes supernaturally successful but more often sub-humanly inept. Sometimes he played like an only moderately intelligent chimp. Horace refused to permit himself to correct his friend's shorting or overpaying the pot when he made his bets. About those errors — which he certainly noticed — he said nothing.

Horace allowed himself to admit that he loved Sonny.

And he'd rather have played poker like Sonny. Sonny took pleasure from those evenings. Sonny acted the buffoon, ate impossible quantities of food, told stupid and inappropriate jokes, teased the other players about their accents and their politics, and sometimes drank so much Sambuca that at the end of the evening Horace had to help him from the car — Horace was always the driver — to his front door. Over the years, Sonny had probably won more money at the games than Horace had, and he'd quite obviously had more fun.

Horace played dutifully and sensibly, but he rarely enjoyed himself. Now that Sonny was dead, Horace thought he'd quit the group. He was waiting until they'd all stopped grieving over Sonny. Which they did by way of speaking sentimentally of him as they played. "Sonny would bet his house and his pension on this hand," someone would say, and they'd snort mournfully. These moments made Horace cringe.

But Horace kept playing to hold onto what was left of Sonny's companionship. Of which there wasn't much.

•

The kiss happens at the conclusion of one of his late Friday afternoon visits to Louise's office — rituals of welcome, he's thought of them — and it frightens him. Horace had intended — or he thinks he'd intended — only a slightly more affectionate gesture than the professionally distant, sideways, comradely, goodbye hug they'd exchanged at the end of their last visit. Horace had thought of that as a collegial hug. This afternoon they've talked softly and somewhat randomly and personally in the little sitting area of Louise's office. Horace has enjoyed the conversation, has felt as if his friendship with Louise will be a pleasure to him in his final years as Provost of the University. The darkening windows of Louise's office tell him that dusk is coming down over the University Green, that it's time for him to go back to his own office. But he feels good. It's a new day in higher education when a provost and a dean can speak openly with each other. He stands up, she stands up, they move toward each other, and then it happens — the kiss on the mouth.

It's shockingly intimate. Has he intended this?

You must have, his little saint replies. *You have to aim a kiss toward a mouth or it doesn't land there.*

Unless the other turns away, Horace protests.

The saint stays quiet.

She didn't, Horace insists, turn away.

·

Mrs. Sydney Graham's attorney is Charles Brady, with whom Horace has been acquainted almost as long as he's worked for the University of Vermont. He and Charles are not friends — he suspects Charles would be as horrified by that idea as he is — but they understand each other perfectly. They dress alike, and were it not for the fact that Charles went to Princeton and Horace to Washington & Lee, people might think they speak alike. Horace's accent is slightly Southern;

Charles's sounds slightly British, from his year of studying at Oxford. The two men both respect the English language. Until it closed, Michael Kehoe's was where they bought their clothes; now Horace drives to Simon's in Boston, and he doesn't know where Charles buys his, but he suspects him of driving to Boston, too. Neither man will ask the other where he buys his clothes.

Mrs. Graham's bequest to the university will be the largest it's ever received. Neither man will give voice to the amount of money. They let the syllables rest unspoken, eight figures written only once into a twenty-page document, copies of which both men have before them, sitting across from each other in the conference room of the President's office. The table between them would comfortably seat a dozen people. It is very quiet today, though Horace knows that all through the offices of this wing of Waterman Building, there are administrators who can hardly wait for this meeting to be over and for the news to be broken and spread throughout the city and the nation — Kroft Matron Makes Major Donation. Horace can see the *Burlington Free Press* headline so clearly that it might as well already have been splashed across its front page.

"You've taken note of how I've written the crucial clauses," Charles says. He's peering over his reading glasses at Horace, who peers back at him over his reading glasses.

"I have," Horace says. "But I'm not an attorney. I'd appreciate your explication of that part of the bequest."

Charles's face shows only the slightest trace of a smile. "Strict interpretation is that the income from Mrs. Graham's bequest can be used only in support of the Religion and Philosophy departments."

"Yes," Horace says.

"Loose interpretation is that under certain conditions, the income may be used according to the Provost's discretion, provided that the Provost determines that the funds are being used specifically on behalf of doubt."

"And how is that to be determined?" Horace is the Provost. He has no choice but to ask the question.

Charles gives Horace what both men would call "a meaningful look." "This document provides no guidance for the determination," Charles says.

"No guidance." Horace says. He's read the passage in question, and this is exactly what he thinks it says, but he hasn't yet been able to believe it.

"Mrs. Graham and I discussed this at some length," Charles tells him. "She thought you were the best person to make the determination. She thought you should make it 'according to your lights.' I believe that was her phrase. 'Doctor Houseman should decide "according to his own lights."' I couldn't disagree with her."

"I'm it."

"You're it."

"But I'm only a year or two away from retirement."

"When you retire, you will have a say in choosing the person to replace you. Indirectly, through that person, you will continue to interpret Mrs. Graham's bequest."

"The Administrator of Doubt," Horace says and gives Charles a smile that he knows is slightly twisted.

"The A.D.," says Charles, giving Horace a smile exactly like the one he's just received. "The old lady liked you, Horace."

·

"You know what's wrong with you?" Sonny liked to ask Horace when the two of them were together, as they often were, driving to poker or meeting for their afternoon cocktail hour at the bar in Leunig's. With this question Sonny so often turned a conversation from one direction to another that it was as if the words themselves instantly transported the two of them into deadpan silliness, a place Horace never visited with any other person.

"No, what?" was his reply, necessary as the "Who's there?" in a knock-knock joke, or Sonny would punish him with a pout and a refusal to go on with whatever it was he had in mind to say. Would hum and look out the passenger side window or at their fellow drinkers on the other side of the bar from where Horace sat. But assuming Horace enunciated it correctly, with just the right amount of innocent hope in his voice, Sonny would begin his performance. It reminded Horace of the way the jazz musicians of the old big bands, when their moment arrived, would stand up for their solos — and keep standing and playing for as long as they could sustain the energy of their improvisation.

"You got too much bare titty when you were in high school," Sonny would begin. "You unhooked all those new brassieres the sophomore girls were just getting used to, and it warped your brain. You thought that's all there was to manhood. That's how you got a premature definition of sex. Back seat of your dad's old station wagon, hand up the back of her baby pink V-neck sweater, you fumble with the damn thing until she instructs you in the basics of it (which she herself probably just learned about two months ago), what hooks to what and how you have to pull with the fingers of this hand and release with the fingers on that hand — which is really, really inciteful — then you've got the silly gizmo loosened, she even pushes your dumb-ass long-haired head down in the direction of her recently blossomed assets, and by God now you've discovered the conjunction of lips and tongue and nipple. Which is really more than you ever even hoped for. Right there where you are is just beyond your dreams. My man, where more hot-blooded boys would have very quickly realized the manifest destiny of below-the-waist and up-the-skirt and gone on to sticky fingers and mutual manipulation and even, Praise God, the magical, transmogrifying deed itself, you the timid one, Mr. Cautious, Dr. Provost, the non-pioneer, got yourself stalled out in West Virginia, stranded on second base. It is no wonder to me that you carry the stink of Saint Agnes wherever you go. When you walk downtown, you are the only grown man I know who looks like he came straight from confessing his sins."

Sonny teaches computer science at Saint Michael's College, he knows Horace is indifferent to religion, but he has the urge to filibuster and improvise, to preach wildly on behalf of the devil. Horace knows he brings out this inclination in Sonny. He can't help it that he reminds Sonny of his own lack of uprightness. To tell the truth, Sonny's ranting like this fills Horace with nervous joy. Sonny is the single person he's ever encountered who speaks to him like this — with headlong and absolute disrespect. Yet there is a delicacy in the way Sonny teases him. Sonny never makes jokes about Horace's family, and around Clara and Hannah he's a paragon of polite affection and consideration. Though Sonny does still tease when he and his wife come over for dinner, it's a more gentlemanly form of making fun. He never tries to embarrass Horace in front of Clara.

"What's wrong with you, Horace, is that you're the victim of a stunted imagination. Who knows what did it to you, but where others recognized that it was their backseat providence to slide those panties down off those hips — and why do you think they buy them in red and black and purple tiger stripes if they don't want you to do exactly that? — you thought you'd better not even think about committing crimes like that. Little old imagination about this big." With his thumb and index finger Sonny shows Horace a distance of about an inch and a half.

"No fixing it?" Horace asks in his straight-man voice. He's come to understand that his role is to keep Sonny soaring along when he pauses or slows down. "Can I not be repaired?"

"Oh yeah, it can be fixed. Repair is possible. There's a great big old American industry that's dedicated to the enlargement and enhancement of the undeveloped mind's eye. I can fix you right up with a sure cure for what ails you. It's the cataract laser surgery equivalent for libido impediments. But I don't think you want that, Horace. I think you like it where you are, sitting all by yourself up in the front row of Sunday school."

He hears something in Sonny's voice. Is he telling Horace a secret or is he offering Horace something that will bring them even closer than they are? A place opens up in Horace. He's never thought of Sonny as needing him or of himself as needing Sonny. But maybe there's a development in their friendship they haven't yet reached. *Here we go*, whispers his little saint. *Destination Delusion City.* Horace ignores the voice, because Sonny is his one true friend in the world, and he thinks he ought to take Sonny up on his offer. And he isn't wrong in his guess of exactly what it is Sonny has in mind as the "sure cure" for what ails him. Horace may have willed himself to be an innocent adult male, but it isn't as if he's been asleep throughout the second half of the American twentieth century.

Better that you had been, says the saint.

·

It's while Horace accidentally observes Clara undecorating their Christmas tree that he makes his notable discovery about her. To keep her spirits up in a task he knows she doesn't enjoy, he's put on the Richard Thompson CD, which has on it "1952 Vincent Black Lightning," a song they both like. It's a ballad about an outlaw with a very particular kind of motorcycle and a leather-jacketed red-haired woman with similar taste; its final verses have the outlaw, shot and dying, handing over to red-haired Molly the keys to his Vincent Black Lightning, uttering his last words: "I'll have no further use for these." The rhyme of "keys" and "these" makes Horace grin, hearing it in the kitchen where he's just finished washing dishes. When he starts back to the living room to help his wife strip the tree of its gaudy baubles and lights, something stops him at the door. Horace stands still a moment, enjoying the sight of Clara lost in her task. That's when he receives an unexpected epiphany: Clara appreciates "1952 Vincent Black Lightning," not ironically as he does but for its romance, a quality Horace finds amusing, albeit exaggerated and tasteless. Unaware he's watching her, Clara sings along with Richard — she's singing expressively! Horace witnesses her face becoming animated, her hand lifting a shiny red globe from the tree, then continuing to lift and fall in time to the music. Clara hasn't kept her looks or her figure into their senior years; instead, she's become what their peers call "a handsome woman." But whenever he's around her, Horace almost always sees the girl and young woman she was years ago. Now he isn't sure he's ever seen her like this — when she believes she's alone. He hasn't meant to spy on her, it's an accident, he assures himself. And the sight of her pleasure in this music moves him in a way he can barely grasp. She has such a feeling for this ridiculous song — a passion for it! It's a feeling that must come from a part of her that she's never shown him, or maybe it's been there all along, and he's just missed it. At any rate, their life together is about as far as you can get from motorcycles and leather and robbing jewelry stores and getting shot and making grand deathbed speeches. Horace hasn't imagined that Clara might have wanted things any other way. As far as he knows, he himself hasn't imagined another life that's half as interesting as the one they've had together. But now he sees that Clara can envision a red-haired version of herself ripping through the open air with her arms and her legs cradling the back of a fearless outlaw on a gleaming motorcycle. He watches her bend to place the little red globe in its compartment of the box of decorations that he'll later carry down to the basement. Should he be stricken with jealousy? He probes that question the way he might touch a tooth with his tongue to see if it's been chipped. Another husband might be wounded by what he's just found out. But Horace — who realizes that he's been half-hiding behind the door jamb —

in this moment feels a thrilling uplift of affection for Clara. How utterly dear she is! All these years she's accompanied him to lectures, panels, receptions, and cocktail hours. She's smiled, and chatted, she's been clever and charming, she's been immensely pleasant to his colleagues and all for the benefit of his career. While her true and invisible self rides with an outlaw on a motorcycle, red hair flying behind her like a flag in the wind. The thought makes Horace cringe with a sense of his own selfishness and Clara's sacrifice. But then he can't help feeling some pride in it, too. She's never shown the slightest sign.

Then she notices him. "Oh, Horace!" She touches her chest with her hand. He watches her face rearranging itself. "I didn't see you there."

"Yes," he says, approaching her with what he knows is too much of a smile. He doesn't want her to know what he's just discovered. "I was just coming in to see if I could help."

.

In his study, in the brilliant sunlight of three o'clock on the first Friday of June, Horace sits back in his desk chair with his fingers steepled an inch away from his nose. He's making himself think hard about Louise Cannizaro. Over the years, his little saint has taught him to recognize his mental evasions. Though he's put plenty of time into thinking about their kiss, he also knows his brain has ducked around the larger issues of himself and Louise. He knows what he has to do. He wants to accomplish it this afternoon.

Louise Cannizaro wears no make-up — at some point in her career she must have decided to downplay whatever prettiness she possessed — but her face becomes animated when she speaks. A single mother of a teenage boy, she's left a higher-paying position at Ohio State and taken this job at UVM so that her son can go to school in Vermont. She's one of those people who, with no visible effort, seems to energize any room she enters. Horace knows he's gotten credit for bringing such a charismatic and contemporary person as Louise into the university's administration. *But didn't you hire her because you found her attractive?*, asks his little saint. Horace shakes his head. *Her credentials were impeccable,* he counters. When Sonny first interviewed her, Louise looked straight into his face with her chin raised almost defiantly. As if to say, *This is my face, I give you the sight of it, but I don't care what you think of me.* Maybe that's how you have to be when you're a relatively young and attractive woman, and you're interviewing to be a dean.

In the months that followed her hiring, Louise has initiated a new curriculum for the honors college, has worked with the deans of other colleges to enhance cross-discipline offerings, and has doubled grant applications from her faculty members. Horace has been so impressed with her that he wishes he had listened to her reports more carefully. He keeps thinking he'll concentrate better when he's more used to her. But maybe he'd only paid attention to Louise to watch her face. This is what he realizes now — he's been studying that face of hers. It's guarded, he decides, as if she's determined not to give away too much. He's pretty certain what she's not talking about has to do with her former husband and their marriage, topics that were off-limits during the time she was interviewing for the job and about which, so far as Horace knows, Louise has revealed nothing to anyone since she's been here. He suspects the break-up of her marriage must have generated a scandal at Ohio State, but whatever it was that she hasn't wanted to reveal, that unknown thing has certainly titillated Horace.

You think it's sexual, prompts his little saint. This isn't what he wants to know about himself, that he's drawn to the possibility of a sexual secret of one of his professional colleagues, but there it is. He's certain he isn't just making it up about Louise, it's something suggested by her manner. As he thinks about it, he decides that he's tracked down what he needs to know about his kissing Louise: It's that withholding quality of her personality that has led him to these conversations in her office and now this intimacy. The withheld thing goes back almost to his first minutes of acquaintance with her. The direct tilt of her face toward his. Even then, there was something intensely sexual about her, something simultaneously there and not there.

Momentarily Horace feels proud of himself for thinking it through and admitting the truth of it. A bit of emotional detective work with a clear answer to the question of what's behind the kiss.

But then his reassurance falls away. When they took up conversation in his last welcoming visit, what Louise had been withholding then became accessible to Horace. In that visit — just before the problematic kiss — she'd talked about her new house, its kitchen and dining room, her garden and the flowers that have come up in it. Her son's guitar lessons and his reading tastes. Their life in that house as it has evolved in their months in Burlington. The dull particulars of how she spends her time away from the office. Louise Cannizaro, forty-one-year-old Dean of the Honors College of the

University of Vermont, takes delight in the trivia of domestic life. *That's* what she's kept out of sight during her interviews for the job. That she is an entirely ordinary person. Better for her new academic colleagues to suspect her of exotic sexuality than know the boring truth about her. That must have been how she thought about it. If she thought about it all.

So she's revealed it to him — who she really is — in their little talks in the sitting area of her office. She has set it out in front of him.

Which insight makes the kiss all the more baffling.

I could give you some advice, murmurs his little saint.

•

Mrs. Sydney Graham, it turns out, penned a note to Horace, the day after his one and only face-to-face conversation with her. Wrote it on her own monogrammed stationery and sealed it in its small proper envelope. Soon after all the papers for her bequest were signed, Charles Brady sent Mrs. Graham's social-size envelope inside his business-size envelope to Horace at his office at the university. Her envelope is inscribed, "Dr. Horace Houseman." Underlined. And the hand isn't shaky.

Dr. Houseman,
    You are, I imagine, chagrined that I have
designated you to see that the terms of the Graham
bequest are honored. Perhaps you will remember
this *New Yorker* cartoon from some years back.
An old man lies in a hospital bed, surrounded by
half a dozen attendees — doctors, nurses, family

members, possibly even attorneys. I wish I had
cut the picture out of the magazine and saved it
to send to you here, but at the time I found it only
mildly amusing; I had no idea I'd be remembering
it in the last days of my life. At any rate, the old
man has a gleeful expression on his face, sitting up
in bed with his Johnny tied behind his neck and
the covers barely covering his lower half. What he
says is something like "As my final wish, I'd like
you all to get into this bed with me right now." Of
course the faces of those in attendance of the old
coot are filled with horror. And Dr. Houseman,
I confess that I was unable to ignore your own
appearance of careful uprightness. Your tie so
carefully chosen to harmonize with your shirt and
jacket, so artfully tied beneath your Adam's apple
and centered within the points of your collar. I
even noticed how closely you'd shaved, and how
your fingernails were properly trimmed, though
not professionally manicured. I took note of you,
Dr. Houseman, and I apologize for doing so; it was
not a disinterested observation that I carried out.
What affected me most was that I saw sincerity in
you. You are a vain man, true, but not a pretentious
person. You do your best, don't you, Dr. Houseman,
and you're aware that in your "will to innocence,"
I will call it, you put a good many people off. In
our conversation, I also understood that it was
not within my power to affect you in any way that
would please me. I thought about pinching you, but
that would have required strength and dexterity

that I haven't had in years. I could have insulted you
or put on some kind of horrifying demonstration
of age and infirmity. Perhaps I should have asked
you to feel my forehead to see if I was running a
temperature. And it certainly occurred to me to
ask you to hold my hand. You would have done
that for me, I'm nearly certain of it, and done it
not merely because you wanted my money to go
to your university. You would have done it because
you'd have wanted to be sweet to a dying old lady.
Which would have poisoned it for me. So even as
you and I were holding our proper conversation,
I began to think how I might make an impression
on you that would require you to reckon with me
personally. To take note of me, as I did of you. An
intimacy, if you will, is what I wanted, and not just
any old kiss on the cheek or term of endearment.
Something to shake you and to last for some time.
On your deathbed, Dr. Houseman, I'd like you to
have at least a passing remembrance of me on my
deathbed. Thus, you must tend to my bequest. I will
be an occasional but ongoing disturbance in your
life. I haven't the slightest doubt but that you will
carry out your duties honorably.

The note is signed "Eleanor." Horace's first reading of it
gives him the creeps. The second makes him feel an aston-
ished admiration. The third twists his mouth into a grim
smile.

•

"Upgrade your manhood," Sonny says when he hands over the black plastic bag. Then he cackles, so that Horace knows Sonny considers the whole thing a joke. Horace feels as if he's suddenly come down with the flu. *As stupidly serious an act as you've ever committed,* says his little saint in the moment of exchange. Horace doesn't argue. It makes him think of the little plastic bags of dog feces he sees dog walkers carrying as they exercise their animals. Though he's never done it — and the idea of scooping up a dog's leavings repulses him — Horace thinks he'd prefer transporting those bags to the one Sonny has handed over to him.

Carrying this bag into his house causes Horace's body temperature to rise several degrees. Clara's car isn't in the garage, and so he's certain she won't be there; even so, he can't help envisioning her coming down the front steps to greet him, smiling in her friendly way, and asking, "What's that?" when she sees that he has something in his hand.

Or Hannah, his daughter, who holds him in such esteem that it embarrasses him — he who admits to himself that he seeks esteem as other men pursue money. What if dear Hannah comes to know about this idiotic manhood upgrading?

Horace stands in the foyer. His house rings with silence. To his left is the dining room, the polished table reflecting light from the windows. To his right is the spacious living room he and Clara have spent years furnishing. *You're an old man,* Horace's little saint informs him, *behaving like an adolescent boy.*

"I guess so," Horace says aloud. "I'll get this over with," he murmurs forlornly.

Horace makes his way down to the basement, to the TV room. So nervous and ill at ease that he fumbles every step of the way, he inserts the first video, witnessing the pictures on its case only from the corner of his eye, reluctantly, and without his glasses. He sits down on the sofa to begin his viewing of the pornography. *When you walk back up those steps, you will not be the same man who walked down them,* his little saint tells him as the first pictures leap onto the TV screen.

"Maybe that's just what I want," Horace snaps back.

But it's as if he's walked in on his own mother fornicating with a stranger. Her backside bobbing in the air sends Horace scrambling to find the remote and turn the thing off.

What did I tell you? sneers his little saint.

•

Now Sonny's dead, Horace has kissed his Honors College Dean, and his little saint has stopped speaking to him. He's sitting in his study, reckoning with all of it. Or as much of it as he can stand to take into his mind at the moment. "I've been a prurient prude," he says aloud, hoping to summon the saint into dialogue again.

The room stays quiet. Beside his left ankle is the wooden crate where he keeps his shoeshine materials — and where he stashed Sonny's videos two years ago. Unseen except for the minute or two of phone-sex advertisement that had assaulted him in his foray into pornography. He meant to return the things to Sonny, but Clara was always in the house whenever he thought of it.

Then Sonny died.

It occurs to him that now they belong to him. They're close enough for him to reach down to the crate and have them up and out and on the desk in front of him. "Last thing

I want to do," he says to the empty room.

Maybe his little saint is dead, too.

He feels awful.

So he steeples his finger and entertains a vision of himself and Louise. They're at the Sheraton. No, they've just stepped into their room at the new hotel down by the lake. They've opened the curtains, and they're standing at the big window, high up, gazing out at the water and the mountains on the other side. Louise leans back against his chest. Horace lifts his hands and sets them gently on Louise's breasts. She crosses her arms and places her hands on top of his.

•

When Horace calls Dean Cannizaro — as he has always done before walking across the Green for one of his welcoming visits — he hears the change in her voice. So he's not surprised when she explains that she's no longer comfortable with his coming to her office. She apologizes for having taken up so much of his time in their last meeting. She goes on to say that as someone new to the administration, she wants to set an example in her professional behavior. "I really want to do a good job here," she tells him.

"Was it that kiss?" He knows he's an imbecile for asking.

"Please," Louise says softly.

"All right," Horace says.

In a moment the line goes dead.

•

It turns out Horace Houseman isn't going to have to live that long after all. His luck is that he's got such a fast-moving cancer that his doctors don't even suggest surgery to him. Instead, they give him prescriptions for drugs that make him more than comfortable, they send him to a hospice house that he surprises himself by liking, and they put him in the care of nurses who treat him with kindness he knows he doesn't deserve. Clara and Eve, his granddaughter, come to see him every afternoon. They're like figures in his dreams. Horace is grateful. Sonny's stroke gave him a death that was too sudden for Horace. For a long time, he tried to take it in but never seemed able to take hold of it. His own death seems easier. A smooth glide out across the evening shadows of Lake Champlain, it's moving at just the right speed. What troubles him is that neither Clara nor Sonny enters his thoughts as he'd thought they would. He'd looked forward to having time just to reminisce over these two with whom he was so close for so many years. But what he can't purge from his consciousness is that business with Mrs. Sydney Graham. The damnable bequest. The silly letter she sent him. He's already spent some years thinking of how he might write her back if there were mail service between the living and the dead. *Dear Mrs. Graham, you have no idea how little regard I have for your wishes about your money. I thought I should inform you that you've been providing generous funding for the Young Republicans on our campus. The little brats are grateful for your support.* Or *Dear Mrs. Graham, You'll be pleased to know that our Departments of Religion and Philosophy have decided to channel the yearly income from your bequest directly to the Committee on Temporary Shelter here in Burlington.* You'd think that he'd have put all that behind him, but now, when he least wants her company, Mrs. Graham is more and more in his thoughts. It's as if she's come to sit at his bedside with her eyes glittering and her iron-haired head slightly cocked, waiting and listening, waiting and listening. His last afternoon, he awakens from his nap to discover that she's pulled her chair closer to his bedside and she's lightly holding his hand. *Mrs. Graham,* he says, *You were joking with me, weren't you?* The old lady gives him a skull-like grin. *All that money,* he whispers. She gives him a bobble-headed nod. *You didn't care where it went,* he says. *And I took you so seriously. You must be very amused.* His words evidently work a spell because suddenly Mrs. Graham is gone. Her absence so exhilarates Horace that he makes a noise. The nurse who hears it as she passes by his door will later describe the sound to his granddaughter as "just the softest little chuckle."

A Thousand Wives

I'M A MORNING MAN — exceptionally alert in the first hours of my day. Lesser men would ignore such pleasures as Yours Truly carefully notes each after the other. E.g., the glories of water sluicing my noggin & shoulders hot as I can take it. E.g., the quiet house, the fresh day. E.g., the future in general. But a proper order is key: Pee, shower, shave, deodorant, brush teeth with the chattering little machine, aftershave, shirt & skivvies, lights out, & out the door. Make the bed, smooth the covers, & transport the body down the steps to the coffee opportunity. All this well before daylight. From every direction assaulted by blessings.

& I'm not ignorant of what's way beyond me. Creation doesn't stop at the inside edges of my brain. Don't have to point at the sky whenever I surpass myself, but I do keep track of what comes to me that I had nothing to do with. What makes me happy when I'm not looking. My mental notebook can't hold it all. So I pay attention. I try to measure up to my undeserved benefits.

Like this morning. I'm sashaying around the kitchen. I'm

orange juice, I'm vitamins & banana & Mister Caffeine Genius, the man who'll put Starbucks out of business when the moment's right. My relationship with my black & chrome machine is so intimate it makes me high every day.

Hannah says I never met a plan I couldn't sabotage. All right, a smart woman is my wife. Hasn't said anything yet that didn't make plenty of sense. But what I reply is one person's aimless & random is another's hidden mosaic. The pattern's just of a larger scope. Got to take two steps back to see it. It's true that I improvise my day, proceed in spontaneous & inspired decision-making: this to that & back to this. One thing shows the way to another, but the one who observes just a link or two may not be able to explain the overall design.

After Eve was born I realized that from some point early on, I'd been working on putting the daily details into place. Baby girl comes into your life, you've got to throw it all up in the air, let the pieces fall where they fall, & start reassembling the whole apparatus. I did it with gratitude. Blood will educate you when nothing else will. Other people's kids are invisible to me, but Eve is my bright & shining. Was from the first I saw of her, swaddled up like they were going to ship her out to Tibet & wanted to be sure she wouldn't come undone. Through the nursery window she was in a line of seven or eight, but she was the baby who glowed in the dark. Floated in a nimbus of light while the other poor little things dreamed about sucking their thumbs. Eve's dreams flew right over the ordinary dreams of newborns. She was generating visions of the spirit mothers.

It was Eve made me see that what I'd been up to was unpremeditated & higgledy-piggledy but design nevertheless. I was Einstein's cousin who hadn't yet realized what his mission was. Make a life out of Tinker Toys. That's it! A city on the head of a pin. Get a baby in your house, you slap yourself twice on each cheek & start self-motivating. Pay attention to the nit & grit of your days.

Which is to say that I may look like I'm playing on ignorance alone, but that is just because most people's eyes are not adequately peeled. I can't tell you how the great galaxy works, because it's beyond me. When confronted with the big picture, I, too, shut up. But I've got a passion for the thumbnails, each & every. I get up in the morning, & instantly my hierarchy pops into focus — Eve, Hannah, Midnight Junior, & next comes either my coffee or my truck.

Tell you about that truck — it's a Honda, & forgive me if I'm a fool for a commercially motivated maker of vehicles. Money-grabbers, I know, but I've been the victim of Dodges, Chevrolets, & Fords. Through the divine inspiration of a TV ad, the Honda came to me. What did it for me was the sound the door made when I shut it, the feel of that resounding tom-tom Thwunk! in my hand, my body, my butt on the seat. That little truck — which is ten years old now, going on 186,000 miles — was the external manifestation of my interior desires. Every little piece in its proper socket, all of it interlocked like the power grid of America. Dependable as moonlight & stars. Open that truck door & shut it, it sounds the same solid ball-in-the-pocket Thwunk! now as it did ten years ago. If I could turn the whole U.S. government over to the Honda Corporation, I'd have done it yesterday.

Few years ago I had this addiction for Burger King Texas Whoppers. Also the large chocolate shakes at Al's French Fries. Jacked the old physical plant up to 225, the waist size to 38 straining toward 40. Looked like I was gonna go down with a heart plugged up by beef grease & sugar fat. One morning my feet hit the floor & I knew that was the end of my life as a pig. Okay, not exactly that instant because when it came to me was when I didn't quite gain my vertical balance. Butt bounced back down to the bed, & I thought for a second I was going to have to call in a tow truck to ratchet me up to standing. Whatever, a fat boy I am not. In my brain I never was. Purged the bad stuff right out of my diet, got myself down to 175, & started feeling like a high school running back again. Even today I'm quick on my feet. Not that I'm about to put the pads back on & ask if I can work out with the JVs. But some cheerful news reached into me: I can combat the negative when it sneaks into my life. Like it likes to do.

I used to have trouble getting back to sleep after Hannah left the bed. Don't blame her, I'm a tosser & a turner, nobody ought to have to try to survive a night under the covers with me. Better to sleep with a cement mixer. Not to mention one night I turned in Hannah's direction & my elbow whammed her in the eye. Three days she was ashamed to go out of the house because of the bruise. "That's it, for you, my man," she said, but she didn't mean she wouldn't start out the night with me. It's just that before one of us nods off she has to slip off to the guest room. For her own safety, she very quietly leaves the bed. I more or less register her departure — but then rise to complete consciousness. Unjust punishment to lie in the dark & the quiet, tired & needing the sandman but my mind ricocheting from duties to omissions to unpaid bills to likely trouble to possible disasters. Wide awake and trapped in my brain.

So I work it out with a not unnatural method — I invite

in the imaginative component. As a teenage boy I learned how the night brain can be turned toward rest & release. Grain of sand to an oyster, all it needs is an object. & fact is, in my daily rounds, I've got hello & how are you status with many a viable lady here in Burlington. This one & that one. Okay, I'm a flirt, I admit that, but as any of my flirt victims will testify, I don't go too far. I just like to chat with the other sex, especially when the other is somebody who pleases my eye. A little hey I like your blouse, it's just the right color for you & oh thank you, my husband advises me not to wear it out of the house, but what does he know & oh well maybe he knows at least a couple things — with a look about chest high. Like that. It comes to nothing. So let's say that at Woodruff Lumber, there's one Linda Ellingsworth of the very stylish raspberry sorbet blouse, one button undone for the sake of customer relations & a schoolboy's dreams. Under the fluorescent lights of the commercial enterprise — & under any real-life circumstance — Linda & I come to no more than some moderately charged chit & chat. But if I can't sleep, Linda Ellingsworth is on call to visit me in the dark & offer no objection to my undoing the next button down. Spare you the complete narrative. What can I say, I got my rest for a month or two with the help of Ms. Ellingsworth, Ms. Appel, & even Sarah Hopper from long ago seventh grade. Also, because the TV encourages me to note the twitching of her derriere when she's about to receive a serve, Maria Sharapova was my night visitor once after Wimbledon and another time after the U.S. Open.

Came a time when I understood there was a profound incorrectness in my methodology. A moral crisis arose in the corridors of my consciousness. I confide it now only because

I moved through & beyond it. I begged the ladies' pardon, apologized for all the unbuttoning & unhooking & sly sliding of the fingers of which I was guilty. I have to go back to my wife, I told them & they sang *That's when those louses go back to their spouses.* It was not without some sadness that I turned myself toward greater mental hygiene. What I found was that I could replace these netherworld narratives with beach thoughts, family trips & outings, great restaurant contemplations, visions of Hannah & Eve & me walking down the Champs in April, the three of us holding hands in the Paris sunlight. I was proud as a monk for making the interior correction. Maybe I'm above-average vulnerable to the negative, but I also have the mental biceps to pry it loose, to liberate myself from what wants to drag me down. I know plenty who can't get loose. See one of those men with three asses waddling down the street, you know it's quarter-pounders got their teeth in the fellow's can't-stop brain spot. Lady in her mid-forties in a mini-skirt & fishnet tights, you know she never got over when she was fifteen & felt the lightning bolt between her thighs.

Which brings me to the topic of Horace's videos. Hannah's dad's dead now, graduated this planet, & as fine a man as I'm ever likely to clink a beer mug with or take out in my truck for a little drive to talk about the family & what we need to do to keep the women from despairing over us. Turns out Horace had a stash of the old-time dirty movies. Most unlikely possession I could imagine that man having. But had it he did, & Horace's women all knew it, Clara, Hannah, & even Eve — they'd known it a long time. But they didn't want to touch those things either. I mean like put their hands on them. So while Horace was still just cooling down to the temperature of his coffin in Green Mountains Cemetery, they send me into his study to fetch out the nasty stuff they know lives in there. Cooperative soul that I am, I do it. A big part of why I get to walk around on the planet on my own two feet is to carry out the wishes of my family. Could have been a salamander, a chicken hawk, or a black fly. Instead, I am the willing if not especially humble servant of those ladies.

I haul Horace's videos out of his Rise & Shine shoeshine box in his study, audience of three silent women watching me take them out. A black plastic bag that I'm ready to transport straight outside to the trash barrel. But I don't because all of a sudden I don't want the rubbish guys to see this particular variety of dirt coming out of Clara Houseman's household. I want to deny the rubbish guys their gloating opportunity.

A zig when a zag was called for.

Forgive me, Honda automotives, I take the black bag of items into the truck with me. Transport it home & downstairs & into my office & insert one into the old TV & VCR set-up I've got down there for purely educational purposes & have myself a look. More education, mind you. See what Horace saw, obtain a new understanding of the man I thought I knew perfectly well.

Doesn't take long to forget all about Horace. Start to finish I watch the first one — two & a half hours dissolve out of my life.

Watch the others, too. Hannah & Eve are over at Clara's house. So I toss the afternoon into oblivion. I observe breasts & butts & vaginas, labia & clitorae, penises & scrotums & buttocks & rectums & tongues, all belonging to an admirable array of ethnically diverse actresses & actors. I become acquainted with dildos in a variety of sizes, colors & mechanical ingeniousness. I witness enough ejaculation to produce a Third World nation. I scrutinize much pelvic gyration & more than a few gymnastic positions. I hear all manner of moans, yelps, curses, prayers, shouts, & lascivious requests — all these elements stream through my eyes & ears & filter into my brain.

When I have reached the end of it, the thought of Horace comes back to me. I blaze with embarrassment to imagine all those things passing before his eyes. But then I start laughing. If Horace Houseman saw what I saw, then no man alive is in fact the actual data you receive by observing him on an ordinary day.

We are all somebody else. Which is not a funny thought.

I've only just now noticed how quiet it is in here. It's a room I use for storage of what I can't quite make myself throw away. Big box of clutter. & none too well lighted. Horace once stepped into this room & got one of his involuntary smiles. "This is the difference between you & me, Bill," he said. "Right here." But I knew what he meant was "Right there." Over at his place. His study over the garage where it's like a home office showroom. Okay, so I'm thinking about Horace & myself & how we're so opposite. Horace always seemed to me like some mutated variety of a holy man, though he never made any claims to being churchy. The holy man had himself some unholy movies. The procreative act repeated again & again — except not for procreation.

I can't really say why it happened, but it was like I got shot right down to the bottom of my own personal Dead Sea. Weighted down with sadness like an iron plate. One of those old iron slave plates I saw in a museum in Williamsburg. I felt like I had one of those heavy black plates just sitting in my chest.

I didn't want to know what I couldn't help knowing.

It wasn't curiosity about what Horace had seen, it wasn't because I didn't want the rubbish guys to see the dirty goods coming out of the Houseman house.

It was me — I'd wanted to see what I'd just seen. Which had been several hundred pictures of hell. Some stinking little piece of myself had wanted to float down that river of pornography bad enough that I lied to myself about what I was doing with Horace's stash.

Now I had it installed in my brain.

& it hooked up with something else in there.

Hannah's coolness toward me. All of a sudden, I saw it. What did I know, I just grew up like anybody, a baby, a boy, a man, & shazam, there I was — knew nothing about love and/ or sex, but figured everybody made it up as they went along, & what was so hard about it anyway? The body finds out what it needs to know. Sure, in our first years of marriage, Hannah & I had sex & plenty of it. The thought occurred to me that maybe she wasn't so happy with what I brought to the occasion. She never said anything. We had a little conversation. "We'll get the hang of it," she said, very cheerful, & I thought she was right about that. But over the years, there was less & less. Okay, as the poet says — little, less, nothing. There wasn't anything lately. The last couple of years. Disappeared from our lives. & the old brain wasn't doing a great job of facing up to the absence & processing it out.

Live inside the elephant, you don't see the elephant.

Hannah sometimes would catch me by the arm & turn

me in her direction & tell me she loved me & look me straight in the eye. & keep, like, searching my face with her eyes. Made me uncomfortable. I'd say love you, too, babe, & go on about my business. But — I saw it now — it was more like she was asking both of us the question. *Do I love you? Do I really do that?*

The question of whether *I* love her, really love her, is not part of this non-discussion, don't ask me why. I guess both of us figure I do so definitely & obviously that it makes no difference. Something out of whack, but here I am, man of the house, husband of the wife, father of the daughter. We're making a go of it.

But at this particular moment in my cluttered & badly lit office — with about enough room to sit as a one-hole outhouse — I give over to several minutes of deep sorrow for our man Bill. What a lousy life, his wife doesn't go for his bedtime manners & methods, & now he's contaminated himself with dirty pictures. Boo hoo hoo.

I bottom out. This is something Horace told me he got from his high school tennis coach. If you're beating somebody bad in tennis, don't let up, don't give him a single point. If anything, play harder. Either he will play worse & lose & maybe throw his racquet & curse & even swear never to play again, or else he will bottom out. He'll figure out what's wrong with the way he's playing & try to fix it. He'll come back & play better & maybe even beat you. But win or lose, he'll be better off for your having given him nothing. If he's got any character at all, he doesn't want your charity. To show you respect him, you've got to try to hammer him down.

Okay, so I see I've been beaten. Don't know who my opponent is, didn't even know I was playing, but now I see I have to put the loss behind me. Ten thousand pieces of this life I've assembled for myself, at least nine thousand, seventy-five hundred are still in place. A few replacement parts, re-think the design, move a few items around, & I'll be good to go.

First of all, because I know I can't go back & unsee the videos, I take the eat-so-much-it-makes-you-sick approach. I put away poor old Horace's black sack, I head out Williston Road to Airport Video, & I rent my own swatch of the nasty things. Five at a time, that's the ticket. In three weeks I watch fifty-five of the things. I'm hiding in the closet of a brothel & watching lady after lady bring in customer after customer. Sandblasters keep working over my pelvic area. I'm in a nightmare of sex education. I meet a thousand naked men & women, most of them people I wouldn't even want to ride on a bus with. I've got my nose right up in these stranger's crotches. The region of hell to which I've been consigned is the one reserved for people who don't know what they did wrong but know they did something & so they've volunteered to be punished. There's this special treatment whereby you're aroused more or less constantly & you hate what you're seeing & what it makes you feel like, but you're helpless to look away.

I don't want to, but I acquire an expertise. I get to know the actors & actresses — many of them appear repeatedly. I know how they carry out their performances. A few of the women I like a lot & wish to advise as to how they could live more rewarding lives. Just about all of the men I despise, some so deeply that I have to grit my teeth to watch their brutal carnal methods. For one or two of the men I can't help developing a grudging admiration. This guy knows what he's doing, I'll tell myself, then take a momentary satisfaction in seeing if his partner is one of my favorites among the women. I find myself paying inordinate attention to settings. There's a swimming pool that I'm pretty certain is somewhere in southern California. There's a house with a winding staircase some director must think is a cool place for people to have sex. There's even a tennis court. Sometimes random people walk by a fornicating couple. Often there is fake sexual moaning in the background. I find that I'm especially alert to the noises & facial expressions of the actresses. Evidently it's the gospel of pornography that actresses should keep their mouths open during every phase of intercourse. Also the ladies rolling their eyes & licking their lips is thought to be appealing to viewers. Choreography varies only slightly from one film-maker to another: begin with cunnilingus, move to fellatio, escalate to female-superior backward-facing genital sex, & so on until the duet ends with the male ejaculating onto the face and/or breasts of the female who dons a mask of joyful gratitude.

Deeper & deeper into illness — fever & scabs, bone ache & dry heaves — I keep at it.

Logistically it's shockingly easy. For work I make my own schedule. Eve's been away at school and out of the house long enough that I'm getting used to it. Hannah does property appraisals for the city, & so she's not here most of the day. Midnight Junior may have wondered why I've suddenly started spending so much time in my basement office, but of course the thing about a dog is that whatever he knows gets translated into barking if he tries to talk about it.

Unfortunately the viewing isn't completely hateful. When I'm not watching the pictures, I have this nagging desire to get back to the task. I'm witnessing the citizens of hell receiving their eternal punishment — unceasing sexual intercourse. My own genitalia is chaffed from incessant arousal provoked by the videos. Again & again I self-flagellate. It feels dutiful, an act of despair. I'm another wretched fornicator. My own face contorts & grimaces in the throes of what is supposed to be pleasure.

Desperate for an end to it, I can hardly step into the sunlight outdoors without feeling pale & sickly. Allergic to life — that's what I feel like when I'm out in the world. My skin feels like a body-size sack of worms. I look at my bare arms & expect to see scabs. All along I've thought that the end would arrive on its own, without my having to do anything. There'll come a moment — maybe in the middle of a particularly intense episode of copulation — when I stand up, snap off the machines, & know I've reached my destination.

Not so. Just a slow, spinning tumble deeper & deeper into the contamination.

Or maybe it does reach its own conclusion, because just at the point when I think I might be the world's first pornography death, the dimmest light begins to glimmer in a far corner of my brain.

I have to do it myself.

I can do it myself.

I do it.

Myself.

I haul the last batch of the things back to Airport Video & don't rent a new batch. Don't even walk inside the place, just drop them one by one into the slot for off-hours drop-offs. It occurs to me that they are merely plastic, light to the hand. For a while there, they have felt like enormous stones that I've carried with me wherever I've gone.

I drive home, feeling righteous & powerful. A feather floating. A balloon rising. My truck doesn't despise me any more.

All this time I've kept Horace's original five down in my office, way back in a filing cabinet full of old receipts.

Turns out not to be so easy. I've accidentally trained my body & my brain. What else is there? Whatever the else is — the *me* of me — has to say no. To my advantage is that I know my life depends on the refusal. The body & the brain want to go downstairs, turn on the machines, slip in the plastic gizmos. Body & brain want it bad. But this little sliver of a thing that wants to rescue me squeaks out its feeble no. Hard Place City — right there's where I have to live for a few days. Major Difficulty Ave. Discomfort Blvd. Not watching hurts at least as bad as watching. I think I'm doing okay, but somewhere inside I've got the shakes. Even so, the feeble no's gotten louder & gained conviction.

It's a weekend, & Hannah's home. She & I are coming up on nearly thirty years of knowing each other. I'm fifty-eight; she's fifty-six. When I come down to the kitchen after my shower, it occurs to me that from little kids on, she & I have both been loners. We don't much hang out with anybody. Which is probably what we saw in each other. & even now that Eve's out of the house, we're still not close, not by any stretch. Nevertheless, I know how she likes her coffee on a Saturday morning, know she likes to drink it while she's reading the newspaper. Likes to take her time getting out of bed, make a slow commitment to the day. So when I hear noises upstairs that tell me she's awake, I bring the paper & the coffee to her. I haven't done this in quite a while.

"Billie," she says with a drowsy smile, rising to her elbows.

She takes a chance calling me that old grade school name. I don't like it in anybody else's voice & even in hers only once in a while. From Hannah, it's a sweet tease, a friendly I-know-you. "Bill to you," I'll snap if I'm busy the way I usually am, a joke with an edge. But I don't this morning. "Say it again," I say, setting the newspaper on her knees & the coffee mug on the bedside table.

She shakes her head & doesn't. I appreciate the restraint. A thousand wives would probably have said it again, but Hannah's the one who knows I like it better unspoken. She's got the bed-head this morning, & her face is puffy. Such eye make-up as she wore yesterday for her property-appraising has smeared down from her eyes just a bit. Not taking her eyes away from the paper, she flaps her hand over on the table, trying to locate her glasses. When I hand them to her, she accepts & puts them on, still without looking away from the front page.

This is another species altogether from the women in the videos. Can't help shaking my head about the difference even though if Hannah noticed I'd have a hard time explaining.

I keep standing where I am. Which I guess is not what she or I expect. I'm definitely a go-about-your-business kind of man, but evidently not today. The room has this scent of Hannah sleeping. Profoundly domestic. Not available as perfume or room freshener except in my exact location. A foot away. She's got on her red & white striped Land's End ripped-shoulder-seam nightgown that she should have thrown away last year, & there's even a little pink line across her cheek from where a pillow wrinkle dug into her skin while she slept. I shake my head again because I know that she really has only two sleeping positions that work for her, & one of them almost always gives her this pink line on her cheek.

She glances over, peers at me over her glasses. Makes a strange little grin. "Where you been, Billie?" she asks in this voice that sort of hides down in her chest & only comes out every once in a while. A Julie London half-whisper.

"Hell's front yard," I say. "Getting chewed on by dogs."

"Manly activities?" she asks. Same voice. Same grin.

I meet her eyes. "Setting off fireworks," I say. "Swimming with the mermaids."

"So you're the young sailor who came home?" She raises her eyebrows. Grin goes up half a notch.

How did I ever find such a wife? "Old Farmer who never went away," I correct her.

Wages of Love

SOMETHING EVER SO LIGHTLY brushes a tender place in her mind. His eyes finding her and not looking away. She blinks but doesn't stop feasting on the sight of him.

At a party. At the country club. Eve's sixteen.

.

HORACE IS A PRICK! Clara prints out the words slowly. A medium receiving dictation.

Horace has been dead for about three hours.

Clara's lips feel twisted tight across her teeth. *Not myself* she tells herself. In her whole life, she's never written or said aloud the word *prick*. In her fifty-two years of marriage to him, she never entertained calling Horace any name other than *dear* or *sweetheart* or — as a joke that offended him the one time she said it aloud in the car after a party at which she'd had a third glass of wine — *Horace Porridge*. Now her hand won't stop. Her fingers press the pen across the magazine page. Her tight lips shape the words as they appear before her eyes. PIG FUCKER. DEVIL'S RECTUM.

•

Eve moves toward him. It feels like sleep-walking. She wonders if she'll be able to keep from touching him. When she's close enough to him to do that, he disables her with a smile. It makes her catch her breath. But she sees it's only incidentally for her. Like he's caught sight of himself in a mirror over her shoulder. She's not too gaga to receive a little burst of understanding. Nothing measures up to the sight of himself. Maybe he can't really see anything else. Her face, her body, her new dress and shoes that she's adored until this moment, even her newly shaved and still slightly stinging armpits are merely a mirror for this boy. He looks at her and sees a plain girl panting and thinks, *Oh yeah, I don't blame her, I'd pant for me, too.*

What she understands doesn't trouble her. And anyway, to walk away now is out of the question. She does what her grandfather has taught her to do with strangers of note. Extends her hand and speaks in a clear voice. "Hello, I'm Eve Collins, I don't think we've met."

•

CLARA IS A WHORE, Clara writes. She feels her eyes widen at the sight of the words. She wants to cry out but the last thing she wants at this moment is for Hannah to come running upstairs to see what's the matter with her. Clara would have to tell her. *I'm a whore. Don't you see what I've written here? All these years I didn't quite know what I was. Now I know.*

The thought of saying such nonsense to her daughter amuses her enough to make her mouth relax into what she thinks might pass for a smile. Maybe this thing that's taken hold of her will pass quickly. It could be just a little step up into proper grieving.

Still. *Whore*. It's something to consider. Never made any money. Seventy-five years old. Had sex with only one man. Even so, maybe *whore* is the name of what I am. What I was all that time.

•

A tongue of flame sweeps across her shoulders and the top of her chest. Because that's where his eyes go when she extends her hand toward him. Down. Away from her face to her chest. "I'm Sylvester," he says. He barely places his fingers into her hand. It's the handshake her grandfather calls the please-don't-hurt-me. Eve can see he doesn't like her making him touch her. He didn't like what he saw of her chest. He doesn't want to be near her.

She laughs at him. Not in a mean way. "Here," she says. "You don't know how to do this." With her left hand, she grasps his wrist to hold it steady, then pushes her right hand forward, firmly grips his right hand, removes her left hand, and gives his right hand three firm shakes. "That's how," she says. Because he's cast his eyes down at their hands, she drills his face with her own eyes. "And look straight at the person you're meeting when you do it," she says.

He still won't look at her. "You're a teacher," he murmurs off to the side. His eyes lift but stop at the level of her mouth. Study her mouth. "So am I," he says. Removes his right hand from Eve's. With the top of his index finger touches the center of her collarbone. Turns and walks toward the punchbowl.

Joan of Arc, she's tied to the stake. Flames blaze up from beneath her feet. Agony and slow death. At the edge of the dance floor in the Burlington Country Club. Fifty adolescent boys and girls moiling around.

His hair is long as a girl's. And he uses conditioner. That hair wafts in the slight breeze of his walking away from her.

.

Clara hadn't asked to be left alone with Horace. But they seemed to think she should be. "Take your time," someone whispered. They left the room. Softly closed the door behind them.

Her first impulse was to open it and step right out behind them. *Wait for me,* she could call. But she stood where she was.

Dead, he's anybody, was her next thought. *What difference does it make what I say? Or do?*

Another thought came, too. *Most alone I've been in my life.* Horace had been her companion. Before him, her mother and father, her sister. All of them gone now. The ones outside, in the hallway — Hannah and Eve and Bill, they were.... She couldn't finish that thought, but they weren't, couldn't be, what Horace had been. As if what she thought, he thought, too. Or something like that.

Here he was. What was left. Which wasn't really him.

She stepped to the bed. They'd — what could she call it? — cleaned him up. Combed his hair. She looked closely. They must shaved him with his electric razor just before she arrived. Arranged his head on the pillow, the covers across his chest and shoulders, the sheets fresh to the bed.

Here he was. She snorted. Here he wasn't.

This was the moment when her hands seemed to receive signals that didn't come from her mind.

Her hand raked the covers down to his waist.

She couldn't say what rose in her at that moment. Or she'd say meanness, except that so far as she knew, she'd felt no meanness since grade school. She'd had no reason to feel it. Then or now.

The hair on his chest had gone wispy, gray, and sparse. His ribs were visible beneath the skin. His chest was boxy. His chin — which people didn't hesitate to tell him was strong — now jutted up from his neck as if he were about to speak some kind of heartfelt conviction. The vague little path of hair that began at his belly button was covered by the sheet she'd disrupted.

She heard herself breathing. She still had her coat on. Ridiculous that she hadn't thought to take it off. She did so.

Whatever it was — meanness, rage or some mutated version of sadness — stayed steady in her.

She wasn't about to throw herself on top of Horace's body and begin to wail. It occurred to her that that's exactly what they wanted her to do, the ones out there or in the reception area down at the end of the hallway. Hearing the first sounds of her grieving, they would nod their heads and take comfort from her noise.

She ripped the covers all the way down. Even off his feet at bottom of the bed.

Not a stitch.

◆

He's all the way across the room, but Eve thinks he knows her eyes are following him. He gives her a look that is no smile at all, jerks his head so slightly she's certain she's the only one who's seen it. She's certain, too, he's intended it for her. Then he steps through the curtained doors out onto the balcony, where she knows the boys go to smoke.

I'm not going out there, she tells herself.

All the while moving that way.

.

A little puff of gray-brown pubic hair, like an exotic forest plant. Penis atop scrotum, the latter tightened, the former relaxed. *No more duties for you, old fellow.*

Horace is thin, and his body looks stretched here on the sheet, as if someone had held his shoulders and another had pulled on his feet. His belly is concave between his rib cage and the up-thrust of his hipbones. His thighs seem to have lost all their hair — they're the shade of white that Clara associates with breasts that haven't seen sunlight. He looks so utterly vulnerable that she can't help imagining awful things being done to him.

You'd like a look at 'im, wouldn't you? Somebody's voice whispering in her mind, she doesn't know whose. It's true, though, she did want to see him. Like this. As, while he had the life in him, she never would have been allowed to see him.

But that's not exactly true. It wasn't a matter of his allowing her to look. Horace would have obliged her if she'd ever asked. He was vain. A dear man, but one who knew exactly how handsome he was and didn't mind anyone looking at him. He'd have said, *Of course you can, my dear.* And lain down naked and stretched out exactly as he is here. Probably closed his eyes so as not to embarrass her.

•

He's alone. He's about to light a cigarette. It's in his mouth. He flicks the lighter just as she steps out. She suspects it's a little show he's putting on.

She walks to him, plucks the thing from his lips and tosses it from the balcony.

I wasn't going to light it, he says. Behind him the stars are out, the black sky milky with light, thin clouds, a sliver of moon. It's cold out here.

Eve Collins, he says. Doesn't say so much as murmur. A little sound only she can hear.

You shouldn't be out here with me, he says. Softer if anything.

She won't speak to him. Won't give him that. Or anything more, she swears.

In one step he's close enough that she can smell his breath. He wasn't lying — he doesn't smell like cigarettes. The cold out here stings her face, makes her feel brave for staring straight at him, refusing to look away.

His own eyes are invisible to her, black sockets of a skull. He has his back to the light, and she knows it makes her face visible for him. It doesn't matter, she won't look away.

Then she feels the lightest touch. So soft a brushing she thinks she must be imagining it. Each nipple through her dress and bra. He wouldn't.

She won't look away or step back.

He is. With the backs of his fingers. Brushing.

He leans toward her ear, murmurs something, the syllables more a silent transmission than sound. It takes her a moment to receive and process it.

You're very beautiful.

She hits him hard, where her grandfather told her to strike if she ever had to hit a boy. In the solar plexus. *Because that will paralyze him, at least for long enough that you can get away,* he'd said and she'd remembered.

The boy goes down. Sylvester. Puppet whose strings got snipped.

She steps back inside. Softly closes the door behind her. Hot in here. Feels her blood rocketing through her veins. Walks among the others who take no notice of her.

I'm not beautiful. Her lips move. *Not even close.*

•

Clara taught him. Taught him manners, taste, books, music, painting. Even tennis. On their honeymoon, they played every day. When he hit a ball badly, he threw his racquet, cursed. Stomped off the court. She doesn't know where she found the patience to put up with him, overlook his roughness, ignorance, self-absorption, errors in grammar, tone-deafness, wrong choices of color and clothes. He's heavy-footed, the least elegant tennis player she's ever seen.

But he listens to her. He learns. He's good at that.

When they were first married, they discovered that neither of them knew how to cook anything more than soup from a can or hamburgers in a frying pan. So they learned together. About matters of preparing food, they rarely argued, because their knowledge was equally thin.

She read aloud to him — Tolstoy, Flaubert, Faulkner, Katherine Mansfield, Jane Austen, T. S. Eliot, Robert Frost, Edwin Arlington Robinson. He was the best listener she'd ever known. He'd ask for the book and read back to her the poem or passage she'd just read.

Music, too. He knew the popular stuff, the big bands from years back. Tone-deaf though he was, he was nevertheless crazy about Elvis and Little Richard and Bill Haley, the Coasters. *Yakety yak,* one would say to the other when that one was talking too much. The other would say *Don't talk back,* and that would make them both smile. But she helped him hear what Bach and Vivaldi could tell him. In the third year of their marriage, they spent evening after evening listening to the Beethoven symphonies, then the string quartets. He had an appetite for it. When he heard *Cosi fan tutte,* it was as if he'd been waiting for years for such music as that. For months, he insisted on nothing but Mozart.

The truth of it, though — the miracle, the secret, the explanation — was desire. Not so much hers for him, which was adequate, at least most of the time, but his for her. He wanted her. She knew that about him almost from the first sight she had of him. It was like a sea breeze, always there, always pleasing to her. Something steady and bracing that had entered her life. At first she thought it would surely diminish, maybe go away altogether. At some point — nine or ten years in — she understood that maybe it wouldn't.

In his sexual attention to her, he was ardent, he was alert, he was (so far as she could tell, which wasn't very far because he was the complete story of her) the most attentive lover a woman could ever have. It occurred to her that she never considered anyone else. Only in his shocking understanding of her body did he became elegant to her. She didn't know how he could have learned what he knew about her. Even if he'd asked her, she couldn't have told him.

Also, his desire for her was so constant and at the ready that it amused her. Hers never rose to the level of his. His was a puppy. They had this little joke that his prick belonged to them both and that it was a "darned dependable piece of equipment."

In that regard, Horace had been her teacher. Or maybe he was just the one who had the aptitude for learning as they went along.

There were plenty of times when she wanted to, but she took some pride in never having refused him.

But there it was. *Whore.*

God damn him!

·

In that year — her junior, his senior — Sylvester takes on a role in their high school life. He's arrogant and feminine and fearless. He's rail thin, and someone has tailored his clothes to fit him perfectly, his jeans tight as a girl's and shirts fit to the waist but big — almost flowing — in the sleeves. Maybe he orders them that way from a catalogue. When he walks through the halls, he gives off the sense of a mannishly-dressed female model striding into a slight wind. His Asian-dark hair shifts and ripples and flows as he walks. His face seems to say that he can't be touched, that he has no need for friends, that he has little pity for most of his schoolmates, that he leads a life of far greater importance than anyone in those hallways, that he knows sources of pleasure that are unreachable by ordinary teenagers, that his future is probably unimaginable to anyone who sees him at this very temporary phase of his life.

Eve can't help watching him. But she thinks her view of him isn't the same as everyone else's.

What she thinks may be ridiculous, but it makes sense to her—he's touched her, he's tried to touch her intimately, and she's dropped him to his knees. Therefore there has been this exchange between them in which she's proven herself superior to him. Thus, arrogant and self-contained as he is, she's seen him otherwise. And he knows she's seen him that way.

Every now and then, maybe once a week or every ten days, he passes by her, sometimes at her locker, sometimes coming up on each other face to face, and she'll hear — or feel — his murmured greeting. *Hey, Eve Collins.* She can never be certain he's actually said it. His lips don't seem to move. His eyes don't fall on her. She starts thinking of it as his no-look hello.

Older boys, jocks, punks of one kind or another, call him names — faggot, girl-boy, Miss Pissy, and of course worse than that, much worse. The names seem not to affect him. Once or twice he gives the name-caller a pitying look. He has a way of walking around and away from name-callers that makes them look powerless and idiotic.

But they laugh about his name. Sylvester.

In the hallway traffic, Robert Alley, the very big boy who's their school's All-State defensive tackle, likes to bump him with his shoulder or give him a hockey hip then point at him say, "Get out of my way, Sylvia!"

She doesn't see it when it happens, but the account comes to her, of Robert Alley's aiming to bump Sylvester but missing because Sylvester sidesteps him — *like a Ninja!* is the phrase every teller of this account uses for Sylvester's footwork — and Robert lurches against an open locker door, gashing a nostril half off his face.

She, and everyone else, expects quick and harsh retribution to come to Sylvester. They keep waiting. Finally one morning Sylvester arrives at school with a heavy bruise around his eye. Two or three boys and even one of the senior girls ask him what had happened. To the boys he merely shakes his head. To the girl, he says, "What makes you think anything happened?" and walks around and away from her.

This is his talent. Walking away.

And photography. There's a class in it, where evidently Sylvester is the star pupil. His pictures are put up in the teacher's lounge, the principal's office, even downtown in the lobby of the Merchant's Bank. Black and white portraits. A boy with his head down in a pout. A girl running to catch a bus with her skirt flapping at her knees. A girl and a boy walking down an empty hallway, very close together, shoulders touching.

Only occasionally does she ever see Sylvester with a camera. She tries to decide if she wants him to take a picture of her. Some days she does want it. Others not.

A picture of Robert Alley standing by his car in the parking lot, sharing a joint with two of his friends, results in the three of them being suspended from school and Robert getting kicked off the football team for the last two games of the season.

A myth arises out of the school gossip — there's been a confrontation downtown between Sylvester and Robert Alley and his friends. The myth is that Sylvester stands his ground and says, "I have some other pictures, Robert. Some pictures that explain how you get your spending money."

They stop calling him names. They leave him alone. He makes no effort to be friends with anyone. Boy or girl. To maybe half a dozen of the members of his photography class, he nods. And that's it. He's the most alone person Eve has ever observed.

Which makes his occasionally passing near her and saying—or transmitting—*Hey, Eve Collins,* the moments of her nearly unbearable sophomore year of high school that she treasures like Aztec coins.

•

Clara was horrified at her grieving self. She could barely stand the company of anyone. Thus she became a master evader of social occasions, or a shortener of those occasions she couldn't evade. Solitude was what she wanted. She wanted to be alone all the time.

She assigned herself to go through Horace's papers. A good excuse for avoiding or minimizing visits. "I'm sorting through his files. I hope you don't mind, I'm right in the middle of something."

People intruded in spite of her tactics. They thought she needed company. Thought she needed to talk about him. About the old days with him. *Would you like to hear about the first time I ever saw his penis?* she thought of asking *Would you like to know what we found out that we both liked? Would you like to know our nicknames for our sexual parts?*

So she was almost always in a state of guilt. *Whore* and *slut* she called herself — and sometimes printed out on scrap paper, a compulsion that seemed crazy to her when she gave in to it. It was as if she were a prosecutor trying to pin a crime on an innocent person — herself. Nothing of her life would testify to her having been promiscuous or a sexual manipulator or even a flirt. But something in her wanted to insist that these names fit her. She went on with it. The name-calling. Which must have been a form of inquiry. She couldn't see an end to it. But that's what she longed for. Not company.

She'd have been willing to be locked up if she could stop feeling what she felt.

She could tell no one what was wrong.

No one could have guessed.

·

In the spring of that year Sylvester starts to sit where Eve sits in the cafeteria. Catty-corner from her. Empty chairs usually around them both. Doesn't speak to or look at her. It's not that they have a table to themselves but that they both take places at a table understood to be for outcasts, losers, geeks, etc. There's little conversation. Kids who sit here are ashamed of sitting here.

Except Sylvester, who, though he says nothing, somehow conveys the idea that he sits here to get away from the trash and riff-raff of the rest of the lunchroom crowd, the popular kids, the jocks, the kiss-ass honors students. It's not so much a smirk he wears as that serene, can't-touch-me, ironic-in-a-way-you-couldn't-possibly-understand, tight-lipped smile.

She makes herself look away from him. Mostly she's successful.

This one time, though, when she does look, he catches her eye.

Doesn't wink. The universe would dissolve into a river of monkey snot if that boy ever winked at anybody.

Okay, so she can't break the stare between them as quickly as she should have.

Next day at lunch he takes the seat directly across from her. Still has nothing to say. And manages not to look at her. So far as she can tell, though he might be doing it when she's successful in her will not to look at him. Good thing nobody's making movies here because these scenes would be funny in a way that would not amuse either of them. Girl and boy determined not to look at each other.

That's where he sits from then on.

One day when he's got his tray down and he settles into the chair, he looks directly at her and says, "Hey, Eve." Like an ordinary boy.

"Hey," she squeaks. Little dormouse. Little blind mole. Little bat baby.

She shakes it off. "Hello, Sylvester," she says in the firm voice her grandfather made her practice with him when she was ten years old. He'd be proud of her for remembering how to speak up in a social situation. Of course he'd be horrified at the boy on whom she's wasted the valuable training he gave her.

·

It wasn't the end — Clara knew that much — but there was a kind of release that came to her in April, when she could go outdoors. The awful words and thoughts didn't come to her when she was bending to pull up the ravenous weeds that had invaded her perennial bed. *It'll get better when I can get down on my knees,* she thought. It was too cold and wet for her to do that now, though ten or fifteen years ago she would have been right down there on the soggy ground. *An old lady has to have a decent day before she gets down in the dirt,* she told herself. A grieving widow.

When she came indoors — couldn't stop herself! — she went straight to the phone pad and printed out CUNT-SNIFFER.

She stood there shaking, wondering if she should call Hannah to come get her and take her to the hospital. Commit her.

Stood a long while. Took a deep breath. Let her hand holding the pen go back to the paper.

BEGONIA, she wrote.

.

Why the kids let them alone she can't understand. Why Hannah and Bill allow it to happen she understands but thinks they should know better. The first boy who's shown an interest in her? Of course they're not going to interfere, no matter how freakish he might seem to them. It's the kids who ought to be mocking them, telling her mean gossip about him or giving him accounts of all the humiliating episodes of her grade school life that most of them know perfectly well.

Everybody stays out of their way. Lets it evolve. Sure, they're interested, Eve can feel the ten thousand eyes on her as she's never felt them in the past. Boys to whom she's been invisible at least now seem to grant her a physical presence. Girls who've treated her with contempt now give her a level stare as if they're trying to fathom some secret she might have, something they haven't previously recognized.

But all it is between them is a little talking. There's no touching. If anything, she can feel him avoiding any contact between his skin and hers. Which — given how he touched her out on that balcony two years ago—seems all the weirder.

Eve knows it isn't a real courtship. Or whatever you call it when a couple becomes a couple. They're a couple, and Eve has a term she's invented for how it makes her feel. She's "tragically excited" all the time. She just wishes she had someone she could say those words to who wouldn't laugh in her face. Or she wishes Sylvester would reach for her hand. If he'd just touch her, she wouldn't mind it so much that she can't discuss him with anyone.

·

A long time ago she'd gradually taken the gardening away from Horace. He'd had no gift for it, but when they first moved into the house on Prospect Street, she'd had her hands full with Hannah as a pre-schooler, and so Horace had dutifully tended to the flower beds. *Tended* wasn't the right word, because she's certain he did more harm than good. *Presided over,* maybe. He pulled up trillium that she knew the previous owners of the house must have treasured. When he wondered aloud why the bulbs he'd ordered didn't come up, she asked him whether he'd planted them with the pointed end turned up or down. And watched his face turn red. Even so, crocuses appeared their first spring. A few grape hyacinths. Old bulbs planted by the previous owner. Later on, the rose bush by the chimney bloomed as if to show them what might be possible if anyone in the house could show some aptitude for horticulture.

"You've got a black thumb," she told him on the day he ran the lawn mower over the little hydrangea bush for which she'd had such high hopes. She'd said it in mild anger, but when she saw him smile, she realized it was funny. From then on, his black thumb was their joke.

The fall Hannah started first grade, Clara ordered the new bulbs and put them in. A hundred and twelve of them. Tulips and daffodils. That first year, she let him dig the holes, but from then on, she even did that work, which was the least pleasant labor she'd ever carried out. "It's a fair price to pay for what they bring us when they come up," she told him.

Horace hadn't ever argued with her. On the second day of May, while she was out in the side yard counting tulip buds, it occurred to her that once or twice he'd fallen into some silent pouting — kept quiet and kept out of her way. But he just didn't have it in him to argue with her. Even when she herself knew she was being unreasonable. The morning sun was warming her shoulders, and she was standing in a trance, realizing something completely obvious about her husband that she should have known all that time.

If she had him back, she'd force him to argue with her. The nerve of him!

Yes, she was crying, and she had to go inside to blow her nose and get her face cleaned up. But he'd had no business treating her that way. Wasn't it a sign of respect if you argued with somebody?

It'd been three weeks since she'd written one of those words.

It's Ansel Adams, Edward Weston, and Alfred Stieglitz he wants to tell her about. Brings art books to school and shows her pictures. Sometimes postcards. At lunchtime, they find a place out on the school grounds where the other kids can't see what he's showing her. Photographs of Georgia O'Keefe nude when she must have been in her twenties. Of Georgia O'Keefe's hands. Of Georgia O'Keefe the old lady with the good witch's smile on her face. Adams's pictures of mountains, trees, snow. Weston's picture of a nude floating face up in a swimming pool. Weston's picture of a nude in an upstairs window, the woman looking down on the photographer with an expression of peculiar seriousness.

"That's how you look!" Eve tells him. "When you're walking through the hallways. Just like that. Like *Who are all these midgets out here getting in my way?*"

He has this way of laughing that's soundless. You have to see his face to know that's what he's doing. "I read this thing Henry Miller wrote," he says. "'I piss on it all from considerable height.' You see me with that look on my face? That's what I'm saying. Words to get me through the valley of the shadow."

She thinks she's been accidentally trained by her father and grandfather to understand the way Sylvester talks to her. Bill seems to talk mostly to himself, and Horace talks like he's practicing a speech. Sylvester doesn't talk a lot, but when he does, he speaks directly and only to her. What he has to say has *drama* to it, like he's confiding something he hasn't told anybody else.

The pictures of Georgia O'Keefe — hands, breasts, stomach, old lady face — make Eve feel strange and secret.

Sylvester keeps quiet when they look at the nude pictures. But she thinks he steals little glances at her face.

•

She liked working through late afternoon into twilight. *Dusk* was a word that came to her when she was out there kneeling and leaning back on her heels to rest her back after a long time weeding. The air turned cool, but she was hot from the work. All around her was the smell of plants, roots, raw earth. *Dusk*, she thought. *Dusk.*

PANSIES, BEGONIAS, IMPATIENS. She was back to keeping her gardening diary. She thought it was as close as she ever came to writing in a real diary. It amused her now to see that this was where she'd taken up printing. Years ago, when she took over the flower gardens from Horace. A way to write out words so clearly no one could mistake them for anything else. DUSK, she printed. OLD WOMAN SWEAT, she set down. STINK, she wrote. And tried to sketch herself on her knees drawing her wrist across her forehead. Amused at how no one looking at her picture would have the slightest idea what it represented. No talent for making pictures. GOOD STINK, she set down, the letters almost as perfect as a typewriter's. She sketched two silly flowers beside the knees of the figure of her unrecognizable self.

•

Toulouse Lautrec isn't anyone Eve knows about, but now Sylvester's absorbed in reading about him. Little French dwarf who painted posters for dance halls. Sylvester has a single page ripped from a book. He shows it to her, a picture called "The Kiss." It makes her skip a breath. The two of them stare at it. They say nothing. "Where did you get this?" she finally asks. He shakes his head. After a moment, he picks it up off the grass where he's set it for her to see, puts it back in its envelope, back in his notebook.

She's knows she's blushing. "It's sex with him, isn't it?" She says it the way Bill would — a question not really asked, just something wondered aloud.

"They're pretty sure he couldn't do it himself," Sylvester says — and this, too, sort of randomly uttered, as if it's okay if she hears him but it's also okay if she doesn't. "Something wrong with him."

Eve isn't about to ask for details.

Sylvester leans back on his elbows. They have only a couple more minutes before they have to go in for their fourth period classes. "But the guy spent a lot of time in brothels," he says.

All afternoon she can't get that word out of her mind. Silently she sounds it. It makes her lips open, then requires her tongue to touch the roof of her mouth just behind her teeth. She looks it up. *Brothel. Wretch, scoundrel, scapegrace, good-for-nothing. An abandoned woman.*

•

Once and once only, she and Horace went outdoors. Their second anniversary. They'd gone to Café Shelburne for dinner, then come home. She knew he was in a state, and that excited her. They'd finished their bottle of wine. In the car, in the driveway, he held her and whispered what he wanted the two them to do. They went into the house without turning on the lights. Took off their clothes in the living room, streetlights shining through the windows. Anyone stopping to look might have made them out in the shadows. He was fast getting out of his clothes. She didn't look directly at him, but she felt him gazing at her the whole time she was taking off her slip, underwear, and stockings.

Then they went out into the backyard. No blanket. No shoes. Nothing but themselves. She believed him when he said they were hidden from sight — a fence, a hedge, the garage, their house, trees overhead. But there was moonlight sifting down through the leaves, plenty of it. They stood half-sideways and kissed such a long time, touched each other with their hands. She didn't want to lie down on the cold grass. He quickly got down there, then turned on his back — a blue-white slab against black nothingness — and raised his arms to her. So she lay on top of him, while they kissed some more. Then she knelt over him, raised her hips, and let him go up into her. She wasn't quite ready for him, but ready enough. Over him that way, moonlight turning them into a pewter man and woman, she could see his face clearly enough to understand he had focused on the sight of her, the feeling of her. The planet stretched out around them, the star-speckled sky and the moon soared overhead, galaxies zoomed out away even farther, and a billion people moved through their lives on islands and continents far away. He was blind, deaf, mindless to it all. Intent on her alone and only her.

She didn't come or even bother to pretend that she had. It was too cold, and the ground hurt her knees, and she couldn't make herself concentrate the way he did without even trying. It didn't matter, this was for him anyway. When he started to shout the way she knew he would, she put her hand over his mouth.

But all these years later, she hadn't forgotten what it felt like to look down on him that way, to know that in that moment she'd made him forget the world and everything in it. No future, no past, nothing. Only her. The feeling wasn't what she understood sex to be, but maybe it was something she liked better. A step beyond sex. Or off to the side.

It was just that once. She wouldn't go outside with him again. She didn't know exactly why. Maybe that feeling seemed wrong to her — realizing she was his entire consciousness. Taking her pleasure from that. It was wrong. And indoors it wasn't possible.

•

He's teaching her about the camera. Eve can tell it makes him anxious. Like she can't even hold it right. She'd stop him and say she doesn't care about learning how it works if her handling the camera is going to make him speak to her this way. But she can tell he's already trying to be patient with her. Even though it's awkward, this is the most intimate he's allowed himself to be with her since that time on the balcony. His hands touch hers as he moves her fingers to the buttons and switches on the camera. Their faces are close. His straight black hair and her slightly curly brown hair hover over the stupid little apparatus. Define a little space around them.

Clara was sitting in his study when she opened a file that contained that old picture of them at Cape May. Her sister had taken it with Horace's Brownie Hawkeye, and Horace had shown it to her before he'd taken the negative to Photo Garden to have the picture enlarged. He'd said that her sister was a genius photographer. The two of them, Clara and Horace, out in the surf. Now Clara stared so hard she could feel the ocean water rising and falling around her legs, splashing halfway up and shocking her thighs. Her mouth was slightly open; she was saying something to him — teasing him maybe. They were both so slender they looked like teenagers. His shoulders seemed broader than she'd remembered them being. But that was something she liked about him, those shoulders he held so straight. She shook her head at the sight of them. What was she saying? She couldn't bring it back. She turned the picture over. In his fine hand, he'd written, *Horace Houseman and Clara Woodford, Cape May Point, June 5, 1953.* That was a year before they were married. She was twenty years old, he was twenty-four. Later that summer he'd ask her to marry him.

Something did come back to her. The night before, they'd walked along the beach until they'd come to a lifeguard stand. They'd climbed up and sat for a long while, not really necking, because she wasn't sure about him yet. People had walked by them, murmuring greetings the way people will do when they're at the beach. Horace had noticed how many couples there were. Old and young. Even one boy and girl who couldn't have been more than ten or eleven, and Clara had refused to count them as a couple, though Horace insisted they were, you could be in love at that age even if it didn't amount to anything. Maybe more intensely in love than when you got old enough for it to amount to something. And she'd asked him, "What does that mean, 'amount to something?'" He'd laughed and said, "I guess we'll find out."

Which was when she knew that he'd made up his mind about her. Even if she hadn't made hers up about him.

·

"An Odalisque," Sylvester explained to her, "was a slave." He shows her picture after picture. Paintings and photographs, some modern, some old, of nudes on daybeds or sofas, with their backs turned or lying face up with their hands covering themselves discreetly. Eve's cheeks go warm as she looks at the pictures. A black-and-white photograph of a woman with large breasts and wearing a hat. A painting of a pleasant-faced woman with a very large derriere that makes her look like she should quickly put her clothes back on. Sylvester talks quickly. He's nervous. She knows he likes saying these names — *Boucher, Ingres, Horst, Degas, Lefebvre, Picasso, Delacroix*. He wants to do a project. "Digital Odalisque." He wants her to help. There's something naked about his face. Or maybe she's just seeing it that way because the pictures have embarrassed her. But she's seventeen. Nearly old enough to vote.

She is, however, a virgin. Very much so.

It comes to her that he is, too. That's maybe what she's seeing in his face, hearing in his voice.

She likes the idea of both of them being innocent.

She's not absolutely certain she's got it right, but she says okay to helping him.

•

Still in his study, with the Cape May photograph on the desk in front of her, Clara came around to thinking again of Horace's dirty movies. The bag of them she found in his Rise and Shine crate. She leaned forward, put her elbows on the desk, steepled her fingers as she'd seen Horace do a hundred times. Here and elsewhere. She'd never tried imitating his pose. Maybe she should go up to his closet and deck herself out in his clothes, come back and sit here this way. See what it would tell her about him. Her husband. A man who'd have a secret like that.

Since his death she hadn't revisited the day she found the movies and made herself sick looking at the pictures on their cases. She counted that day among the worst of her life. She'd called Hannah, which was a stupid thing to do. But she'd thought that since Hannah and Horace were so close, Hannah would be able to explain it to her in a way that would help. She wasn't crying or hysterical when she talked with Hannah. And Hannah was shocked, too, that her father would have those things hidden away. Though she couldn't say much because Eve was in the room when she took the call, Hannah had had sensible advice: *Talk to him*, she'd said. And Clara probably would not have talked to him about it if Hannah hadn't advised it.

So she did.

On a Saturday afternoon, she'd knocked at the door to the study. He'd invited her in, very pleasant and sort of mock formal about her visit. He gestured to the chair in front of the desk. She sat down, and she told Horace what she'd found. "Right down there," she'd pointed toward the crate, which was within kicking distance of Horace's left foot. "I know what kind of filth you have down there," she said.

She was proud of herself for her composure. Her voice had had an edge of anger to it — just the right amount — but what it hadn't revealed was how afraid she was of where the conversation might take them. Dirty movies weren't another woman. But they did, if you were the wife who found them, tell you that your husband wasn't the man you'd thought he was. The man about whom you'd thought you knew just about everything — and now this! It wasn't a huge leap from that piece of knowledge to a mutual acknowledging that maybe they shouldn't be married at all.

She didn't want that. And whatever he said after she'd accused him could take them right there in an instant. *Maybe we shouldn't be married.*

He'd sat as she was sitting right that moment. Elbows on the desk, fingers steepled against his lips.

As she'd spoken, he'd looked straight at her.

In his face, she'd seen fear, too. The same as hers. Or maybe because she felt it so powerfully in the silence that followed her little speech to him, she projected it into how she saw him. She couldn't know. But she had to trust what she thought she saw.

He never looked away from her. Never turned in the chair. He did, however — when he was sure she wasn't going to say anything more and it was his turn to speak — take his hands down from in front of his mouth.

"They're Sonny's," he said. "I tried to look at them, but

I couldn't." His voice was level. His eyes didn't move away from her face.

She let the silence stretch. Because she thought that would be a proper test. Let his words hover in the air.

Finally she said, "I don't believe you." Because it was a preposterous answer. Anyone would think so.

He let some silence pass, too. But then he said, "I think you do, Clara. I think you do believe me."

That, too, was preposterous. And she wasn't about to tell him that he was right.

After a moment, she got up and left the room and closed the door behind her.

They didn't discuss it again.

Their lives went on.

.

Sylvester lives with his grandparents, the Dusablons. It's a new house, a big one in the development just across Dorset Street from Vermont Country Club. Eve and Sylvester have driven here in Bill's old truck, which he's given to Eve for her last two years of high school. It's Friday afternoon. From school, Sylvester has directed her to the house, Dusablon Manor, he calls it. She's wondered where he lived, and now she knows. Also she knows his parents are in Montreal, and they've sent him to live with his grandparents. He doesn't say why. She doesn't ask.

He instructs her to park diagonally across from the front of the house. "That door," he tells her, pointing. Tells her she's to enter without knocking, to walk straight through the kitchen and the dining room. "You'll come to a hallway. On the other side is the living room. There'll be double doors that will be pulled to but not all the way closed. Open them, pull them to behind you. You'll see the camera on the table in front of you. I'll tell you what to do."

She sits still, heart crazy in her chest. She studies him. He won't look at her. Instead keeps his eyes fixed on the house. She wills herself not to blurt out that this scares her. That she's afraid to trust him. That it worries her, how she's made him up in her head, but the person she's made up might not be him at all. She hopes he'll look at her.

He doesn't. She knows he's deliberately evading her eyes.

"Your name is Dusablon, too," she says softly. "Like your grandparents."

He nods. "In Montreal," he says, "you say you know Sylvester Dusablon, people will know who you mean. They will give you respect. Except they will think you mean my father." He laughs softly.

This little bit of new information and his laugh make her feel no better. *I might not show up,* she thinks of telling him but doesn't. But it's how she thinks of it when he gets out of the truck. "Tomorrow," he says, giving her just the flash of a look through the passenger window before he turns to the house. Then she's driving back into town, wanting to speed but forcing herself to obey the speed limit. "I might not show up," she says aloud. She has time to decide. The thought of being a no-show and him waiting for her is a comfort. Something to help her stay calm from now until then. When she's supposed to be back at Dusablon Manor.

·

Clara knew a lot of time had passed since she first sat down here at his desk. *I'm about to dissolve,* she thought. The Cape May photo remained face down on the desk. *Horace Houseman and Clara Woodford, Cape May Point, June 5, 1961,* the reverse side told her whenever her eyes flicked down to it. As if the handwriting were some kind of message.

Clara Woodford is as dead as Horace Houseman, she thought. Deader. *What we have here is Clara Houseman,* she thought. *And who might that be?* came the question.

Something she'd seen very recently touched a switch in her mind. Made her stand up and turn to the open drawer of the file cabinet where she'd found the folder with the Cape May picture in it.

The ever orderly Horace. That folder was marked merely *Personal*—which is what made her want to see what was in it in the first place, to see what he'd designate as personal. But of course there are other folders there, but they're named. *William Collins. Eve Collins. Hannah Houseman. Hannah Collins. Clara Houseman. Clara Woodford.*

That was the one she took out now. She sat down again and set it on the desk in front of her. *Clara Woodford.*

Hesitated to open it.

But did.

Pictures of all sorts. Newspaper clippings. Snapshots. Clara's senior picture taken for the Northfield yearbook. A family portrait that must have been taken when Clara was confirmed — twelve and in a white dress with a huge collar. Clara looking proud and happy with her Northfield tennis team, each girl cradling her racquet by its head, as no tennis player would ever hold a racquet. Clara with her toes pointed and her hands raised above her head on a diving board. Clara receiving an honor at summer camp when she's nine. Clara in her prom dress. Clara at a restaurant raising a champagne glass on her twenty-first birthday. Some of these pictures were very old, but she remembered them all. As if they were portraits of a friend she hadn't seen for years.

Then this one. Which she had never seen. A black and white taken fairly close to the subject. Clara asleep. On her side. A summer nightgown, lopsided and slipped off her shoulder. The beginning of her breast. A sweet look on her face. Lips very slightly parted. It was a compelling picture. Clara in the study couldn't stop studying the sleeping Clara's bare shoulder. Her breast wasn't exposed, but the slipped-down nightgown at the center of the picture insisted that the eyes take note. There was the shape underneath the flimsy cotton. Maybe even the shadow of her nipple.

But you had to look hard to see the shadow. The girl looked sweet. It was a nice picture.

She knew it was at Cape May that same summer. He was there with her family in the big house they rented. Otherwise well-behaved, he'd been a little obnoxious with that camera, taking pictures of them all when they just wanted to enjoy themselves. He said they didn't have to smile, just to go about their business and not to mind him.

She thought she'd seen all those pictures.

This one meant he'd slipped into the bedroom she shared with her sister. Or now that she thought of it, there were two nights when her sister had gone to Philadelphia to stay with a girlfriend. This was late enough in the morning that he didn't need a flash to take it.

It was an unusual picture. Something about her own sweetness caught like that — in a way she never could have seen in her waking life — made her smile at the girl she was then. Though that girl was certainly old enough to be considered a woman.

Again, she sank into such a trance that she lost track of where she was. A memory surfaced. Waking to Horace in her room. *I was just coming to tell you breakfast is ready,* he had explained, with a wry smile on his face. She never thought to doubt him. Even though he had that camera in his hand. So he must have taken this picture just before she opened her eyes. Maybe it was the camera's snap that had wakened her. But he'd never mentioned taking it, never shown it to her.

She picked it up with her fingers — it was like something he'd stolen from her. What did it mean that he'd kept it like that? A little secret.

She can't ask him, of course, and nothing she knows about him tells her the answer. But she can't help smiling. To think she'd printed out such names for him. And for herself. From the dead he's whispered to her, *Just look at this pretty girl!*

·

It's dreamlike, following his directions for parking, entering the house, moving through these rooms. Until this moment she hasn't questioned that this is his grandparents' house. But it could belong to anyone. Kidnappers. One of those men who captures girls and chains them up in a basement torture chamber. Maybe Sylvester —

The double doors are ajar just as he said they would be. The house is so silent she thinks he must not be here as he said he would be. But those doors standing ever so slightly open reassure her. If he's here, then he must know she's out in the hallway. She stands still just a moment before opening them and stepping into —

He's there on the sofa, turned away from her, the pale skin of his back lighted extraordinarily within the shadowy living room. The curtains are pulled against the sunny spring day outside. But she can see how he's arranged the lights to make a bright oasis in the middle of the shadows. *He must have borrowed them from school, she thinks.*

"Pick up the camera," he tells her, his voice as conversational in tone as if they were chatting out on the school grounds. "It's on automatic but without the flash, and so you don't have to do anything except focus, and then snap it."

She picks it up and steps forward.

"Stand right there and take the first one," he tells her.

Through the viewfinder, he's a figure at the center of a picture. Shining length of a boy's back in the light of paradise. She focuses and snaps.

I understand this, she tells herself. It's at least half true — she does understand it, and she's so greatly relieved that he hasn't pulled some awful trick on her. Even so, that he's completely nude — this is the word that comes to her instead of the crude one, *naked* — has her in a state of mild outrage. But then she thinks, *If I had thought about it, I would have known this was what he had in mind. This was what he was telling me he wanted to do.*

"Now down there," he tells her, pointing toward the table at the foot of the sofa. "Take at least two shots each time," he says. "Take enough shots, one or two of them are bound to be good."

She knows he's talking to her to help her move through

the shock he must know she's feeling. But then she thinks, *I can do this. He knows I'm perfectly capable.*

And she is, though it jacks her blood pressure up a couple of notches when he turns over and presents the whole front of himself to the bright lights. Eve's only seen pictures of male genitalia.

"Are you okay?" he asks. "Because if you aren't, I don't mind covering up. But I'd prefer this to be straightforward."

"I'm fine," she says. Saying this helps. She even steps forward and focuses. The viewfinder helps, too. *A penis is just a penis*, she tells herself. And Sylvester's could hardly be less threatening. Pale thumb of flesh in a nest of ink-black hair. Pinkish scrotum. *There it is*, she thinks. *Nothing to it.*

Two snaps. A third for good measure.

•

On the last day of his life, Clara visited Horace at the hospice house and met her granddaughter just as she was leaving. "How is he?" Clara asked, but Eve shook her head and wasn't able to say anything to her. When Clara opened her arms, Eve moved against her and hugged her so hard Clara thought she might have to ask her to let go.

So she knew this would be the day. Eve had divorced her husband before there were children, and she'd come back to Burlington to be close to her family. Clara knew it was Horace she mostly meant by family. That child had loved her grandfather, and she thought it would probably go harder on Eve than it would on herself when Horace was gone.

Before she went in, the nurse told her she'd just helped him back into bed.

His eyes were on her when she entered the room. She took her time closing the door behind her back, holding Horace's gaze all the while. He nodded very slightly and watched her take off her coat. Didn't try to smile. Watched her while she pulled the chair up beside him and sat down.

Still, neither of them spoke. That whole week Horace hadn't been strong enough to say more than a sentence or two at a time. Less each day.

"A nice visit with Eve?" she finally asked.

He nodded. Even that was an effort.

She was quiet. It was all right to sit like this, just saying a word or two every now and then. They'd both gotten used to it.

"Do you think," he began. And swallowed.

Clara waited.

"… she'll be all right?"

She had no choice but to tell him yes. But then she said — and the thought came to her in the saying — "She's been through the worst of it. She'll be fine. She's lucky she's had you to talk to all these years."

He nodded, and she thought she saw a little smile come to his lips. His eyes were half closed. But then they opened and turned directly to her. "You?" There wasn't any sound, but there was no mistaking what he'd asked.

She bit her lip and felt herself shaking her head. "I can't answer that," she said.

And stood up and leaned down to hug him. Gently enough to tell him how much she cared for him but hard enough that he'd know how much she'd miss him.

•

Eve hasn't counted the shots, but when he asks her to hand him the camera so that he can switch it to black and white, she thinks maybe she's already taken thirty-five or forty. And then she takes almost that many again in the new round. She has no idea how much time has passed. By the time he says he thinks they should stop, she feels as if she's driven to some distant place, a journey that started yesterday afternoon and has taken most of the night.

"Do you mind waiting for me in the hall while I put on my clothes?" he asks. He's kept his place on the sofa, but he's picked up a pillow and covered himself with it.

She grins at him because she's amused that after many minutes of lying there nude in her presence, he doesn't want her to watch him get dressed. But she takes it that he's being thoughtful of her. "Not a problem," she says.

Such intense sunlight washes the hallway that it makes her blink. She feels dizzy. And stands in front of the big mirror by the front door. Considers the thoroughly unremarkable person staring back at her. Brown-haired girl in a sweatshirt and blue jeans. So-so complexion, eyes neither brown nor green. "Strong chin," her father once said of her at a holiday dinner. "And her grandmother's lovely high forehead," chimed in her grandfather. Eve's still studying her otherwise nondescript self when Sylvester steps out, blinks, even raises a hand in front of his eyes.

"I left a robe for you. Just on the chair in there. You'll see when you go in. In case you want it."

She turns to face him. A boy in jeans like tights and a fitted black shirt. Long hair black as midnight and eyes so blue they could cut you like razors. Anybody looking at him would wonder what's up with this kid. She knows her eyebrows are raised.

"Your turn," he explains.

She says nothing. Just stares at him. Knows her mouth is slightly open.

"You knew, didn't you?" he asks. He's not quite looking at her. "I thought you'd figure it out," he murmurs.

She still doesn't say anything. But now that he's said it, she realizes that she did know. At some level, like in some hidden room deep down in herself, she had already figured it out. She did know. *But I don't have to do this,* she tells herself. *Nothing can make me.*

Then he meets her eyes.

And after a moment, she nods. Takes a breath. Steps through the double doors.

.

She knows they won't bother her as long as that door is shut. Or they'll knock before they come in.

She places her index finger against the cool skin over his rib. The short, last rib at the bottom of the cage.

She takes away her finger and stands like that until a drop of water falls onto his forearm right beside her stomach. *Where is that coming from?* she thinks. Then she knows.

Half Man

STEPPING OUTSIDE WITH HIS BROTHER that first spring night called up something inside Bill. He was smiling and as full of energy as a little kid slipping out of the house to play hide-and-seek with the other little kids in their neighborhood.

"You don't have a clue, do you?" Robert asked with a worldly shrug. Bill replied, as sarcastically as possible, "Yes, big brother, of course I have a clue. This has to do with girls. Isn't that right?" And Robert nodded. But he gave Bill a condescending look because he knew that Bill didn't know the details. Bill had some crazy suspicions — like maybe Robert had arranged to set him up with Frannie Leland, who was supposed to be a slut, but then again, he couldn't imagine Robert doing something like that. He knew Robert to be a quiet fellow outside their family, not really the type even to say hello to Frannie Leland, let alone make a wild arrangement with her.

They lived on River Road, the oldest and poorest neighborhood of their village. There was also Station Street, the in-between part of town, and then Hilltop where the new people built their houses and where the doctors and lawyers and bankers moved when they'd made enough money to build new houses. Hilltop was the direction in which Robert started walking. They took the shortcut, a path off their road that had probably been carved into the hillside by old Mr. Levesque's cows before he sold his land to the O'Haras, who started building houses up there. It was a clear night with a sky full of stars. There was even a hint of barnyard fragrance in the air, though perhaps Bill just imagined that smell because of thinking about Mr. Levesque's farm. He knew about it only because their father liked talking about the old days in White Brook. No cows had been pastured on that land since before Bill and Robert were born.

Robert led Bill up the hill to a high hedge, which they followed until they came to an opening. Easy as that, they stepped into someone's yard. Robert lifted his hand and they came to a stop, facing the back of a house. A flickering light came from a TV in a downstairs room. After a moment Bill could make out the silhouette of the head of a woman watching TV. A brighter light shone in an empty kitchen. Upstairs was another light in what must have been a bathroom, but though they stood still at least five full minutes, they saw no one else. For all the movement she made, the woman in the TV room might as well have been dead.

Robert tapped Bill's shoulder and led him back through the opening in the hedge and around a garage. Now they were on an access road behind the houses along Hilltop Drive. Whenever they came to a house with a lighted window, Robert and Bill stopped on the road and stood still for some moments. Though they didn't talk, Bill nevertheless liked being out there with his brother. He and Robert ordinarily had little to do with each other — over everybody in the family Bill was closest to his sister Katie, who sort of worshipped him — but now he had this peculiar sense of Robert's being a lonely boy who might have appreciated his company more than he'd imagined. The night had cooled down considerably, there was a three-quarters moon showing just above the horizon, and the sky was huge and just amazing with its stars. The rear ends of houses had begun to bore Bill, so that he was paying more attention to the way the moon shone on the grass, how the dark trees made darker shadows, and how the town made a pattern of lights down in the valley. Then Robert tapped his shoulder again and pointed toward an upstairs window. They made their way through a metal gate into the back yard of someone's house.

Upstairs, behind the scrim of a curtain was the profile of a girl or a woman whose shoulders were bare but who seemed to be wearing a slip or a bra. She sat — perhaps on a bedside — and held quite still, either lost in thought or more likely studying her reflection in a mirror, which wasn't visible to the boys. Their view from the cool darkness below her was tantalizing. Though her hair was short and dark, they couldn't make out her face enough to know how old she was or if she was pretty. Had her shoulders not been bare, Robert and Bill probably would have gone on their way.

Suddenly — as if she'd realized they were outside staring in at her — she stood up, stepped directly to the window, and pulled down the shade. In the two or three seconds Bill had seen the front of her, he realized that it was a bra she had on and that she was one of their mother's friends. If he thought long enough, he'd probably remember her name, but he didn't really want to put his mind to that task.

"Ha!" Robert said under his breath. He gave no sign he'd recognized the woman. "What do you think of that, Billie boy?"

"I don't know," Bill whispered. That was the truth. To see a lady in her bra was a thrill, but it was horrifying to know she was somebody he might run into in town the next afternoon, somebody he'd have to speak to politely if he happened to be in the company of their mother.

"That's nothing," Robert said, turning back toward the access road. "We can do lots better than that. We'll finish doing the scouting, find out which places are good. Then it'll get really interesting."

Without saying anything, Bill followed him. He was happy enough being in his brother's company, though it began to bother him that he probably wasn't getting what Robert thought he should be getting out of the experience. He wondered if he would ever get it or if maybe there was something wrong with him. And if he did actually get the right thing, how would he know he had gotten it? Would Robert realize and tell him that it had happened?

For the next several nights, Bill thought of making an excuse to Robert about why he couldn't go out. At the same time, the outings began to seem a personal test, something he had to do, aside and apart from what Robert thought he was supposed to gain from it. As Robert had prophesied, their scouting did lead them to narrow down the number of houses they visited. The tour became more interesting. They witnessed several ladies undressing and slipping their nightgowns over their heads. They saw Stacy Mercugliano sitting on her bed in her underpants, but since Stacy was only eleven years old, Robert turned away without saying anything and Bill felt embarrassed. They moved on to Station Street, and they even scouted out a couple of houses on River Road, but they didn't want to be caught spying in their own neighborhood. So it was when they went back up the path through the former cow pasture to Hilltop that they found what Bill apparently needed to see: Nadine O'Hara.

Because her father and grandfather were the men who started developing that part of town, Nadine lived in one of the first houses built in Hilltop. She was a junior, a couple of years older than Bill but a year younger than Robert. And Nadine was a geek. That's how everybody in school thought of her — a tall, drab girl who wore glasses, didn't wash her hair, and got A's from all her teachers even though she was too shy to ever do more than mumble an answer to a direct question. She was in their sister Katie's class, and even Katie — who had to be one of the shyest and kindest people in their whole school — would have sadly agreed that Nadine O'Hara was a geek.

Something Bill learned from those outings with Robert was that households have habits. More or less at the same time each night, the people of a house eat dinner, wash the dishes, sit down to watch TV, turn out the lights, and go to bed. At the O'Haras', night in, night out, they did it by the numbers — TV off at 10:30, lights out, Mrs. O'Hara trudged upstairs to join her husband in the master bedroom. Downstairs, at the opposite end of the house at 10:30, Nadine sat at her desk doing her homework until she heard her mom call goodnight to her. Years ago the O'Haras had hired an architect to design their house, and maybe if he'd laid it out differently, Robert and Bill wouldn't have had such a clean line of sight from the backyard shrubbery through Nadine's shades-up downstairs bedroom window. But then if the house had been laid out differently, maybe Nadine would have never gotten started with what she did. Evidently she had known for some time that once her mom trundled up to bed, she was not going to be disturbed.

Bill knew a little something about private rituals invented and refined by people who think they're alone. Because he and Katie spent so much time with each other at home, and because there were three kids in their family, he almost never got to be by himself. From his first moment of spying on Nadine, he was envious of the privacy she believed she had.

She stood up from her desk and stretched — a long, luxurious stretch. To Nadine it probably meant *At last I'm free to do what I really want to do.* And to Bill it meant *Now I'm going to see, I'm really going to see!*

Reaching far back into her closet, Nadine removed a large navy-blue shirt on a hanger — surely it was a man's shirt, and Bill had in mind that it must have been corduroy. She took it off the hanger and arranged it on her bed, unbuttoned and facing upward. She moved quickly and efficiently. From the top of her bed she removed two regular pillows and two smaller ones, setting them carefully onto the open shirt. She stuffed the smaller pillows into each sleeve, pulled the sides of the shirt up over the regular pillows, and began buttoning and molding the thing into the shape of a torso — that of a man with an abnormally thick chest and shoulders. When she had it shaped as she wanted, she tied up the shirt-tails to hold the pillows in place. Then she propped what she'd made up against the bed's headboard, turned on the lamps at either side of her bed, and turned off the ceiling and desk lights. Removing her glasses, she set them on the desk, quickly stripped down to her underpants, stretched a thin arm to pick up one of the shirt-cuffs, smiled, mock-curtsied, and spoke to the headless shirt. From having watched her lips at least half a dozen nights, Bill was certain that her words were, "Would you care to dance?"

Nadine's half man never refused her invitation. She held him close to her and, stealing occasional glances into the mirror over her dresser, she moved slowly and gracefully around her bedroom. The waltz she danced required the partners to chafe their chests against each other. Gradually Nadine's steps slowed and shortened until there came a point when she stopped moving her feet and stood still, pressing her partner against her chest and pushing the thing down her body and against her pelvis while she stood there shuddering. Finally she took a deep breath, flung her bed-covers aside, collapsed backward onto her bed with her pillow man, and quickly stretched one way and then the other to snap off the lamps on either side of her bed.

That was it — the show was over. Robert and Bill weren't tempted to step closer to the window to see if Nadine disassembled her pillow man and used his parts to cushion her head or curled around him and held him close as she went to sleep. By silent agreement, lights out in her room was their signal to turn away to walk down the hill to their own part of town. To himself as he grew older, Bill argued that he and Robert did no harm to Nadine because they were never caught, and she never knew they were out there. Eventually the two boys stopped going to her window.

One night it rained hard enough to keep them from going out. The next night Robert gave Bill a look and said he had some reading he wanted to do, he thought maybe he'd give Bill's education a rest. This was around the middle of June, full summer just coming on. Bill had nothing he wanted to read, and he doubted that Robert did either, he'd probably just had enough of seeing the same show every night. But that wasn't the case for Bill. He was restless, and he hadn't gotten enough of Nadine. So when the hour came around, on his own he left the house and took the path up through the field to Hilltop. Without Robert walking ahead of him to lead the way, he felt much more illicit.

From the first night he'd witnessed it, Nadine's ritual had aroused Bill. It must have aroused Robert, too, but they'd never spoken of that and had in fact discreetly avoided looking at each other while they were watching her. Because Robert had always been there before and because he'd always behaved modestly (so far as Bill knew), Bill had never even brushed his hand against the outside of his pants. But without Robert there, it was natural enough—it was almost an innocent act—for Bill to grab his erection at the moment when Nadine removed her blouse and dropped her skirt to the floor. And it wasn't even a decision to unzip and to take his cock out of his pants, he just did what occurred to him to do.

For the rest of his life, it would amuse Bill to remember that he and Nadine came together. They had a mutual orgasm — it's just that he was the only one who knew there were two of them. And that's what put an end to his life as a backyard spy. At the exact moment he fired off his little barrage of sperm into the O'Haras' pachysandra bed, Bill knew he wasn't coming back. It wasn't so much because of shame as it was Nadine's face. Geek though she may have been, when Nadine took off her clothes, she was a pretty girl. She had shapely breasts, a dancer's long legs and arms, and her back was a wonder of curves, dimples, ridges, and ripples. Without her glasses and with her face aiming to please her pillow man, she just wasn't the same little geek of their high school hallways and classrooms. Still—and Bill didn't know why this was the case — it had been mostly her body he'd gazed at when Robert was with him. The one and only night he came to her window by himself, it wasn't her body but her face that held his attention.

Maybe because the stopping point of her dance put her face in his line of sight, Bill couldn't break away from staring at her eyes and her mouth. Her excitement and his simultaneously began to crescendo. She appeared to be returning his gaze, but of course she wasn't. Literally those hooded eyes of hers were seeing the reflection in her window of herself and her dressed-up pillow model; however, what she must have been seeing in her mind was the back of her big-chested dancing partner. From a distance of maybe ten feet, Nadine and Bill were staring directly at each other, and in their separate journeys they were perfectly synchronized. Yet he might as well have been standing in China. The distance between them, however, was not what disturbed him.

He saw himself in her face. What had taken him to that window in the first place was the need to see the other sex— to see his opposite. But that little jolt of Nadine's jaw muscles and gritting of her teeth showed him exactly what he felt in his own body and mind as his ejaculation rose up in his groin and shot out of him. Bill felt tricked — tricked by whatever had driven him to be there doing what he'd done. Nadine, of course, was just as driven as he was. But at least she was seeing only what she wanted to see — her imagination held her in its spell. At the very moment Bill least wanted to see himself, a mirror sprang up in front of him. Years later, he'd think it was like paying to get into a strip show, then suddenly seeing *himself* up there on the bar, grinding to the drumbeat, undulating and licking his lips.

Well, of course, he was only a boy, and the situation — standing in Nadine O'Hara's back yard with his thirteen-year-old dick in his hand — didn't exactly encourage philosophy. But with his whole being Bill felt it — *This was not what he wanted! This was not it!*

Hannah Outside In

SHE ENJOYED READING WITH HER MOTHER, CLARA. Well before she entered kindergarten, Hannah was capable of reading, with a little help, a first-page article in the *Burlington Free Press*. And she enjoyed playing board games with her father, Horace, who had a gift for explaining subtle or complicated principles of the games in such a way that Hannah immediately understood them. They moved quickly from Chutes and Ladders and Go Fish to checkers and dominoes. When she was a second-grader, Horace introduced her to chess and was gratified to see that she was more than ready for the challenge. Because she so loved the pieces — and the look of them on the board, the phalanx of Pawns guarding the King, Queen, Knights, Bishops, and Castles — chess instantly became her favorite game. Of course her father was the only person with whom, as a second-grader, she could play it.

> With me, what you see is definitely not what you get. I
> never really meant to do it, but I just started out
> cultivating an appearance that conceals the truth about
> who I am. So far as I know, from infanthood on, I was

working on the mask. I heard on NPR the other day
that autistic people really like systems, and maybe this
is my form of autism — perfecting the system of an
inside person and an outside person. Or God knows,
maybe I've got some flukey version of Tourette's where
all the tics and cursing and inappropriate sentiments
are on the inside. Whatever it is with me, I've evidently
polished up the outside so well that even my family
members don't have a clue.

As she moved through elementary and middle school,
Hannah continued to enjoy being around her parents, because they treated her with respect she received from no one
else and most especially not from her peers. Clara had been
thirty when she gave birth to their daughter, Horace nearly
forty. They cherished the child perhaps more than they might
have if she'd arrived when they were five or ten years younger.
Horace and Clara were decorous people, not inclined to be
invasive in their relationships with others and particularly
wary of bullying their daughter's consciousness to mold her
to their liking. Also, from her first days out of the womb,
Hannah impressed them as a creature of integrity — a rare
being, as if a cardinal or a dolphin had taken up residence
with them. They merely wanted their daughter to become
what she seemed destined to be, a bright and capable person.
A woman of substance. "She's already perspicacious," Horace
told Clara the night after Hannah had first beaten him at
chess. "When she grows up, she may turn out to be a female
Gandhi." "God forbid," murmured Clara from her side of the
bed, and they both chuckled.

For one thing, when it comes to other people, I have intense likes and dislikes. And you talk about snap judgments — I'm Queen Snap herself. I meet somebody and instantly I've got an opinion, like I just read the biography of this person. Sometimes I try to figure out what it is about somebody that impresses me one way or the other. It's not like I'm correct in what I decide — plenty of times I've thought so-and-so was an angel sent down from heaven only to find out that so-and-so is actually a full-time employee of the devil. Even then I have a hard time changing my mind. But I did figure out that my parents are pretty much my measure of everybody I meet. I never went through that stage of rebellion some kids go through, where they want to be around anybody who's *not* like their parents. My parents listened to me, they talked to me, they helped me, they made me understand that no matter what I did, I was okay with them. So if I'm a screwed-up person, it's not my parents' fault. I'm sure of that. I'm also pretty sure that I've done only one awful thing in my life, but it wasn't because of any harm Clara or Horace did to me.

The adult Hannah found most exciting was her father's friend Sonny Carson. A computer science professor at Saint Michael's College, Sonny Carson had a charismatic personality and a reckless way of talking. He gave the impression of knowing all there was to know about contemporary culture — and he seemed especially astute in his understanding of how digital technology was likely to globalize U.S. culture. Sonny Carson also had a pleasantly caustic attitude toward the humanities, in the value of which Horace Houseman passionately believed. The conversations of those two men — Sonny a word-slinging iconoclast and Horace a skilled rhetorician — were stirring to Hannah, not only for the sound of the language but also for the conflict and affection that constantly played between the two men.

When Horace and Sonny were on their second cocktail and just warming up to their favorite topic— the Catholic Church — for me it was like the circus had come to town. I wanted to be nowhere but sitting near enough to them to take it all in but not close enough to distract them. I knew they were, at least to some extent, performing for me, but I'm pretty sure they understood that most of what they said was going right over my head. So the best part was when they forgot about me — I learned to have my nose in a book and maybe to be sitting on the floor or off to the side when they were in these sessions. Sonny and my father didn't really disagree with each other all that much about the Catholic Church. They both thought it was pretty awful for the way it harbored child abusers, preached against birth control and abortion, wouldn't let women into the priesthood, didn't tolerate homosexuality — all of that stuff. But my father stood up for the positive influence of the church in the advancement of literacy and human rights. And Sonny Carson liked nothing better than going off on "the real story of the church and human rights." I must have been listening to those old guys carry on that argument from the time I was about seven or eight, and I went right on eavesdropping on them when I got into high school. The odd thing was that even as much as I adored my father, I was pretty much on Sonny's side of the debate. The Catholic Church was a total mess, yes indeed, I was right there with Sonny on that. Of course I knew almost nothing about Catholicism, but the way Sonny described the church — making everything look pretty on the outside but hiding "a plethora of sins, a veritable nest of snakes," as he put it, on the inside — made me understand what was going on with me personally. I don't know why, but I found it a comfort that the way I understood myself to be could be described by Sonny talking about something else. And even though he tried to make it sound awful, I wasn't put off by that. To me a nest of snakes was pretty darned exciting, and I didn't mind imagining that I had something like that inside me. As long as I didn't have to tell anybody.

Thus the child, the girl, even the very young woman into whom Hannah Houseman was evolving, received a remarkable (even if somewhat peculiar) education in academic discourse. She heard two very intelligent and informed men speak with passion and wit on subjects that fascinated them. For them, those exchanges were an entertainment. They couldn't have imagined that for Hannah their conversations were deeply compelling.

As a very young child, I thought a lot about doing painful things to people. I don't know how far back it goes, but the first time it surfaced was at a birthday party my mother took me to before I even went to kindergarten. At this party, there was an unnaturally pretty little girl, my age, my size, but with very dark hair and eyebrows and skin so pale it made me think of vanilla ice cream. The instant I saw her, I was infatuated with that child. Greta was her name. Until then I'd never experienced anything so intense as what I felt for Greta in the first hours of my being around her. And she seemed to take an interest in me. She wasn't a talker, but she gave me a smile that made me blush. When it was time for cake and ice cream, I sat beside her. I picked up her arm — she allowed me, curious, I suppose, to see what I was up to. I studied that arm for a moment — the loveliest pattern of tiny blades of dark hair angled across its creamy surface. Then I lifted the arm to my mouth, put my teeth to its warm surface, and began to bite. At first I was so gentle that Greta must have thought I was giving her a special kind of kiss. But I gradually increased the pressure of my teeth into her skin, all the while watching her face to see how I was affecting her. All these many years later, I see that moment as vividly as if I'd just lived it this morning — Greta's angel face changing from curiosity to worry to serious concern to outright horror and outrage. The funny thing was that Greta didn't think to pull her arm away from me. She certainly could have, but she didn't. For a long moment she was collaborating with me in my project of hurting her. But then of course she shrieked and cried, and the grown-ups separated us, and I began to realize how much disgrace I'd brought down upon myself. My mother was very embarrassed, but she wasn't seriously angry at me, because she was certain I was too young to know any better. She was wrong about that. I knew.

And I learned a couple of questionable lessons from
the incident. One, biting Greta came out of the passion
I felt for her and watching her face as I increased the
level of her pain was the thrill of my life up to
that point. Two, I didn't ever again want to get
caught doing something like that.

Hannah Houseman was ideally prepared — or educated
— to encounter Professor Jerome Cummings of the Religion
Department at Skidmore College. Thirty-five years old, Professor Cummings was a relatively young man for a scholar
but because of his disheveled clothes, his beard, and his un-
kempt hair, he looked much older. His social manner was
mousy, irritatingly egoless, absent-minded, only marginally
articulate and/or coherent, and geeky. But he'd gotten tenure for two compelling reasons: In the classroom, he spoke
with such brilliance that the number of Religion majors at
Skidmore had tripled since his arrival on campus, and his
one published book, *Columcille and the Cult of Saints: Con-
textualizing the Vassals of God*, was famous for being a spell-
binding treatment of a boring topic. He was about to be
promoted to full professor. As a junior, Hannah sought and
obtained Professor Cummings's permission to enroll in his
seminar, "Seeing the Sacred: Vision in Early and Medieval
Christianity."

Jerry Cummings patiently listened to me explain why
he ought to give me, a junior, a place in his senior
seminar. I was most certainly bullshitting him, but
I did so in the grand tradition of Horace Houseman
and Sonny Carson, men who generated intellectual

conversation as a recreational act and loved long but grammatical sentences. Cummings had agreed to talk to me about his seminar, but everybody knew he only took seniors. In that year I was into the heroics of despair. I'd hoped that college would be the place where I found classmates and professors who would excite me, but by Thanksgiving break of my freshman year, I realized that hadn't happened and wasn't going to. By applying only to small colleges within easy driving distance of Burlington, I'd denied myself access to the very people who might have saved me. Had I gone to Columbia or BU or NYU, I'd have had a better chance. The kind of person I wanted to be around went to big schools in the city—I figured that out my freshman year, when it was too late. But I'd resigned myself to the oblivion of Skidmore and Saratoga Springs, I'd developed an attitude of making the best of my isolation and boredom but doing so in the spirit of irony. I knew Professor Cummings wasn't going to let me in, but I'd reasoned that it would be cowardly not to ask him. Short, squatty little guy wearing just about the worst clothes I'd ever seen on a grown man, he seemed to me, in that first meeting in his office, a living symbol of my disappointment in college life. I had nothing to lose, and so I just sat there and improvised on the Catholic Church—Horace and Sonny's old beloved topic. I had looked up a saint or two, because everybody knew Professor Cummings loved to talk about the saints. I threw a fact or two into my monologue. I made it clear that I was a serious atheist. "Belief of any kind," I remember saying to him, "seems to me both simple-

minded and irresponsible in the twenty-first century."
My stifled hopes rose exponentially when I noticed
a little smile squirming around under the professor's
beard. But then he raised his hand to signal to me that
I'd said enough. I knew he was about to tell me that he'd
love to have me in his seminar next year when I got to
be a senior. He'd thank me for coming in to talk to him,
and blah blah blah. I was standing up and reaching for
my backpack to make my exit when he said, "I'll be
happy to have you in my class, Hannah. Bring me the
form from the Registrar's office, and I'll add your name
to the class list." I got out of his office fast, so as not to
make a fool out of myself. I also managed to thank him
without getting down on my knees and trying to kiss
his hand.

Second semester of her junior year, Hannah requested
and received a single. She was relieved to be out from under
the oppression of a roommate. Disappointed though she was
in the intellectual — and though she wouldn't have said so,
the *spiritual* — climate of Skidmore, Hannah nevertheless
exerted herself in her studies and tried to be a good citizen
in class. She didn't try to be unfriendly around her peers,
but she found it difficult to become interested — and stay
interested — in them. If she'd followed her real wishes, she'd
have driven back to Burlington every weekend to be around
her father and hope to get lucky and sit in on one of his conversations with Sonny Carson. She was homesick for their
"palaver," as she called it when she was teasing one or the
other of those gentlemen about their habit of extended and
intimate social debate.

When he walked into our seminar room, Jerry Cummings underwent a transformation that was like nothing I'd ever witnessed. It was the astonishing fairy tale of Skidmore College — every Thursday afternoon at 3:30 the troll transmogrified himself into a prince. Since I saw it occur only once a week, I never quite got used to it. I swear I got chills the first meeting of the seminar. The man shuffled in, sat down at the head of the table, arranged books and papers in front of him, looked up — straight across the room more or less in the direction of the blackboard on the far wall — and began to speak in this voice that you couldn't really imagine until you'd heard it. Baritone, yes — which shocked me because from our conversation in his office, I'd have figured him for a tinny and monotonous tenor — but also sonorous and musical, a voice that filled the room and resonated around each one of us. The closest approximation I can think of is Bach's suites for solo cello. What was weirdest of all was that I felt like Jerry was speaking to me personally. Of course he wasn't — and his eyes only occasionally strayed toward me — but that's what it felt like, and only after I'd been out of the classroom for a day or so was I able to be objective and tell myself that everybody in the seminar must have felt the same way — *Professor Cummings has singled me out today, and he really wants me to understand these ideas.* That first afternoon, he talked about Saint Francis and the painting called *Saint Francis in the Desert* that's in the Frick Museum. Saint Francis holds his arms away from his sides, looking upward and receiving the Stigmata. Jerry talked about the way that we've sentimentalized Saint Francis, how we all have this general idea about Saint Francis and the animals, birds on his shoulders, a deer nibbling something from his hand, but that it takes a painter like Bellini to remind us of his suffering and isolation. Jerry talked about how the imagination is the only way we can understand the idea of a saint or a god and especially the kind of God proposed by Christianity but how we resist what the imagination can tell us. He said suffering and isolation are just words until something sparks the imagination. He talked about that painting hanging in the Frick — and he had a book that he passed around so we could see *Saint Francis in the Desert.* He talked about going to see it and standing there in the museum gallery and facing the painting until he just lost track of time. He said he noticed people edging away from him and he wondered why they were doing that until he realized he was holding his arms out and making these little moaning noises. He even made the moaning noises for us, and we laughed softly. "I'm certain that before that day I'd never really grasped the kind of internal torture that Giovanni Bellini made so real in that Saint Francis." He paused as if he were searching for words that would get through to us. "And even that was just a glimpse," he said slowly, "of what it felt like to be utterly alone and filled with almost unbearable aching." The rest of that class was more of a musical experience for me — Jerry's voice made sounds that comforted me, and he even invited discussion so that there could be a kind of community chorus, but I confess that I took in very little of what he or anyone else had to say. I was just so certain

that Jerry had been talking to me about my life and that
he wanted me to understand that much of what I felt
was pain, even if I was afraid to call it that. He knew I
was all alone with feelings that I could hardly bear.

Hannah Houseman's life had been one of high privilege.
It's fair to say that on the surface, she was advantaged in every possible way. More to the point, she had undergone sufficient moral evolution to understand her good fortune and
to feel some responsibility toward others. To her credit, she
was grateful that she'd not been burdened with beauty, as a
fair number of her classmates (both women and men) were,
but that her appearance was pleasant and her personality,
when she wished it to be so, was appealing.

Vassals of God galvanized my life. Suddenly everything
made sense. Not only did Jerry Cummings speak to me
more deeply than anyone ever had, the reading for the
seminar also showed me issues I hadn't realized were
at the center of my thinking. I hardly knew what to do
with myself. It took will power to give much attention
to my other courses, but I did double and triple
readings of the assignments for Vassals of God. In
retrospect, I see that I underwent a conversion experience, but at the time I didn't see it that way. I continued
to consider myself an atheist but one who had opened
up to what Christian theology had to say. This was fool-
ish, I suppose, because I actually took up praying, my
own personal version — *I want to be humble on my walk
this morning, I want Horace and Clara to take some joy
from this day, I want to pay even closer attention to*

Professor Cummings in class tomorrow, that kind of thing.
I might as well have been chanting *Lord have mercy
upon me, Christ have mercy upon me,* etc. But real prayer
offended me because it seemed completely selfish. I
also knew it offended Jerry Cummings because he as
much as said so in class. But when I stepped into that
seminar room, I was as much an acolyte as any Catholic
nun ever was, striving to believe ever more deeply. In
reality, I entered that room clothed and normal looking,
guarded in my expression, reserved in my comments,
but figuratively, I was utterly naked and opened to Jerry
Cummings, filled with desire for him to fill me with the
truth toward which my entire life, up until that point,
had been directed. When I left that classroom, I felt
as if I walked with a soft nimbus of light all
around me. I was twenty years old.

The change in Hannah was quickly evident to her parents. Her letters and telephone calls were filled with news about the Vassals of God seminar. Horace and Clara were pleased that their daughter had suddenly become passionate about her studies. But they were both concerned that Hannah might be vulnerable to what could turn out to be another of those crackpot cults. Horace even checked out Professor Jerome Cummings by way of the academic grapevine and was reassured by the news that the young scholar was brilliant but quirky and harmless. And Hannah was quick to assure him that if anything she was more skeptical than ever of all religions. It was simply a matter of her having discovered a way to utilize the superior intellectual offerings of religious thinkers. In a late-evening phone conversation she told Clara "You don't have to be religious to get something worthwhile out of Thomas Aquinas and Marcus Borg." Clara thought her daughter sounded so sensible that she instructed herself to stop worrying. Hannah would be fine.

Though I've done it only that once, during my Vassals of God spring, I know how suddenly one can step into an alternative life. That spring it was as easy as slipping a new dress over my head. Or taking off an old dress and everything else and walking out into the world without any clothes at all. One can do that, of course but one will be quickly stopped and very likely institutionalized. In my case, I felt as if I'd found — or stumbled upon — a way to give myself over to the whole force of life. Best of all, I could be naked like that and no one would notice, no one would know. Except, of course Jerry Cummings, who — and I don't think I was making this up — knew and understood what was happening to me. He was my true and only witness. The papers I wrote for him and the weekly journal entries we passed in for his inspection received extensive and warm responses from him. He annotated our manuscripts in a tiny spidery handwriting that my classmates joked and complained about. My impression was — and this may have been delusion — that he took special pains with what he wrote to me, because even with a fast glance at his little clumps of paragraphs in the margins, I understood every single word. But I found myself saying less and less in our seminar discussions. I was aware of having too much to say, and if I got started, stopping would not be easy. For a while I had enough

judgment to know that it would not be in my best
interests to alert my classmates to the intensity that
informed my every moment.

In fact, her classmates and acquaintances seemed to notice very little change in Hannah. All along, she hadn't been
someone who stood out in a crowd or even a small group.
True, she had impressed one or two students and professors with her ability — demonstrated only occasionally — to
speak articulately and with unusual poise. But another skill
she'd perfected from childhood was taking on the appearance of everyone else. Instinctively she was a social chame-
leon, so much so that she probably wasn't even aware of the
extent to which she chose her clothes, her speech patterns,
how she wore her hair, even her manner of walking and her
posture while sitting and standing, with an eye to camou-
flaging herself. Skidmore of course had its nuances of style
practiced only by Skidmore students, but if there had been a
class or a test in such matters, Hannah would have been the
one who received an A+. She had no particular loyalty to,
or even liking for, Skidmore, but no one would have looked
more quintessentially Skidmore than she did.

It's my opinion that I was out of control no more than
about ten minutes. A shrink would probably say that I
started losing control at the beginning of the semester
and that I didn't start regaining it until late in the summer. But I think the real insanity was just this one
episode. In the seminar, we were talking about the
Gospels and their differing accounts of the crucifixion.
Jerry had begun to speak about the resistance in our

contemporary culture to Christ's agony on the cross, and how that resistance stands in stark contrast to the values and attitudes of those who actually witnessed it. "For most of them, it was entertainment," he said in his softest, deepest classroom voice. Then he stopped speaking, as he sometimes did when he wanted us to absorb what he'd said. And I was off. I had had no intention of speaking, and though I was surprised to hear myself start talking, I was pleased to note that my voice was calm and that my demeanor seemed appropriate. Worrisome, though, was that I felt as if I'd suddenly spiked a fever so high that it might kill me if it lasted very long. "If there were a case to be made that Christ was divine rather than human," I began, "it might be that that level of slow and excruciating pain, inflicted for the sake of a public spectacle, is just about the only force that could cut through the spiritual deadness that victimizes us more and more as civilization removes pain from our lives and injects pleasure in its place. I don't know anything about the kind of suffering that goes on all over the world, but let's just say that a child starving to death in Africa is not likely to think Christ's agony is more exceptional than his own pain and despair. But to the people who are walking around Mall of America, or our parents at home, or even the kids downstairs in the snack bar right now, Christ on the Cross is just about the only thing that could stop them in their tracks. I personally know a girl who put six thousand dollars worth of clothes on her father's credit card before she came here to start her freshman year. Every detail of our lives works against our taking in that story. Not a single one of us wants to hear it, and I put myself at the head of the line of those of us who want to shut down anybody who starts preaching about it. But you know what? It won't go away. No matter what drugs, what incredibly expensive houses and cars and hotels and casino and spas and parties and food we come up with, here comes Christ on the Cross, sneaking in under the doors and through the seams around the window sills. I understand why evangelists and even serious theologians are ready to buy into Christ's being part of God. But that's just another way of defending ourselves against Christ on the Cross. Make him part of God, and it just doesn't hurt nearly as much. It's a story about a man!" I banged my fist — lightly — on the seminar table and went on. Sweat came onto my forehead and oozed out of my scalp. I blinked away what I suppose were tears. I sat perfectly still. I looked into my classmates' eyes. More than once I looked straight into the face of Jerry Cummings. Each time I did so, I understood — even though I resisted the thought — that he adored me and that he wished I would shut up.

If she'd had a close friend or family member in whom she confided, Hannah would have said that by upbringing, temperament, and intellectual inclination, she was undersexed. She had no such person. Within herself, she understood her restrained manner and appearance as the way she kept the monster under control. Both Clara and Horace Houseman, though certainly not prudes, firmly believed that sex was a private matter. Clara had carried out the obligatory discussion of sex with Hannah not long after her eleventh birthday, an occasion that embarrassed both of them — though not so much that they weren't able to joke about it a few years later. But Hannah's period didn't arrive until she was nearly fourteen, her figure remained "understated," a word Clara used for it that was a comfort to Hannah during her high school years. Hannah wasn't so much shocked as puzzled by the brazen appearance and behavior of many girls in her classes. She understood the point of wanting sexual attention, and she supposed that maybe — if her figure ever became a little less understated — there'd come a time when she wanted boys to look at her as they did the most audacious girls of her class. And she did always have a low-simmering interest in this boy or that one — there'd be one whom she found herself observing with particular care. But her interior life had a way of processing those boys through her imagination and then tossing them out. She was reluctant even to start daydreaming about a new one because pretty quickly she'd see that boy's face twisting up when she'd handcuffed his hands behind his back and begun twisting a piece of flesh from his chest or the thick part of his shoulder or even his thigh until she made him yelp. The monster she knew herself to be could take a perfectly decent boy — who'd done her no harm whatsoever, probably couldn't even have imagined hurting her — and in an evening's pre-sleep fantasizing turn him into a sniveling crybaby. It was, Hannah joked to herself, a hateful magic trick. She'd wake the next morning filled with contempt for a boy whom yesterday she'd thought pretty attractive. Mercifully she rarely remembered her dreams, and the boys themselves didn't have a clue as to what had transpired between them and her monster.

Jerry Cummings rode with me on the last leg of my trip into crazyland. At the time it didn't occur to me that he, too, had entered a heightened state of consciousness. I just thought that he had the capacity to understand me. That he was attuned to me for reasons mostly having to do with my father and Sonny Carson's accidentally having trained me to carry out intellectual discourse while I was still a child. That his brain had in it that whole library full of theology and church history and probably just about everything that had ever been written about saints and martyrs and religious phenomena, and he appreciated my excitement in discovering all that. What didn't occur to me was that he found me romantically or sexually attractive. He was married and a professor; I was a student who didn't even date. He was a grown-up, and while, at the age of twenty I wasn't legally a kid, I'd only taken a few practice runs at thinking of myself as an adult. I confess that I had received so little of that carnally charged kind of male attentiveness that I probably wouldn't have recognized it, no matter who it came from. And bless his heart, Jerry wasn't somebody who had any sexual presence whatsoever. Sweet, smart, funny, exciting in the classroom, but sexy? Not even slightly. Then all of a sudden — Shazam! My Christ on the Cross monologue in the seminar room set us in motion, and our destination was so inevitable we knew we had no choice. I thought that then. I think it now.

After she'd finished speaking about Christ on the Cross and the girl on her hall who owned twenty-two cashmere sweaters, Hannah walked straight from the seminar to her dorm room, locked the door, and sat at her desk until dark. Then she went to bed. She hadn't been able to sleep, cry, or eat. The one course of action she could imagine was going to Professor Cummings and apologizing. She focused on that vision so intently that when she actually carried it out, the experience seemed no more real to her than any one of the dozens of times she'd imagined while curled under the covers of her dormitory bed. Shortly after daylight that morning, she was the only person on the campus when she walked across it to the Humanities building, but she didn't question the dreamlike quality of the emptiness all around her. She had no words for what it felt like to be herself in those moments, but if she had tried to put the feeling into language, it would have been something like *What is is what has to be.* Fate itself was moving her, showing her the way, opening up the future with each step she took. When she finally came to it, Professor Cummings's office door was closed, though the thought never occurred to her that he might not be in there. When she knocked, she heard a soft noise that she took to be his directive to her to come in. But when she tried the door, it was locked. She heard scuffling. Then suddenly the door was open, and Professor Cummings was there, his eyes red and his clothes disheveled. The two of them began to speak almost in unison, "I'm sorry…" But then a clumsy pause clunked down between them, and they stood like wooden figures carved on a clock on some European church steeple or a tableau of lifelike museum statues entitled *Encounter of the Wretched.* Indeed they'd neither of them changed clothes from the previous day. Neither of them had thought to look in a mirror for many hours. It was just after 6:30

a.m., though neither of them had any idea what the time was. Professor Cummings stepped aside. Hannah stepped through the door. He closed it behind her, turning to her as she turned to him.

> I hadn't imagined physical contact with Jerry
> Cummings, maybe because I'd been afraid of what I
> might do to him in the chambers of my psyche. More
> likely was that I just didn't think of him in that way, and
> I'd probably have been grossed out by the thought of my
> body touching his body. So I can't account for the jolt
> of energy and excitement — arousal, I might as well call
> it — that hit me when we actually put our arms around
> each other. However unattractive he might have been
> to me before that moment, the spell I was in converted
> him into something else entirely. Or — what can I say?
> — maybe I'd denied desire for so long and with such
> determination that all it took was the spark of my body
> pulled hard against his, and I flamed up like a stack
> of logs soaked in gasoline.

"Shouldn't you leave a note or something?" Hannah asked him. It was a Friday, and she knew he had afternoon classes. He shook his head, looked directly at her, and let her see him straight on.

> Face of a saint, face of a fanatic, face of a homeless
> person — Jerry was really and truly a fright — his hair,
> beard, and clothes looked as if someone had come along
> and jerked pieces of him out of place. He widened
> his eyes at me, as if my appearance startled him,

too. Looking at each other like that just elevated the
intensity of what was pushing us to move, go forward,
fling ourselves into the future as hard as we could.

By 7:30 that morning they were in Hannah's car heading
for the Albany airport. Jerry knew there'd be a Holiday Inn
or some kind of motel out there, and of course he was right
about that.

When Horace and Clara and I had traveled, we'd stayed
in such rooms. My memory had them saturated with
sunlight, a swimming pool outside that I was hot to get
myself into, and a huge bed all to myself, upon which
I could bounce until I was so exhausted I would sleep
deeply into the morning. Jerry and I kept this one dark
as a tunnel. One light on in the bathroom, the door
cracked slightly open so as to allow a faint signal
of basic orientation.

Between them, there were long stretches of silence. Then
outbursts of conversation, a rapid clatter of words, sometimes the two of them speaking at once and nevertheless
hearing each other and responding, the talk a wild mesh of
sentences criss-crossing, repeating and soaring off. Years later, Hannah would remember it in almost symphonic terms,
a composition by a mad old maestro who'd be filled with joy
in one movement, then plunging into despair the next, but
never in any hurry to reach a conclusion. If anything, delay-
ing the end. Her sense of those hours was that she and Professor Cummings were among the musicians — maybe the
second horn player and the first cellist — two players among

the many so passionately caught up in performing the piece.

First sex I suppose is probably strange for everybody.
Had Jerry and I been ourselves — as opposed to the
extraterrestrials into which we'd been transformed — it
would have been the saddest of times, the most forlorn
efforts to "make love" ever carried out by two human
creatures. Even in our heightened states, we had to
struggle through immense clumsiness and ignorance.
But the thing of it was, body and body, we kept being
impelled toward collision and after collision. Trying to
get to ecstasy was part of it, but much of what we did
and tried to do was — okay, Jerry said it aloud — "Fuck-
ing ridiculous!" Shocked by such a word coming from
Jerry and delighted at the aptness, I laughed for the first
time in what felt like months but was probably only a
day and part of a night. It wasn't really funny, though.
Bold and worked up as we were, we were evidently
incapable of reaching climax with each other. Jerry said
he knew that nobody ever gets back into paradise, but
he hadn't realized that what you get for attempting it is
just sadness and frustration. I didn't take it as hard as he
did, though. When we finally went to sleep, I cupped
my body against his back and wrapped an arm around
him. It wasn't an orgasm, but it was at least half an
answer to the question of what I thought I was doing.

The next morning Hannah and Professor Cummings
decided they'd burned through the madness and maybe
they could start talking about how to reassemble their lives.
Hannah invited him into the shower with her. This she'd

learned from Horace and Clara whom, as a little girl, she'd overheard from her bedroom, chattering away in the bathroom while the water ran. She remembered the specific moment when she figured out that her parents were in the shower together and that it had brought out a gaiety in their voices that she'd never heard from either of them anywhere else.

Jerry and I decided that it wasn't the Christian God that was pulling the strings attached to us on this trip, it was the old-fashioned gods — "the bad-assed, mean ones," Jerry said a little grimly. Desire took hold of us again while he was washing my back, and it turned into his washing my breasts and moving downward. Desire caught us when we thought we were through with it, and it yanked us hard. We left the water running, we stepped straight from the shower to the bed, wet and without even taking a towel with us. Then we were at it again, and this time Jerry's hands made their way to my throat — I put my hands on his and even pushed them to make him squeeze harder. All of a sudden I was dizzy, but I was also rising and shuddering, and that's when I heard him rasping out that he wanted me to hit him. I did! I slapped his jaw as naturally as I might have caressed his cheek. The sting of that hard slap in the palm of my right hand took me that much higher into my climax, so that he didn't even have to ask me to strike him a second time. I felt him come into me, as he must have felt me shuddering around him. We stopped moving and stared at each other, a pair of wild-eyed wrestlers pinned together and suddenly turned to stone. "Jesus Christ," Jerry finally murmured. And I gasped, "No. I don't think so."

"The drive of shame," they called it as they made their way back to Saratoga Springs. Hannah and Professor Cummings were so shaken by what they'd found out about themselves and each other that they'd needed several hours of talking in the motel room to begin to feel that they might at least attempt to go back to what they'd left. They had little disagreement over some basic points. They'd been profoundly unwise in their behavior. That they hadn't used condoms probably wasn't an issue since Hannah had been taking birth control pills to regulate her period for a couple of years and Professor Cummings hadn't ever had sex with anyone but his wife. Around noon, he called his wife—Jane, Hannah heard him say the woman's name as the first word he spoke into the receiver—to tell her that he'd be home that evening and that he would explain to her where he'd been. Hannah couldn't make out what Jane was saying on the other end of the line, but she picked up the frantic tone of the woman's voice, and it made her cringe. Hannah and Professor Cummings agreed that they couldn't see each other again anywhere but in class. And if what they'd done came to light at the college, if there were a scandal and they were questioned, then they'd both have to be honest and tell it exactly as it had happened.

Jerry said he thought that even as awful as we had been, we'd nevertheless done what we had to do. "A necessary spiritual errand," he called it. I wasn't sure about that, but I agreed with him that to lie about it would be a desecration. Not to mention that we

wouldn't get by with lying anyway. Jerry also said that
he thought his marriage probably wasn't going to
survive the lightning bolt that would strike when he got
home and told Jane what he'd done. I thought that
lying might be a kindness to Jane, but I knew better
than to say that to him. I knew he wouldn't anyway,
and I didn't really want him to.

They got quieter and quieter as they headed back up the
Northway. As Hannah drove, Professor Cummings rested his
hand on the seat between them.

I kept trying to figure out whether any part of what I
felt might be classified as desire for him. I was also
trying to guess whether he might still have some shred
of desire lingering in his feelings for me. Would it be
possible for it to take hold of us again the way it had in
the shower? I hoped that no was the answer to all those
questions, and I was pretty certain that all the no's
would become definite once we got back to campus.
That was the good news.

The bad news was that now Hannah knew exactly what
she wanted. She knew it might be hard to find, but it was out
there somewhere.

If I'd found it once, I could find it again.

Or it could find her.

And I wondered how I was going to live with that.

Helga After Midnight

A FEW DAYS AFTER HE MET HANNAH, his wife-to-be, Bill spent a night with Caroline Pinard, who was semi-famous. His mind was full of Hannah — within minutes of entering his sight, she had begun to generate a pleasant disturbance in his thoughts — but he and the actress had made their date weeks ago.

Caroline had a one-scene part in a low-budget movie that had just come out, and she'd impressed just about everybody who saw it. A *Village Voice* reviewer praised the powerful but restrained emotion of Ms. Pinard's performance. Some months ago, they'd been seatmates on a plane from Detroit, they'd struck up a lively conversation, and before Bill got off in Burlington, she'd invited him to visit her in Boston. They liked each other. They had a lot in common. When he'd called her, she'd said the invitation was still good. Bill didn't break the date with the actress, because he thought he might find out something that would help him settle his thoughts about Hannah. And Hannah's mostly downcast eyes had given him little evidence of having more than a passing interest in him. He'd tried to charm her, but he didn't believe he'd gotten anywhere with the effort. So of course he went ahead with his date with Caroline and drove down to Boston.

Bill's reading and personal experience had led him to believe that for women desire was way more complicated than for men. A couple of times in his twenty-two years of life he'd been desired by women strongly enough that they made fools of themselves — one of them embarrassed him by getting drunk and feeling him up in public, while the other one pretty much scared the hell out of him by casually showing him the knife she carried in her purse. The semi-famous Caroline Pinard was the opposite of those women — restraint wasn't acting for her. She was a genuinely modest person. During their conversation in the restaurant, Bill had thought he heard some attraction in her words, but he also knew he could be wrong. And he was young enough that he didn't mind taking a chance. So later that evening in her apartment, the two of them sitting in the middle of her sofa and kissing sociably, Bill murmured, *Can I stay?* He kept his voice low, his tone conversational, his words an ordinary little question.

When she gave a nod to his question, it was such a slight movement of her head that he could easily have thought she just wasn't saying anything. If Bill had asked her to say the words out loud, her answer most likely would have been, *No, I don't think so.* This was during a snowy night in Cambridge, and he'd driven all the way down from Vermont. It was late. They'd had a nightcap. So that little nod of her head might have translated out to *Why not?* He would have bet a small amount of money that *Why not?* was her thought. But of course now, forty years afterward, the night is deeply buried in layers of time, and there's no telling. Bill thinks it's better this way — he still savors the iffiness that hovered over the whole ten or twelve hours he and Caroline spent together. Fate did not decree what they did. If anything, fate — which had so recently and tantalizingly introduced him to Hannah Houseman — shook its head at them and whispered *No* when they stepped into her bedroom.

In Bill's memory it was a very sweet night that seemed to go on for a very long time. It was also more than a little bit strange. It's been years since he's shared a bed with anyone except his wife, and he thinks the first time a person shares a bed with another person must always be peculiar. But this was more than peculiarity, which Bill attributes to Caroline's being a movies person and his being a kind of blue-collar businessman. They were collaborating on some kind of project that wanted to be art but that kept on slipping into regular life.

Caroline's apartment was in a quaint building with tilted, dark-stained floors, drafty windows, and obsolete plumbing. There was, however, plenty of space; there were even a couple of rooms she wasn't using. Bill was already sufficiently involved with real estate that he noticed such things. Her bed seemed big enough for four or five people.

Earlier in the evening, Bill and Caroline had talked about their parents. He'd told her that as a little boy he'd overheard his parents having sex from his bedroom across the hall and that he thought it might have affected his thinking about sex — when he was around couples, he found himself imagining them in bed. She had told him that she never saw her parents even touch each other, let alone give any sign that they actually had sex. She was certain her parents' distance from each other had affected her thinking about sex. When she was around couples, she tried to imagine them in carnal scenes and almost always found it difficult. Over coffee, he and Caroline had grinned with each other, pleased with what they'd confessed, with the symmetry of it. When they went back to her apartment, it made perfect sense that they sat down and started kissing.

After the conversation and the kissing, fate's disapproval notwithstanding, what choice did they have but to make their way into her bedroom? Bill remembers standing up from the sofa and following Caroline down a hallway, the fingers of one of his hands holding onto the fingers of one of hers. He remembers feeling his whole body softly vibrating, as if it were a chime that someone had lightly tapped.

He thinks it was nice to make out with Caroline in her big bed, the slow, awkward taking off of their clothes holding them back even as it moved them along. Patience gradually overruled urgency. It wasn't really foreplay, because that word implies a mutually understood destination. Bill thought there was an extra thrill to his not being all that sure they were going to have sex. So maybe it was foreplay with a toe on the brake pedal. And maybe there was a point when he absolutely did know it, but of course until there was penetration, *no* was always a possibility, and of course their bodies had a say in the matter, too. Bill thinks there were probably a lot of reasons for intercourse not to happen that night.

Even when it did become certain, when sex was actually happening, and they were in it, and it was just fine, why even then, wasn't it possible for one of them to do or say something that just completely put the other one off? He could have whispered a little endearment that reminded Caroline of a very bad past experience, and she would have had to say *Stop, this isn't working, I'm sorry* — oh, awkward and painful moment! Okay, that didn't happen. If anything it was the opposite. They got deeper and deeper into each other and what they were doing, what they were making. Not really love, as Bill has come to know it in the decades he's had with Hannah, but a good enough approximation. A collaborative effort. They finally did reach orgasm, first her and then quickly afterward him, but it took a long while to get there, and by that time they'd each learned most of what the other liked. They weren't exactly on the same page, but they were closely enough matched that they could have had a future as lovers. Over time, they'd have refined it. In the aftermath, when they were lying side by side and letting their heartbeats slow back down to normal, their damp skin to cool, Bill found himself feeling a ridiculous welling up of affection for Caroline. *Thank you,* he said, and he knew he should have explained what he meant, because the tone of her *You're welcome* translated out to *Can't you say something more interesting?* But he couldn't say *Thank you for the affection,* and so he let the silence stand. He didn't have the will to try to add any subtlety to what he'd said. Maybe what it came down to was just *Thanks for the fuck,* maybe it was no more complicated than that.

The crassness of his thinking brought Hannah's face flashing into his thoughts, her eyes meeting his and her eyebrows lifted as if to ask him what he thought he was doing. *Research,* he told her in his mind. *I'm trying to find out something. Maybe something about you.* He felt his mouth make a wry smile.

There wasn't much talk then. Caroline got up to go to the bathroom. She wasn't self-conscious about being naked, and that surprised him a little — he'd have thought she would be. Her body was farm-girl sturdy and appealing in a healthy way. When he remembers it now, Caroline's body makes him think of Andrew Wyeth's Helga, or what Helga's body would have looked like ten or fifteen years before Wyeth painted it. One afternoon at his in-laws' house, Bill once spent an hour leafing through an oversize book called *Andrew Wyeth: The Helga Paintings* — the pictures kept making him think of Caroline.

When she came back to bed, Bill got up to pee. They passed each other coming and going, naked man, naked woman, scene out of the Bible. It made them both sort of snort. That, too, he took as mutual acknowledgement that they were in a state of accord that was way beyond where he was with Hannah. He thought the odds were high that he'd never get to such a place with Hannah. But he knew it meant something that Hannah wouldn't stay out of his thoughts.

When Bill came back to the bed, Caroline had settled toward the middle, with the covers on one side open for him. He remembers their saying nothing much, but she gave him a smile, and he responded with a friendly caress and a tender, only slightly lingering kiss. Then he was gone, plummeting down into the deep depths of sleep.

Sometime in the pre-dawn dark, Bill woke up and saw her standing at the window. If he'd been more awake, he'd have been startled by the sight. She was still naked and holding her arms across her chest, as if she were cradling her breasts, though they weren't substantial enough breasts to need cradling. Also she was chewing her lip, which he took not to be a good sign. Who chews her lip in the middle of the night does so out of anxiety — he was only twenty-two, but he knew that much.

His sleeping position had been such that on waking up all he had to do to see her was open his eyes. There she was. He thought he must have blinked a couple of times, because the sight was dreamlike but very vivid. Streetlights or moonlight turned the room into a black and white movie set. He had no urge to move even slightly. He just wanted to see exactly what he was seeing for as long as he'd be allowed to look. He sort of wanted Caroline to glance over toward the bed and catch his eye — he wanted to see how that would play out.

She stopped chewing her lip, touched it with a finger. Then her face took on this half-rueful smile. Which Bill translated to mean *Well, here I am again, a man in my bed I only half like.* And he didn't get his wish, she never looked his way. But he did get something else that has stayed with him all these years. He thought it could only have happened in a room lit only by streetlight, only with him lying curled where he was, spying on a young woman standing naked at her window. The thought came to him that he didn't know her very well at all. Immediately — almost as a kind of correction — he, William Collins, was granted access to the brain of Caroline Pinard.

It wasn't what he might have expected. It was this peculiar amalgamation of a memory from her childhood and a real-time, semi-humorous meditation on her acting career. The childhood memory Bill might have constructed from having seen her movie, the part where the grown woman, who's been abused by her father as a child, encounters this little girl on a tricycle in a neighborhood like the one where the woman grew up. In the movie, the point of view suddenly shifts to the child looking up at the grown-up. The child sees the woman leaning forward about to speak to her, about to ask her a question. The child says, *Excuse me,* and just wheels right around and past the grown-up lady. She looks back once, and their eyes meet, which makes the child turn her head forward again and pump her tricycle even harder up the sidewalk.

Bill still trusts the revelation that was given to him. He felt what Caroline felt at that exact moment, racing her tricycle up the sidewalk — to escape the prying adult but also for the sheer exhilaration of it. That child body knew it needed just to get the hell out of there.

The meditation on Carline's acting career came through to Bill much less clearly, and he suspected its origins were in his ordinary low-level paranoia. She was thinking about the director of her movie, a fellow named Freddie Morrison, he remembered from the credits, a movie person of some prominence in those days. It was with considerable bemusement that Caroline was interrogating herself about why she never let Freddie fuck her, whereas she'd let this doofus more-or-less nobody — Bill! — not only fuck her but had actually let herself come with him. *Maybe I should sew it shut,* she told herself, a thought her college roommate had expressed at breakfast one morning after a particularly squalid encounter the previous evening.

All right, maybe Bill projected this vision, these thoughts and words, onto Caroline as he observed her. So be it. Even so, he'd argue that every now and then somebody gets a glimpse of what it's like to be somebody else. Even as a young man Bill believed in that possibility. Nowadays he thinks that something similar must have happened to Andrew Wyeth—Wyeth caught a glimpse of Helga in some innocent moment, maybe the fully clothed back of her at a kitchen sink, and he became her for a little sliver of time. So he was able to paint Helga again and again as he saw her posing for him, of course, but also as she saw herself. Bill thinks that's the secret of those pictures—they're about a man seeing a woman, but they're also about how the woman sees her own life.

Bill didn't find it an alienating experience, seeing—or imagining—how Caroline thought of him. If anything, those moments made him all the more affectionate toward her. It wasn't love for her. He's certain of that—probably because he was aware of love starting to come at him from another direction. He also knows that affection was really all he'd hoped for from Caroline. Maybe he'd have been flattered if she'd fallen in love with him, but he couldn't have responded in any acceptable way. He'd say that at that phase of his life, he was not sufficiently strong or large-hearted enough to meet the duties of love. Affection he could feel. Affection he could handle.

Bill doesn't remember her coming to bed. Consciousness came to him next when, standing at the foot of the bed, Caroline had hold of his ankle and was shaking it. "Get up," she said. "I've run us a bath." She was still nude, but her demeanor conveyed such alertness and sociable humor that she might as well have been fully dressed. She'd begun her day, and naked or not, she was proceeding with it.

Grumbling a bit, Bill got up and let her lead him to the steaming tub she'd prepared. He stepped into it gingerly—the water was on the verge of being too hot, but after the first shock on his skin, he realized the temperature was just about perfect. Caroline stepped in, too, and they sloshed around a bit, arranging their bodies to sit facing each other.

Settling in, they were much amused with themselves in the big bathtub together. Caroline had her hair up, which made her appear surprisingly practical. It was Sunday morning, and so, skootched down, with their legs tangled and with the water up to about the level of their collar bones, they talked about how their families had behaved on the Sunday mornings of their childhood. Caroline had had no church experience whatsoever. "I come from a long line of atheists," she told him. Though it occurred to him later that maybe she threw out that sentence just to see if he would ask her for more information, he didn't question her. Instead, he talked about his own boyhood martyrdom, of being taken to a Methodist Sunday School where the big boys mistreated him, and of going to church camp in the summer, of singing in the choir. Somewhere in his talking, he realized that he'd moved away from the openness of mind and heart he'd reached in the early morning hours. As his monologue went on, he felt himself returning to his selfhood, burrowing deep down into who he was. Signals were reaching him — the bathtub water was cooling, Caroline's face had taken on such a jaded expression she might have been trying to remember her multiplication tables. But Bill didn't stop babbling for quite a while. Something was moving him to do it. He kept talking well after he realized that he needed to shut up.

There were options, of course. He could have just suddenly said, "Hey, what were you doing up last night, standing at your window?" Such a question would have thrown them into having to talk a lot more intimately than they had been doing so far that morning. He could have wound down the religion-in-childhood confession and just said very quietly, "Caroline, I have such a strong feeling for you. What should we do about it?" That would have been an honest blurt of a thing to say, a definite clumsiness, but one that would have invited her to break through to an honesty of her own to offer in reply.

So Bill knows it must have been that he really didn't want to stop his and Caroline's downward spiral. He wonders if it's not always like that. People know when they're drifting away from someone else — it can be a lover or a friend, but it can also be a brother, a parent, a child. *I need my space* is a thing people say that generally applies in a social way. But the truth is that people — no, he has to reject the *we* here and just speak of himself — throughout his life, William Collins has turned away from affection, generosity, sweetness, love, understanding, all those emotions that he needs from other people — well mostly, from Hannah and Eve — and that they were willing — sometimes eager — to extend to him. He's turned away because he can't bear the duties that he imagines come with the gift. He wants to hang his head now that he's thought it through. The word that comes to him is *cowardice*.

Well, he doesn't want to make too big a deal out of this particular moment in the bathtub. He and Caroline had eventually stepped out of the water, they'd put their clothes on, they'd said and kissed goodbye, all the while engaged in smart, funny, and very nicely paced repartee, the two of them again collaborating on a work of art/life, a movie scene, a piece of a regular late morning that seems important when it happens but that probably isn't.

Bill thinks there was no imbalance in his and Caroline's liking for each other. Their goodbye kiss did not rekindle any of the previous night's energy, but the hug that came after the kiss was strong and of a sufficient length that it said, for both of them, *I'm glad we did this.* But of course that's Bill's translation, which he can't help distrusting. He is, however, pretty confident that he and Caroline both took some pleasure from having made those hours right in their own terms. He can't explain it, but he believes he'd never have made his way to Hannah if it hadn't been for Caroline.

He hasn't lost track of Caroline; he's kept an eye out for the movies she's done. In spite of the rave notice she got for that first film — the title of which was *Color of Darkness* — she always plays the part of an interesting but minor character. To tell the truth, Bill thinks her work, though certainly professional enough, isn't distinguished. At first it was sort of creepy to see the person whose interior life he'd accessed so intimately up on the big screen acting like someone else. But then he got used to it and stopped being so aware of her pretending. She was in a play or two in New York, one that survived on Broadway for several months, but by then he'd married Hannah, and he never thought of going down to the city to see the play. Or Caroline. By that time, she really would have been somebody else.

A month or so after their night together, Bill got a postcard from Caroline from Göteborg, Sweden. On it she'd written a note that he read over and over again. *I sat in Liseberg park all morning, though it was so cold I felt like I was in a dream of being frozen. But there were so many children to see, and they all seemed happier than I ever remember being in my life. I don't know why this made me think of you, but it did.* She'd signed it, *C.P.*, without a *love* or a *fondly* or even a *your friend*. Bill thought she must have been trying to tell him something important. He thought it had to do with when they were in the bathtub. With all those words spilling out of his mouth — and none of them, really, for her.

Snow Day

HORACE THOUGHT HE MIGHT FEEL DIFFERENTLY about himself had his boyhood not evolved as it had. His physical development was slow; his body remained childish up into his junior year of high school. He compensated for this physical embarrassment by being articulate — as a teenager, he possessed dazzling verbal skills. Only occasionally was he picked on by anyone for being small and pale and hairless. But in the spring of his junior year, he underwent a growth spurt — from five-foot-five in February to five-eleven in mid-June and to six-foot-one at the beginning of his senior year. His classmates didn't know what to make of him — he wasn't sure what to make of himself. For a little while, he was frightened that he might be changing into the opposite kind of freak from the one he had gotten used to being, from midget to giant. As it turned out, the growing stopped, and his voice deepened sufficiently that he impressed his schoolmates with his baritone resonance. Everyone looked at him in a new way.

During Christmas break of Horace's senior year, his new

maturity gave him the confidence to make a bold move on a girl he'd have been scared to speak to in the previous year. She was a junior and the one serious ballet dancer in the whole town of Barre. Three times a week her mother drove her into Hanover for dance classes. As a little girl, she had actually had a role in a New York City Ballet performance of *The Nutcracker*. Lisa Swain was too pretty, too tall, and too self-possessed to have had a boy make a bold move on her before Horace dared himself to risk it. Half joking, he walked up to Lisa at her locker and intoned in his newly deep voice that he wondered if she'd like to go to the movies with him sometime.

She was impressed. For one with such a sophisticated background, Lisa was surprisingly innocent — but, as Horace discovered in the weeks to come, she was also in a mood for sexual adventure. Their intimacy progressed. As was the custom in those days, Horace and Lisa took to parking out by the granite quarry. In the back seat of his parents' Buick, they quickly moved through the early and middle stages of petting. At a certain point, however, Lisa put the brakes on. There were limits as to how far she'd go in a car, she explained. "I'm too tall," she said. "It would be comical. Not to mention humiliating." Horace was thrilled with her frankness. He understood then that she envisioned the sexual act in terms of choreography, blocking, performance. He respected her for it.

Before Lisa Swain, he hadn't ever intimately touched a girl. Now he had undone the clasp of a brassiere, and he had felt a small but definite breast and an erect nipple in the palm of his hand. Lisa's breast put him in such a fever that he could hardly believe his luck when the McCleods a few houses down from the Housemans on River Road asked him to housesit for them. His one duty, aside from staying in the McLeod house, was to look after their dachshunds, Popeye and Olive. First his growth spurt, then Lisa and the pleasures of the family Buick's back seat. Now the McCleods' house was to be his for two whole days. Popeye and Olive would be his guardian angels.

Horace and Lisa worked it out for their rendezvous to begin on Saturday. She had to be home for dinner, but the morning and afternoon were entirely theirs. And she thought she could probably manage to come back to the McCleods' house that evening. Friday afternoon after school Horace purchased a carton of two dozen condoms, which he hoped would be enough to get them through the weekend. The fever was in him. He had very little perspective.

Early Friday evening a classic Vermont snow of some four or five inches fell, then during the night the sky cleared, so that Saturday morning, the air was sharp, there wasn't a breath of wind, and sunlight whitely resurrected every house and tree and shrub on River Road. When Lisa knocked on the McCleods' door, Horace opened it to behold beneath a parka hood the rosy-cheeked face of a girl in a state of snow-day exuberance. She and Horace were both so giddy they might have dashed straight for the master bedroom, had Lisa not noticed the grand living room just off the front hallway. "Wait," she said, pushing Horace slightly away and stepping toward the room. "I want to look at this place."

In that neighborhood, the McCleods were famous for their living room. Big as a milking barn, it had a cathedral ceiling and four enormous exposed beams. There were grand sofas and elegant chairs; the floor was polished cherry.

Rumor was that Mrs. McC. had said she didn't care if the rest of the house was ordinary, she just wanted a living room in which she could throw a decent cocktail party. Horace's father said what she really wanted was to have the governor come to one of her parties — the McCleods gave a lot of money to the Republican Party in Vermont. Horace's father said that eventually Mrs. McC. would get her wish, they'd keep on donating money until a Republican governor would have to set his foot in her living room, sip a gin & tonic, and nibble a cheese-cracker. Then the woman would have to find a new goal in life.

But nothing about the McCleods' living room had so much bearing on Horace's story as the floor-to-ceiling panes of glass that made up the entire southeastern wall of the house. On this morning of snow and sunlight, no room in America was so blazingly illuminated. As Horace and Lisa stood just inside the doorway from the hall and her eyes took in that brilliant space, he could feel the energy of all that light channeling into Lisa's mind. "Let's stay in here awhile," she said. Her voice was whispery, as if she'd just received advice from an angel.

Horace stayed quiet. For some reason he knew to sit down at the edge of the room and pay attention to Lisa.

She shed her parka, tossed it behind her into the hallway, unlaced her boots, and tossed them back there, too. Then, in her winter socks, she stepped into the room and slowly paced toward the center window. Out there, the McCleods' back yard sloped down toward a stand of spruce and cedar swathed in the new snow. That morning Lisa wore what any Barre girl would have worn on such a day, blue jeans and a sweater. Horace hadn't ever seen her in these long-legged jeans before, and they fit her with stunning precision. The sweater wasn't new, but it was one he'd told her he liked, a loose-fitting pink cashmere with a big fluffy neck. She'd shampooed, conditioned, dried and brushed her nearly-black hair so that in the room's sunlight it gleamed down her back like liquid obsidian. For some moments Lisa stood at the window with her back to him, her shoulders profession-ally and heartbreakingly straight. He had a notion of how many hours of training had gone into her posture at this moment. He was enthralled.

Finally Lisa turned from the window and walked direct-ly toward him with that deliberate pace of hers. She stood over him a moment, before taking his hands to pull him up to a standing position. They were the same height, and he knew she liked it that she could look him straight in the eye, though she did not do so now. Instead, she placed her hands lightly on his chest, and as if she were his valet, she helped him off with his jacket and tossed it back into hallway with hers. She waited a moment and seemed to smile to herself before she knelt to help him with his boots, tossing them out into the hallway as well. All the while she kept her eyes turned down, allowing herself only the flicker of a smile and saying nothing. Horace wasn't tempted to break the silence.

Lisa took his hand and led him to the arrangement of fur-niture at the center of the room. On an impressive rug were a huge black sofa and two matching easy chairs; a low cof-fee table was at the center. Danish Modern is what Horace imagined the pieces were, the sofa and chairs low and thick in a black fabric, the coffee table a blond wood, and the rug a dramatic royal blue. Lisa stepped him around to the front of one of the easy chairs. Still silent but at least slightly smiling, she put a hand on either side of his shoulders to fix him where she wanted him to stand. Then she moved around to the other side of the low table so as to face him. Hands at their sides, they stood opposite each other with about a body's length of space between them.

Guardians of the coffee table. Soldiers of the great room. Horace was aware of the sunlight washing over them.

When Lisa suddenly pulled the pink sweater up over her head and dropped it to the chair behind her, Horace was startled — he realized that she must have planned that dramatic gesture all along, but he wasn't prepared. Her movement had a magician's flare and efficiency to it, but now, in her brassiere, she stood perfectly still except for the rise and fall of her chest. Her expression was expectant, as if he should know what to do.

He didn't. He merely stared at her upper torso — as, in his opinion, any boy in his socks would have done. Not that Lisa was a buxom girl — she had a dancer's slightness. Horace was certain she had more in mind than merely showing him her breasts. He took the revelation to be general. He took note of her collarbone and her shoulders. He took note of her very pretty pink bra. After a moment she pointed and motioned with her hands so that he understood he was to remove his shirt. He did so, though because he had to address buttons, had to manage untucking, wore a T-shirt underneath his regular shirt, and hadn't yet come into complete possession of his coordination, Horace's exposé was notably — and comically — less dramatic than Lisa's.

But he suddenly got it — the plan she had in mind: In silence the two of them were to undress for each other. She would take off a garment, then he would follow. Shirt for sweater, blue jeans for blue jeans, socks for socks, T-shirt for bra, boxers for panties — he even understood how the symmetry of it pleased her. Already he knew that she'd take it slow, she'd make it something he'd never forget. Impatient and eager though he may have been, Horace couldn't help appreciating how she had elevated the occasion. It wasn't just her virginity that they were tossing into history, it was his as well. Quite a girl, that Lisa Swain, and there she was, tall and shapely, giving herself to him, allowing him to feast on the sight of her in a grand room full of sunlight.

But even as excited as he was by the sight of Lisa — and maybe nobody would ever see her so vividly again in all her life — Horace felt a current of anxiety flowing through him. From early childhood, this girl had trained her body to be carefully watched, whereas he was unschooled and unprepared. Pulling off a sock, he nearly lost his balance. Getting his jeans off, he stumbled and had to hop around on one foot and then the other. His body had recently increased itself by about ten percent, he wasn't used to it yet, and anyway physical grace wasn't high in the Houseman genetic code. When Lisa put her hands behind her back to unclasp her bra and let the straps slip slightly down her shoulders, there could never have been a more charming set of movements. So he came to understand that his part of the duet could only be to provide comic contrast to the high drama of her disrobing — he understood and accepted that. Lisa appeared to be sufficiently absorbed in her own performance that she might not even notice his clumsiness. Even so, he worried that in his excitement he might entangle himself just getting his T-shirt off.

Looking back on that boy after some forty years, Horace

shakes his head. He can only admire the kid's silly courage, naïve pluckiness, or whatever those long-disappeared parts of his character were that rose to save him in that enormous room with Lisa Swain. Given what he knows nowadays about sex and dignity and humiliation, Horace wonders that he didn't run from the room or collapse into weeping in the chair behind him or walk into the kitchen to phone his mother. He did none of those things. Clinging to the hope that something wonderful was about to come to him, he went on playing fool to the queen.

When Lisa removed her bra, Horace experienced an uplifting of his spirit. Nowhere in Vermont could she have found a more appreciative boy. And again, he understood that what she had bestowed upon him wasn't merely the sight of her breasts, or her ribcage and solar plexus, which he also found extremely appealing. He understood this moment she was creating to be one of intimacy and aesthetics. Lisa was lovely in a way that was perfectly suited to the morning, the snow outside the bright windows, the warm sunlight streaming into the spacious room. She absolutely stopped time. Had Horace come upon her in a museum gallery — one whole white wall all to herself and a printed caption "American Girl in Pink Underpants" — he could not have savored the sight of her any more.

They might have remained frozen there. Horace thought — or imagined — that they were both reluctant to move on. But finally Lisa signaled him with the slightest flick of her fingers. He pulled his T-shirt over his head. *Smoothly,* he thought. *I did it without a hitch,* he thought.

Something changed. For the next forty years, Horace would take it as evidence that stunningly complex communications pass between human beings without the slightest sign or sound.

At first there was nothing different in Lisa's face.

Then there was.

He didn't quite know *what* it was, but the change made him glance down at himself.

He couldn't quite account for this. He could only say that it was a result of boyhood — of the craziness of his growth spurt, the chaotic changes that were occurring in his life too fast for him to process them. And of course there was just plain old youthful obtuseness. There were explanations having to do with his always sleeping in his T-shirt and with his body's antics making him reluctant to take a good look at himself in the mirror. Most likely no other boy would have had such a thing happen to him. At any rate, he hadn't taken note of what now seemed to him — as it must certainly have struck Lisa — shocking.

He was the hairiest boy he had ever seen. From his neck down, he was almost as hairy as a chimp. In his quick look down his body, he thought the effect must have been caused by the way the light in that room made everything exist at some higher level of intensity. In regular light, he was certain he wouldn't be nearly so hairy. He looked quickly back at Lisa.

She tightened her lips at him. It was the very slightest of constrictions, but he noticed it. And she noticed him notice it. "I'm sorry," she whispered. Then her face contorted, and she was openly weeping. "I'm really sorry, Horace," she blurted. She squatted down to the floor, where she quickly managed to put on her bra and her sweater. She stood halfway up and got to work on her jeans and socks while he stood where he was, looking down again at his chest and stomach. Twisting to try to get a view of his back. Taking inventory.

His legs were hairy, too, but he thought he'd noticed that at home. He seemed to remember it. And with his boxers on, his legs didn't make the impression that his upper body did. He supposed another boy in his situation right then might have been paying more attention to Lisa, but the fact was, his own body was too interesting to ignore. So he was a really hairy guy! He wondered how that was going to play out in his life. He could more or less anticipate how it was going to play out with Lisa, and he'd certainly say that he was ready to feel bad about that. The funny thing was, though, he actually felt sorry for her. She was crying in such a slobbery way that he took her to be genuinely upset. Also he saw that she'd gotten a bad deal — everything about him with his clothes on suggested that with his clothes off he'd look normal. Now that he thought about it, he realized that all that hair didn't bother him, but he could see how it would her.

He felt something for her that was very similar to compassion.

When Lisa finished with her socks, she came over and stood in front of him, head bowed. She didn't touch him, of course, but she stood near enough that either one of them could have reached out and touched the other. "I'm a horrible person," she said.

Of course Horace told her that she wasn't anywhere close to horrible. While he put his clothes back on, he did his best to cheer her up, and pretty quickly it started working. By the time he was fully dressed, he sensed that it would be okay to give her a hug. Her body felt stiff, but he didn't object to that. And she submitted to his hug enough so that he knew she wanted the physical contact — or at least wanted to want it.

After a while Horace and Lisa made their way to the Mc-Cleods' kitchen where they brewed tea and played with Popeye and Olive and actually had a sort of quiet and cozy time. They'd been through something remarkable, and it was only 10:30 in the morning. They both must have wondered what they were going to do with all the rest of that day. Suddenly the question occurred to Horace: What was he going to do with all of those condoms? He excused himself and went to the master bedroom to fetch them from the bedside cabinet where he'd stashed them. He brought the carton in and without saying a word, set it in the middle the kitchen table. Then he sat down and folded his hands around his tea mug. When Lisa put her hand to her mouth, he thought she might have been about to cry again. But it was a giggle she was trying to stifle, and that set them both off. They sat there laughing and laughing.

You might think such an experience would scar a boy, but Horace didn't think so. Illumination is how he thought of it. It wasn't too much later that he encountered a girl who didn't mind his hairiness. He lost his virginity in a much more conventional fashion than he might have that morning with Lisa Swain at the McCleods' house. A good deal later on, he met Clara Brodkey, who not only didn't mind his hairiness, she actually found it among his most appealing qualities.

What Horace learned with Lisa Swain was that his body needed to be a secret but that it was a secret he rather enjoyed. Look at him in the expensive clothes he wore in his academic career, and you'd never guess what he looked like in the shower. And the truth of the matter is that he never was quite as hairy as he appeared that day in the McCleods' living room. It was mostly a trick of light. Even so, after that morning with Lisa Swain, undressing was never again a thoughtless act for Horace Houseman. Which, as he grew older, was more and more how he thought things ought to be.

High on a Hill

Sonny's just met Horace and Clara, but instead of moving through the crowd, he's stayed with them, talking for the past ten minutes. "Don't tell me you didn't know it was going to be like this," Sonny semi-shouts, flapping his hand at the frantically chattering people. They're standing in the twelve-walled President's Dining Room. "Sure, this is Roanoke, Virginia, but this is what faculty do all over the world — drink cocktails and make godawful boring conversation." From the walls, past presidents of Hollins College smile down upon them — there are also portraits of the founder, Edward Clemens Nelson and his regal-bosomed wife. Sonny tells the Housemans what he just found out a few minutes ago, that campus wits speak of the founder's wife as Margaret Herearemytits Nelson and this room as the Dodecaheadroom. Horace smiles, and Clara blushes, but she laughs, so that Sonny's impressed with what a good sport she is. In the days to follow, Sonny and Horace and Clara will each explain to someone on campus, "We took an immediate liking to each other." For some weeks to come, they will go on trying to explain to themselves the speed and intensity of their affection for each other. Clara and Horace think of the relationship as almost comically wholesome. Sonny doesn't imagine himself as wholesome, but he keeps that to himself. Thoughtful and mannerly Horace is the big brother he wishes he'd had growing up. And Clara's damned cute.

Horace is a couple of inches taller than Sonny, but otherwise not that much bigger. Horace can see that Sonny isn't put off by his size — or by the way he thinks through what he's going to say before he says it. Here at the reception, Sonny stands slightly to Horace's right side and a little closer than most men like to do. Horace decides it's a familial impulse on Sonny's part. He likes it. He also likes it that Sonny knows a lot of facts. He knows, for instance, that the money that founded Hollins College was Pendleton money, from Margaret's family. "They essentially built a college for Edward and made him the president," Sonny tells Horace and Clara. "Her money," Clara says and lifts her champagne glass to Sonny. "I like that," she says. Horace savors the way Clara's presenting herself to Sonny as a faculty wife — this is new for her. He also thinks he's a dummy not to have looked into the history of the college before he signed on to teach here, but then he forgives himself because he's never been one to do his homework if he didn't have to. He gives Sonny a grin and lifts his glass, too. "I appreciate a man who does his research," he says. "What else do you know about the college?" he asks.

Sonny's a little swimmy-headed from the champagne and from the way Clara's eyes widened when she lifted her glass to him. He doesn't think she's flirting exactly — every few minutes he's seen Clara or Horace touch each other on the sleeve, the hand, the shoulder. Sonny knows what's what with all that touching—but there's also an energy she sends his way. If he doesn't know what the name of it is, that doesn't matter; evidently it pumps a little air into his tires. "What did you say?" Sonny asks Horace. Horace smiles and repeats himself. "Oh yeah," Sonny says. "Well, what fascinates me is that Margaret kept a diary that's like an unofficial history of the place. I got interested in her diary because of the numbers. She was Hollins's first statistician. Evidently she liked numbers even more than I do. She kept track of how many students, how many horses, how many faculty members, how many service people. She also kept track of the money in those early years. I wouldn't have wanted to marry her, but she had a mind I can appreciate." He looks Horace in the eye as he speaks, but then turns his attention to Clara when he's finished.

"To Margaret Pendleton Nelson," Clara says and raises her glass to Sonny then to her husband. "To Margaret!" they say almost in unison and loud enough to turn a few heads in the crowd of reception-attenders surrounding them. Then they laugh at themselves and at how ridiculous they must seem. "We're already a clique," Clara says. She's giddy with the look of the room, the grandness of the party, the dressed-up citizens of the college—and the fact that Sonny seems to be so comfortable in her presence. She was worried she and Horace wouldn't fit in—and maybe they don't, but it doesn't matter as long as Sonny stands here and talks with them. His ruddy face pleases her, his city accent, his confidence—but what pleases her most of all is how he and Horace have taken to each other. She can see how both men are animated. Clara's a worrier, has been since childhood, and she's learned to keep her worries mostly out of sight. The new anxiety that came to her on their honeymoon is that she won't be able to hold Horace's interest. He'll get tired of her, he'll come to see that she isn't any kind of an intellectual, she's just become what her parents wanted her to be, and even now she doesn't really know what she wants to do with herself. Here at the President's party, with champagne and laughter quickening her pulse, she recognizes how Sonny has enlivened both Horace and herself. With people like Sonny in their lives, Clara won't have to worry about what she and Horace will find to talk about during the thousands of hours of companionship that await them out in their future. She won't have to put forth any effort at all.

·

Newly married, he's intoxicated with Clara's body — which she treats as if it means so little to her that she's surprised by how moved he is by it — and she's perfectly willing to share it with him as much as he likes. He appreciates the round-the-clock availability of sex of course, but occasionally the thought ambushes him that maybe he doesn't want the sex as much as Clara does. "This is what I've been waiting for," she says one morning after they've done it almost before they're awake. She's glancing over her shoulder at him on her way to the shower.

Their sex is a project they seem to have taken on without saying so, an ongoing refinement of how their bodies seem to suit each other. Or of what works best for them. A way of communicating arises that's both primitive and subtle — a groan says *keep doing that*, a yelp means *too hard*, a sigh slyly suggests *turn over*, a low humming translates as *nothing but this, only this, please just this.* To Horace it feels like their bodies are teaching them another language. They're getting somewhere, moving toward something. There will come an ecstatic unfolding of their wings when they'll rise skyward in tandem. Horace snorts with bemusement.

Another thought that twists his mouth in private moments is that maybe it's demons they're on the verge of becoming — hellish creatures with raw scraped flesh they'll have to keep rubbing against each other forever. Silly as that idea is, Horace understands there's a side of their sex he can hardly bear, he doesn't know why. He imagines it's the same for Clara. At first, as a joke, they start keeping track of how much time they spend in the bedroom of their new apartment. It's a lot. But then they start having sex in the living room, then Horace's study, the bathroom, the kitchen, and all that time counts, too. They bicker pleasantly over the time calculations and the locations of their intercourse. Out of breath from just having had it on the staircase, he says, "We haven't had it in the patio yet." Now Clara's the one to snort. "I think we'll be in trouble, if we do that," she says. "That'll be the end of us if we do that," she says. "Let me up, please."

Well, so Clara has her limits, but he has his as well. In the writhing of their bodies, there are moments when Horace wants to leave the bedroom, leave the apartment, leave his body, fly cleanly and entirely out of his life.

•

Sonny doesn't know what he's getting into. He knows he's flirting, but he's doing it in a correct way. He's twenty-six years old and entirely aware of being a little too smart, too good looking, and too confident. He can't help knowing what he's got. So he makes an effort to be a modest person. This he knows to be hypocrisy or deception or something more or less despicable, but he thinks the effort to be modest is necessary. He doesn't want to be a jerk, or he doesn't want people to think he's a jerk, but he's afraid that deep down, being a jerk is his nature. So in his opinion he has no choice — he has to try to nudge himself in the direction of modesty, humility, sensitivity to others.

It's because he's sensitive to his new friend and colleague, Horace Houseman, that he makes it his project to be Horace's friend. Being Horace's friend also obligates him to be the friend of Horace's new wife, Clara. And this is precisely where the friendship has become problematic for Sonny. In spite of being small, slender, and very modest in her way of dressing, Clara Houseman radiates an energy that transmits straight into Sonny's erotic imagination. He's certain Clara intends nothing beyond mannerly hospitality. How she provokes him is a collateral effect of the way she and Horace are locked into each other's frequency. He can see that, he can feel it. And he isn't jealous of it. That kind of exclusive focus on a single other human being is exactly what Sonny is not looking for. Also, he really likes both Horace and Clara — they're charming, decent, generous people. He wants to be a good friend to each of them. Even so, he wakes up one night convinced of Clara's presence, so vivid and immediate he feels it in his palms, his fingertips, his tongue. She has snuck into his bed and persuaded him to have sex with her.

Don't tell Horace, she'd whispered just before he'd waked.

From the dream, Sonny realizes Clara dresses the way she does to understate the fullness of her breasts. This is when he recognizes himself as a bad friend and — in a part of himself over which he has little control — a vile human being. He isn't about to avoid contact with the Housemans, and he isn't going to be able to ignore the effect Clara has on him. What he can do is cultivate the appearance of having no interest in the woman who has evidently taken over his interior life. Mild and disinterested affection — that's the facade he needs to present when he's around the Housemans. Not an easy task with the wild pressure of his feelings, almost as if she's whispered a secret to him — *I have big breasts, but most people don't notice it.*

·

Horace's field was the American Modernists. His dissertation at UNC had been on Faulkner. More particularly, it had been on the evolution of Faulkner's syntax in the Snopes Trilogy. Horace had been born and raised in New Hampshire — and so the South was essentially another country to him and Southerners were foreigners whose language was similar to American English. His professors at Chapel Hill were impressed with the kinds of observations Horace the graduate student made about Faulkner's prose. "It's a deliberate improvisational overflowing," he'd observed in the *Absalom, Absalom* seminar one afternoon; afterward word spread around the department that the kid from New Hampshire was a genius. Horace knew it wasn't the case. He knew that what those Southerners considered insight was merely his ability to hear the sound of a Faulkner sentence or paragraph with innocent ears. Extravagance of language was alien to his family and the people of the little New Hampshire valley where Horace had grown up—and yet those rural Northerners had everything in common with the Ratliffs, Varners, and Snopeses of Faulkner's Mississippi. Horace heard—and read—Faulkner with both an understanding and an objectivity that no Southerner could bring to the texts.

So Horace wrote his dissertation more or less out of common sense, with enough research thrown in to make it sound properly academic. He left Chapel Hill suspecting that he'd stolen his Ph.D. And later on, after not very many years of teaching, he would be relieved to move over to the administrative side of academia. He would think that finally he wasn't going to be exposed as a person who knew only a very little bit about literature. First, though, he was hired to teach English at Hollins College. That summer he married Clara and honeymooned with her for the two weeks before he had to show up in Roanoke, Virginia, to teach at an all-women's institution. He and Clara moved into an apartment across the main highway from the college.

The first morning Assistant Professor Houseman walked into his Am Lit I class, he found twenty-five students waiting for him. Seated, composed, sweatered, skirted, ear-ringed, barretted, loafered, and fragrant, they might have been quietly sitting in that room an hour or more. In graduate school Horace had led discussion groups, but he'd never had a class of his own. A wave of anxiety very nearly pulled him back out into the hallway. Their faces were heartbreakingly alert. His own heart hammered, but he pressed forward. There was a podium upon which he spread his papers and the stack of syllabi he'd brought to hand out. He made himself survey the room and try to look directly into the face of each young woman. He hoped he would have a voice when the occasion demanded that he speak.

Walking through the rows of seats to distribute his syllabus one at a time was a way to remain quiet and to get his bearings. Then he was finished with that. As he walked back to the podium, he took note of the squares of sunlight beaming down through the high windows. It helped to be reminded of the world and the day outside. He pronounced the words "Good morning," floating the words out into the room over their heads, then was much relieved to hear the soft murmur of good mornings that answered him. So, doing his best to accommodate the energy crackling between him and the room full of young female students, Horace set forth upon his lifelong career.

•

Sonny's bachelorhood carries with it some free tickets. It's 1960. He is, as they put it in those days, "eligible" and only five or six years older than the senior girls at Hollins. His academic field is statistics, but Sonny knows a lot about many fields, and he knows at least a little bit about girls. He helped raise his younger sister, and from his Grandma Baumen he received intense schooling in the dark side of the weaker sex. He was brought up Catholic and in Queens. Though he admits he's something of a jerk, he isn't a sexual predator. Sometimes he thinks he's a fool not to be. If he were more aggressive, he might harvest the favors of half the senior class.

But he also isn't a prude, and so on a couple of occasions,

he does sleep with a Hollins girl — one night in a motel with each of them. They aren't students from his classes, but they are Statistics majors whom he sees around the department. So Sonny finds himself summoned to the Provost's office a week after the second episode, to receive a brisk indoctrination into the rules and customs pertaining to carnal experience between students and faculty at a southern all-women's college. The Provost is a pleasant and worldly person with a tight permanent who's been at Hollins her whole career. She makes it clear to Sonny that by her standards, his transgression are mild and entirely ordinary; if, however, a similar report comes to her before he is granted tenure — assuming he will be granted it — he'll be dismissed from his position and not likely to be employed by any other reputable college or university in the country. She's very chipper as she speaks, but Sonny is shaken and embarrassed. He's also shocked that what he thought to be a discreet dalliance was within forty-eight hours a topic of discussion in the dormitories and a rumor that made it way to the Provost's ear.

Sonny knows he likes sex, though he also knows it's a complicated subject. But he likes women in general, and he thinks there's nothing complicated about that. He just likes them. He attributes the liking to his having spent so much time looking after his sister when they were kids. He became intimately acquainted with Katie's struggles to hold onto her dignity. He'd tried to protect her from being picked on and insulted at school; he'd pleaded with his parents when they treated her harshly or unjustly. He'd protected her against their grandmother's perverse efforts to diminish Katie's innocence and inject sex into her consciousness.

In his late teens, just after her death, Sonny went

through a phase of hating Grandma Baumen. But then he found himself finished with the hating and, against his will, more or less forgiving the old woman. The passing time had made him understand Grandma Baumen was driven and didn't really know what she was doing. This occurred just as he'd begun to understand himself to be driven. He thinks it's likely that he, too, doesn't always know what he's doing. Or doesn't know all of it. Even so, Sonny gives himself moderately high marks in his alignment with women. Sure, he gets uncomfortable when a date or a girlfriend seems to have a plan to impose her will on him. He doesn't like the controlling aspect of some women he's known, but Katie wasn't like that — even as a really little kid, she'd been a grand companion. And he thinks he'll eventually make his way toward a relationship like that with a woman. He's in no hurry to get there, but that's how he sees his future.

So it's both a happiness and a trouble to him to spend time with Horace and Clara. Clara's told him he has a standing invitation to join them for the evening meal whenever he's in the mood. Horace told him he has a standing invitation to ring their doorbell any time day or night, and they'll let him in. These invitations were extended late on a December evening after a long dinner in the Housemans' apartment during which the three of them had consumed four bottles of wine. So Sonny knows the Housemans' words were not to be taken literally. But he values them anyway.

What's problematic is that that was the same evening when he also understood that he'd been thinking about Clara way more than he was thinking about Horace and that he was thinking about her in a boyish crush kind of way. He was dreaming about her — wet dreams, for pity's sake. Also when he was around the two of them, he received flashes of insight into Clara's thoughts and feelings. He saw moments when she was proud of Horace, when she was worried about him, when she resented him, and when she felt he'd unjustly humiliated her.

He knows where he stands with the Housemans as a couple. He knows where he stands with them individually, and he thrives on the warmth and generosity that flows back and forth between him and them. But in an unofficial and — Sonny knows this very well — unhealthy way, there is an invisible connection between himself and Clara that no one can see or know about or even imagine. He knows it's entirely in his mind, but it evidently has its own life. Even so, what harm can come if he keeps it to himself? He's already developed a habit of turning his eyes away from Clara when he catches himself wanting to stare at her. And of course he can always just stop having anything to do with the Housemans.

•

In that spring of his first year at Hollins, Horace begins to take regular walks around the loop that circles the college. He knows himself to be a person who needs daily exercise, but in the first months of his marriage, he spent most of his non-working hours with Clara. And they'd taken some walks, but they were so leisurely and slow-paced that Horace couldn't count them as exercise. When Clara took a job in the Roanoke city planning office, Horace started walking the loop with a pace that suited him.

He likes it that the two big hills of the campus make

his pulse accelerate but that he has the stamina to take them without slowing down. He likes the gradually warming weather, especially the clear days after a rain when the mountains on both sides of the campus become so hugely visible that they're like some uncommon form of animal life. And — when she comes home from work and the two of them are in the kitchen having a cocktail and fixing dinner — he likes telling Clara what he's seen that day. Hollins has plenty of bird life, and there's a small creek that runs alongside the campus where ducks live and where a heron is said to show up occasionally. Also there are turkey buzzards that greatly interest Horace. "They were doing that high altitude swirling today," he'll tell Clara, and then he'll describe how they seem to have flight patterns of rising and falling and moving out of and returning to the swirling circle — patterns that are dance-like. "I think there's a turkey buzzard choreographer up there with them," he tells her. "Merce Cunningham Turkey Buzzard," he says.

He loves it when she smiles to herself over something he says. He thinks he likes her smiling silence even more than her companionable laughter.

On his walks Horace finds himself repeating some patterns of his own. At the top of the big hill along the front side of the campus is a graveyard surrounded by a brick wall. It contains members of the family of the Hollins founder, Edward Clemens Nelson. He's counted the graves — there are eighty-seven of them. The little cemetery also contains plantings of boxwood and half a dozen very old, western-looking cedar trees that appeal to Horace. He likes entering the side gate of the graveyard, then following a path of his own design around the grassy back area then straight up through the shadows and gravestones to exit at the front. That way, when he comes out the front gate, he's headed directly toward the barely visible roadway that goes straight and level along the hilltop to a slope for some four hundred yards before it curves down to the hard surface of the loop road.

From the two tracks of this straight gravel-and-mud roadway, Horace can see blue and bluer layers of mountains into the far distance, forty or fifty miles out beyond the other side of the city. On either side of him rise the mountains that border this part of the Roanoke valley — Chinquapin Mountain directly alongside the campus is such a notable presence that it comforts Horace as it seems to comfort almost everyone who pays attention to it. Along a stretch of the roadway there sit bales of the hay that was cut from the hillside field the previous fall.

On his first exploration of the campus, when Horace walked up the path through the high grass, dozens of goldfinches rose up out of the green stuff before him and flew out away from him in rising and falling loops. It was like walking into a shower of riches. From that afternoon of the goldfinches, Horace felt buoyed by rare luck. "Hollins is a good place," he told himself that day.

The hilltop is also the place where Horace established what he likes to think of as a personal relationship with the turkey buzzards. On rainy days they're often perched in the trees that border the field, a dozen or so on the bare limbs of several trees, black blobs that aren't especially skittish of humans. He's taken to calling out to them, albeit softly, whenever he sees them like that. "Hello, my friends," he'll say, and it amuses him to think of such allegedly mournful creatures as his friends. Horace discovers that he can walk close enough to their trees to make out the red heads of the birds — instead of being frightened of him, they seem almost interested.

It's above the big hillside field that Horace sees the buzzards' high swirling — and the way a circling formation sometimes shifts gradually over the hillside and off toward the mountains on the far side of the campus. Sometimes it looks as if there are more than a hundred of those big-winged gliders up there, though Horace knows the number is closer to forty or fifty. In the big field, too, sometimes a few of them will sail down to perch on the hay bales or even land on the ground in groups of six or seven, where they look ungainly and common. Most remarkably they sometimes glide very low over the hill, slowly and gorgeously maneuvering close enough for Horace to imagine they're studying him as he studies them. When they coast in close and silent, Horace sees how they use slight slants of the feathers at the tips of their wings for their turns. When he views them from below, the feathers at the backs of their wings appear startlingly white — and in late afternoon sunlight those feathers turn the brilliant reddish orange Horace associates with Lakota war bonnets.

•

Since Sonny lives alone — and has done so since his junior year at Washington & Lee — it comes naturally to him to speak aloud when he's in his little house on campus. With or without company, either way, he speaks. He's not one to sing in the shower, but he likes to fill his spacious living room with semi-musical bellowing — *O sole mio,* or *Oh my love, my darling* are among his favorites for the moment when he steps into the room stark naked to cool off from his morning shower which he likes so hot he can barely stand it. He also likes recitations from the Doo Wop songs of the past decade, such as *My darling, I need you,* and *Can't see a thing in the sky / I only have eyes for you.*

Sonny's an early riser, and so his moment of stepping naked into the living room and unleashing an operatic profession of love occurs just around daylight. One whole wall of the room is glass, on the other side of which is a slight hill that looks down onto student dormitories. The lights are off in this room when Sonny enters and saunters in his cooling-off circle that leads him back to the steamy bathroom to shave. But almost every morning the thought occurs to him that if a student happens to catch a glimpse of Professor Carson in his morning mode and reports him to Security, well, then there he'll be, sitting in the Provost's office again, trying to explain why, and to whom, he presents himself naked every morning. *It's my own living room, ma'am.* Perhaps he'll tell her that he also sings to his living room around this time every morning. *You don't have a problem with singing, do you, ma'am?*

This particular morning, after his living room performance and his shave and putting his clothes on, Sonny enters his kitchen to make coffee, and he's thinking about one thing and another, talking his way through what's on his mind. *Maybe the thing to do is give you a nickname, Clario, Clarina, Cleopatra, something just to get a little distance. Clean it up, Cleo, cauterize it before it gets out of control. Change it up. Same face, same sweet smile, same eyes that say things to me they don't even know they're saying — but different name. That way if you come to me in the night, it'll just be us strangers under the covers. Nothing wrong with it if you're Corinna and not Clara. Clara lives over there on the other side of the road with my good pal, Horace. Keeps her clothes on, sleeps in a big nightgown. Corinna makes her way over here to my house, takes her clothes off the minute she steps in the door. Corinna and I got something going here that don't want to stop. Clara wouldn't have a bit of what's happening here —*

Sonny gazes out his kitchen window, speaking to no visible person, waiting for his coffee to finish brewing, when he's utterly stopped in his conversation because a Hollins student is walking up Faculty Avenue in her riding pants and riding boots, carrying her helmet. When she and Sonny are maybe ten yards from each other, she turns her eyes toward his kitchen window and sees him soliloquizing while he watches her. It's way too early for a student to be out there, but the riding students are a peculiar lot, maybe not as peculiar as a professor who talks to himself in his kitchen, but Sonny blushes with getting caught doing what's entirely customary and private to himself. The good thing about it is that he knows the student rider is also blushing from having seen him and having met his eyes in this moment. *Lonely, lonely, little life I got here, Corinna,* he sings in his Elvis voice. *Good thing I got your titties to meditate over all day, sweetheart.*

His coffee is ready. When he pours it into his big mug, it comes to him that what he really loves, what he really, really, couldn't ever possibly give up is exactly this loneliness he's got here. Exactly this.

•

One afternoon Horace overhears his students talking among themselves about something they call "ring night." Though he isn't curious enough to ask them about it, he gathers that there is some kind of forthcoming campus-wide ritual associated with the juniors receiving their college rings from the seniors. The students' voices suggest to Horace that ring night is something they've looked forward to and that there's some naughtiness associated with it. He imagines a party with drinking, singing, and dancing, but he also has the impression that the ritual involves neither boys nor faculty members. His imagination takes him no further in envisioning ring night. From his months-long acquaintance with them, he's come to understand that Hollins students are mostly innocent girls and that they're almost comically less jaded and worldly than the undergraduates he knew at the University of New Hampshire and UNC. What they do among themselves is none of his business, and anyway, lately he's been thinking about the heron. He had caught a glimpse of it the day before, just a quick sighting of its wing and tail feathers as it silently maneuvered up along the narrow flight path between the tree branches that hovered above the creek. After the only evidence of its visit was a bobbing limb over the water's surface, Horace told himself, *Eventually I'll see it.*

The next afternoon, on his customary walk around the loop — after class and before he goes home to start supper — Horace notices unnaturally bright-colored feathers here and there along the hillside as he walks up toward the graveyard — splotches of scarlet, royal blue, yellow, orange, and green. They're scattered, and there aren't a great many of them; even so, Horace's mind begins trying out stories that would explain their presence on this uniformly green hillside. His mental project proceeds almost without Horace's choosing — but then it also amuses him. The feathers are somewhat mysterious, but they're mostly just silly. The only explanation he can come up with is that maybe some mother on campus gave a child a birthday party that involved costumes or a game. Horace doesn't think that was likely, but he isn't eager to waste his thoughts on such a paltry topic for his walk today.

As he comes up onto the flat hilltop, he sees a cluttered and trampled area in the field, just a few steps off the parallel tracks of the roadway. Here there are more than a few of the tawdry feathers scattered in a circle in the grass that seems singed, though there is no scent of a fire. Horace steps over to the darkened place to try to make out what the other things are that he's seeing. He finds discarded containers of chocolate syrup and whipped cream. He finds marshmallows, many of which are coated with chocolate syrup, strewn around the grass and mud. And of course he finds clots and clumps of the many-colored feathers. With what feels like considerable satisfaction — *Aha! There's more!* — Horace's mind seizes upon these details. Suddenly he's witnessing a circle of chanting young women surrounding a smaller group of girls huddled together to withstand the shower of syrup and whipped cream and marshmallows pelting down upon them.

Horace blinks at the scene coming into focus in his mind. The girls of the inner circle have stripped down to their underwear. A couple of them are students of Horace's — he knows their faces well. They're wailing in real or pretend suffering. The faces of the outer circle are twisted with pleasure. One of those girls with a squirting can of whipped cream steps into the inner circle to smear the stuff into the hair of one of Horace's students. Another of them darts back and forth to the inner circle of suffering ones, smacking their bodies with clumps of feathers that stick to their skin.

Horace turns and walks briskly toward the brick walls of the graveyard a hundred and fifty yards away. He's emotionally stirred up, but there is no clarity to what he feels. Of course he disapproves of the behavior of the students — the outer circle of seniors — but that condemnation is only a small part of what he feels. He also registers some physical nausea, but this, too, isn't of much note. Walking ordinarily helps Horace sort out his thinking, but now each step seems to move him deeper into confusion. He's pretty sure what he feels is guilt. An intensely piercing variety of guilt. But how can it be that? He hasn't done anything. Has he?

•

Okay, Sonny can face the truth when he has to. He's even got a joke about it — *Don't get enough abuse from anybody else, try abusing yourself. Funny?* He went through phases of blaming it on Grandma Baumen for starting him out thinking about sex when he was way too young and on Father James for turning away from him when he needed somebody to talk to about sex, but the truth is that everybody gets configured a certain way, and Sonny's way is mostly mono-sexual. That's just how he came into this world. Even when he's had girl-friends — and he has, he has, plenty of ladies take an interest in somebody who's smart and got the gift of gab like he has and somebody who might be a little bit of a jerk like he is but who's nevertheless making an effort to be good. *The ladies like me,* Sonny assures himself, and that's just as true as the fact that over the years he's spilled a lot of seed. But even in the two semi-relationships he's had with women who wanted sex just as much as he did, Sonny found himself looking for occasions to be with himself. *To get off by myself* — that's how he would put it. No reason for wanting that or doing that because he couldn't have been horny if first Barbara and later on Sue Ellen was giving him all the sex he could handle. But there it is. From around age nine or ten, Sonny's truest sexual fidelity has been to himself. He's close to twenty-six now, and doesn't see it ever being any different.

It's not so much the *self* part of it that troubles him, it's the *others* part: He moves through a lot of *others*. Barbara had been in the final stages of moving in to his apartment, and they'd both been excited about presenting themselves to their friends as a couple, when they got into an argument over whether to leave the dishes to be washed next morning or do them before they went to bed. It was their first and last argument — Sonny ended it by telling her, "Look, these dishes are not the problem; *you're* the problem. I'll help you move your things back over to your place in the morning," and Barbara's saying, "Hey — why wait till tomorrow? Let's do it right now." And in silence, they moved her stuff — four carloads worth of it — out of his place and back to hers. End of relationship. Sonny admits to himself that it was eighty — maybe ninety — percent his fault and that it's ongoing evidence of his being a jerk.

With Sue Ellen (who was probably the sweetest young woman he's ever known), it hadn't even gotten that far when he told her that much as he enjoyed sleeping with her —

she'd been over to his place three nights in a row — he didn't like her taste in clothes. Just like that. She just looked at him with her lip trembling. Did Sonny feel bad? Hell, no, he couldn't wait for her to walk out of his apartment. To get her sweetness the hell out of his sight. Which she finally did after six tears — yes, Sonny counted them — rolled down her cheeks. He shut the door behind her, walked straight into his bedroom and commenced his solitary ritual. Fulfilled his true desire. When he thinks hard about the kind of life he's evidently constructed for himself, he makes himself more than a little sick.

Okay, the worst he didn't realize for a while, because it was located in a territory where Sonny deliberately turned off the analytical mode of his inner life. It had to do with the pictures Sonny used for what he called his "inspiration." The pictures mostly came from the mainstream skin magazines, *Playboy* and *Penthouse*. Sonny had subscriptions to both of them. And yes, he did occasionally read the articles, but he never tried to persuade anybody that reading was his main reason for taking those titillations into his life. It was the pictures; it was the inspiration. When a new issue came to him, Sonny found occasion to turn the pages front to back so as to carry out a quick inventory. Then he'd set it aside and come back to it that evening. Without running it through his conscious mind, he'd know exactly which picture he wanted for his evening's pleasure. Sometimes a Miss June or a College Girl of the Midwest would inspire him for as many as three occasions. More likely, she'd endure only once, and then maybe he'd come back to her after a week or so. He had an archive of dependable images he'd return to after many weeks and some that were no longer functional but that out of sentiment he couldn't bear to throw away.

And here it is: Sonny's hooked on turnover. When that insight arrived — which was not long before he came to Hollins — Sonny knew absolutely A) that no matter how hard he tries not to be, he's doomed to be a lifelong jerk and B) that he's certainly unfit for a "real" relationship with a woman. No matter how much she cares about him, understands him, admires him, et cetera, he doesn't have it in him to stick with somebody. So is everybody a discard? Sonny really doesn't want to think so, but he behaves as if that's the case. He understands himself to be a mutation. *Jerk* is precisely the right name for what he is. *Jerk*. Just sounding that single harsh syllable makes Sonny's lips curl in bemusement and self-loathing.

●

The next two days Horace takes his walk up through the graveyard, then down the mud and gravel roadway to the place where the girls carried out their ring night antics. His heart thuds as he approaches the place, and he can't keep himself from stopping there, or pacing around the edge of it and staring at the scattered debris. He's up there alone, in a high place where he can see for miles to the west and north, and the weather's warm now — full spring has arrived. Horace opines that it was a seasonal force that impelled the young ladies of Hollins to carry out these perverse ceremonies. He can feel the pleasure it gave that tall senior girl to squirt whipped cream over the shivering junior girl's shoulders and smear it down her back. "Turn around, bitch!" he hears the tall one shout, and the power of her voice seems to proceed out of his own chest. "Push your bra down!" the tall one orders just before she squirts the chocolate sauce over the junior girl's chest. He hears the laughter of the other seniors, seven or eight of them up here in the deep night to amuse themselves with pretend torture. This is a thing that can happen only up here where people usually don't go after dark. A thing that can happen only one night a year, because these girls can't stand to show this hateful part of themselves more than once in their four years of college.

"Get down on your knees, bitch! You made me spill this nasty stuff on my foot. Now I want you to clean it off with your tongue. And you'd better be fast about it." This is when Horace feels his dick stirring in his pants. The junior girl has got down on all fours, bending her head almost to the ground to lick the senior's foot. This tableau is so horrifyingly compelling that Horace has to force himself to turn away from the desecrated place. He makes himself lift his head and continue his walk. He's facing the clean distance out to the southwest where the sunlit blue mountains seem to promise what Horace wants for Clara and himself. Not a pious life, but a correct one. A life without meanness of the sort that he knows darkened that area of grass he's walking away from. He'll come back tomorrow, he'll bring a big plastic bag with him, and he'll clean that mess up. The thought pleases him mightily. Nobody will see him; he won't have to explain it to anyone. Almost immediately he's looking forward to restoring his hillside field to what it was before ring night.

·

This is new for Sonny. Every night this week he's gone to bed with Corinna. He's felt no desire to go to his archives for Miss Montana or page 143 of Holiday in Amsterdam. He needs nothing but his thoughts. His concentration. His strong right arm. He feels oddly pure and righteous. As for Corinna, when she asks him if he'd like her to dance for him, he says sure, and he especially requests that she do the shimmy for him — it's what he really, really wants. So while he watches her, Corinna discovers that she enjoys shaking her boobies, inspiring him this way. *All these years, I've been keeping these babies out of sight,* she told him. *Wow, I never knew what they could do!* This is nothing like the way he hears Clara speak when she's around Horace. Another language. Sonny thinks he and Corinna will probably get around to talking dirty and that she'll find out she likes that, too. But he isn't about to rush it. Mornings when he wakes up, he lies in bed a few moments to take inventory of his libido, to see where desire will lead him later in the day or evening. *Corinna, Corinna — looks like it's you again, my dear. Whaddaya thinka that?*

•

Horace is glad the plastic bag fits into his jacket pocket. He doesn't want to be seen carrying it up onto the hillside field, nor does he want to be seen cleaning up the ring-night aftermath. On the other hand, he wants the trash still to be there when he arrives at the area. He'd thought that the students might come back to clean it up, but he knows that by this time — the fourth day since they fouled the place — they've forgotten about it. The students rarely come up onto the hill anyway, which suits Horace just fine. He likes having it to himself, as he almost always does. He often chides himself for thinking the field belongs to him in any way other than as one tiny part of the planet that he deeply appreciates. But then he feels himself bristling whenever he sees anyone else up here. One day an art teacher brought her class to the graveyard to do some sketching, and he'd hated that. But he knows he shouldn't have.

Today is cool but sunny, with a little breeze. Horace begins by picking up the mostly empty containers of whipped cream and chocolate sauce. Then he works on gathering the feathers, which stick to his fingers because of the chocolate that seems to have touched everything in the area. Horace knows he has the stuff on his shoe soles, and he hopes it will wear off before he gets back to the apartment. It would be just too strange to try to explain to Clara why he's tracked chocolate onto their wall-to-wall carpeting. Finally he picks up the marshmallows, which have an obscene, slippery feel to them from the wetness of the grass and weeds and of course from the chocolate. Horace breaks into a sweat from the constant bending over and standing up. When he looks at his watch, he realizes he's been working almost an hour, and he still has the outlying wind-blown feathers to gather up. It won't do to leave any trace of the ring-night ritual if he can possibly help it. The longer he works on it, the more certain he becomes. The clean-up must be absolute.

◆

Sonny runs into Clara outside the college post office. They're face to face before Sonny has a chance to prepare himself.

She's almost a foot shorter than he is, and so he has to look down at her, which means he takes special note of her very dark, shiny, and slightly tousled hair. He's about to say he likes her hair this way — though the truth is he hasn't made up his mind about it — but such a comment would be just so sophomoric. So he ends up just opening his mouth and closing it again before he gets caught in a trance of staring into her face. Which is an act that feels deeply wrong — it's exactly what he's trained himself not to do when he socializes with the Housemans. He tries to wrench his eyes off to the side.

"Hello, Sonny." Clara's mouth forms a little restrained smile, which makes Sonny realize that she's used to his providing her with humor, or at least lively conversation. That's what he does in the company of Clara and her husband. It's the only way she's knows him to be. Also, he realizes that he's never been around her by herself, just the two of them. Now she's waiting for him to say something really smart or to tease her as he always does when they're around Horace, and all he can think to say to her is that he's never noticed how tea-cup pale her skin is and how there's almost a shade of blue where her hair borders her temples and that these tiny dilations of her nostrils are just the most darling features imaginable. He says nothing. She's dressed more casually than he's ever seen her, a sweatshirt, old blue jeans, and sneakers — which make him want to ask her if she's doing some painting at the apartment or going for a hike or what. But then he realizes he shouldn't be scanning her body up and down this way, and so he does a little side step to begin moving around her, at the same time he says, "Hello, Clara," and moves toward the post office door. He sees disappointment wash over her face — he's certain he's not imagining that, and it makes him all the more uncomfortable. So he exerts himself to rescue the situation and blurts, "Great to see you," as he slips through the door into the foyer. With his hand raised in a wave to her through the glass door, he backs toward the area where his post office box is located. He's pretty sure she shakes her head ever so slightly before she turns away.

There are students milling around Sonny when his mind snaps him through a crackling sequence of thoughts. Clara possesses very little bosom at all. Clara sees Sonny as the jester who hangs around her royal husband. Clara has just landed in his discard pile. And Sonny is a jerk — which is of course no news at all but which in this moment he understands to be the part of himself with which he's most comfortable.

◆

While Horace leans against the brick wall of the graveyard, half a dozen turkey buzzards gradually come swirling and gliding down from high up in sky, lower and lower over the hillside. The day is sunny and breezy, so that the big birds hardly have to move their extended wings to drift through great swatches of space. In the past he's stood and watched them, sometimes turning his body to follow the flight of one of them swooping low over the grassy flank of the slanted field. Now he finds himself doing it again — pivoting slowly in one place, his eyes riveted on a single bird. The buzzards seem aware of him; they coast low and veer away only after they've given him a detailed view of the white undersides of their wings. *I'm not dead,* Horace says aloud to them. *I'm many years away from that, my fine feathered friends.* It feels wonderful to speak to creatures who couldn't care less what noise he makes, to say these words with no human being near enough to hear them.

Then Horace does something that feels both strange and right — he lifts his hand above his head, arrows his fingers toward one slowly sailing over to his left. As if it has received a command, the bird turns in his direction and drifts downward. It comes so close, then seems to float a long moment at a point about ten yards above and directly in front of Horace. He watches it with such intensity that he feels buoyed upward. The bird's crimson head angles down toward him. For one exultant moment Horace thinks it might actually touch his extended fingers. But of course he knows that's a silly thought. The buzzard evidently thinks so, too, because it slowly wheels away and soars down over the hillside. Reluctantly Horace lowers his arm and turns his body to track the bird's flight path away from where he stands.

◆

Just at twilight Sonny has stepped out of his house and begun walking the loop around the campus. He's never done this before, mostly because he considers himself an indoors person. But he likes this hour of the day because it puts him in a reverie over Vespers and how he and Katie walked together to Saint Stephens in Queens for the Vespers services during Lent. They'd held hands. Brother and sister, they'd walked and held hands and hadn't even thought about it, because they were children.

Horace is out here, too. He's walked the loop a hundred times or more, but it's unusual for him to be out at this time of day. Clara has been invited by a friend from work to attend a concert in Roanoke this evening, which has made them both rather proud of her. In these first months of their marriage, she's spent all her evenings in the apartment. Horace has occasionally had to be out for meetings or dinners with guests of the college. Right now he's absorbed in how this half-light changes the landscape. He won't be seeing turkey buzzards, though he knows they roost in the trees over behind the graveyard.

Sonny has walked past the riding barn and the tennis courts. Now he's approaching the place where the road runs parallel to the creek. In his nine months of teaching at Hollins College, he's heard students and colleagues mention Secret Creek, but he's never seen it before. He might have walked by without noticing it now, except for the sudden fragrance of water in the air. Sweet as rotting wood, that smell makes him think of a girl he met at Jones Beach, with whom he once ran through a thunderstorm. He can see her face, but when he tries to remember her name, it won't come back.

Horace has taken his usual path through the graveyard. He's heading straight across the spine of the hill. He can't see the mountains in the distance, but the sky is lavender, and a few stars are out. If Clara were with him, she'd love this soft air and light. He gets a little stab of guilt for never having brought her up here. But he knows she'd want to linger, to savor the mood. Some of Horace's pleasure comes from moving briskly through the landscape. He's striding down the hill. Soon he'll reach the creek — which he's loved since his first day on campus.

Along the water's edge, twilight is the hour of greatest creature activity. Catbirds, jays, bluebirds, and sparrows flit among the trees. Turtles graze the bottom. Insects dip and hover over the water's surface. Suckers rise to take nymphs, leaving quickly disappearing circles.

The light has faded enough that Sonny's paying almost no attention to the creek, the trees, even the road he walks on. He's obsessing over what happened with Clara. He knows it's ridiculous, but he's actually grieving over the loss of her. *Coulda been faithful to you, Corinna,* he murmurs to himself. *Why'd you have to ambush me at the post office?* Then it occurs to him that at least now he can stop torturing himself when he's around Horace and Clara. Guess *I ain't torn no more,* he says. That's when he catches sight of it.

Horace isn't used to this absence of light. He strains to see his usual points of interest. Along the road and in the parking lot, streetlights switch on, so that he sees a man approaching him, some poor man caught up in his troubles, walking with his head down. When the man stops in his tracks, Horace recognizes his pal Sonny. Then he looks over where Sonny's looking. It's what he hasn't ever seen before, and the sight of it freezes him in place.

Sonny can't stand to stay still and keep his mouth shut any longer. "Great Jesus—what are you?" he shouts at it. He knows it's stupid, what he's said.

The heron is a ghost rising from the water, and though its wing strokes are silent, they're powerful. In a few seconds it's a hundred yards upstream.

"Not Jesus," Horace says as he walks up to Sonny. He's irked at his pal for scaring the bird away, but that dissolves when he sees Sonny's face.

"Hey, Horace!" Sonny's beaming. The sight of his friend fills Sonny with irrational joy. He grabs Horace's sleeve.

For that single moment the heron was still and one-dimensional as a paper cutout, and in the light from the street it shone like platinum. To the men who witnessed it, it looked so wildly sculpted that it might have tumbled down from the moon into Secret Creek. This particular heron will never again be seen by Horace Houseman or Sonny Carson. They may never see another heron in a natural setting. But for now, under a streetlight shining down on them, these two freshman professors at Hollins College grasp each other's arms awkwardly and step in a circle. If a student saw them, she'd think they were drunk and laugh out loud. But of course they're sober, and they'd both be embarrassed if they thought anyone had seen them.

Volunteer

WHEN SONNY STARTS TO ENTER A ROOM, kids begin streaming out of it. When he tries to leave a room, kids on their way in jam the doorway. Murmuring, "Excuse me," "Oops," and "I'm sorry," Sonny moves against the flow, his arms slightly lifted, his eyes looking down into upturned faces and onto the tops of amazing heads of hair. Who knew the hairstyles of children were miracles of cosmetic engineering? And their voices make a high-pitched, fast-cadenced music Sonny can't imagine ever getting used to. This is his first day at the King Street Youth Center. He's sixty-one. He's never before volunteered. He hopes he'll get through the afternoon.

No children of his own, Sonny fought his first two wives to keep from having them. It's not an issue with Louise, his third. And anyway she has two by her ex, both grown and keeping their distance. Today he realizes he's underestimated his ignorance of children.

So far, Sonny hasn't found a way to get a kid to speak to him. Or even to stand still and look directly at him. "Hi," he says as he approaches one sitting at a computer off by himself. The boy glances up at him, stands up and walks out of the room. Sonny hopes no one has seen his first exchange with a King Street Youth. He sits down at the kid's machine. The boy was playing something called "Love Hina Sim Date RPG." Sonny blinks at the screen. Professor of Computer Technology at Saint Michael's College, he hasn't encountered anything like this. He's being advised to "Go to the university school and hit on hot chicks there get to know them and fight them." He's tempted to lift his hand, move the cursor, and click on the button.

When Sonny was a boy, he couldn't have imagined a world where he might have faced a machine like this that would invite him to hit on hot chicks and get to know them. The most exciting thing in his life at that boy's age was Father Hirschfield. Father Richard. Richard Hirschfield is probably the reason Sonny is sitting in this too-small chair right at this moment.

Sonny grew up in Queens about as Catholic as you could get. German on one side, Irish on the other, and both sides what Sonny privately terms "heavy Catholics," meaning that as a kid he felt like he carried a weighty chunk of the church on his back all day every day. Meaning that Father Richard constantly whispered in his ear: *You must be kinder than your friends. You must take care of your sister. Each day a chance to do some good. Everyone suffers — remember that before you speak in anger. Harm no one.* Fifty years later, Father Richard still whispers to him on a daily basis.

With this remembrance of Richard Hirschfield, the basic complication of his life comes back as well — Sonny's old grandmother. Whenever she comes to mind — though she died when Sonny was nineteen — the old woman makes him shake his head. Grandma Baumen was like the family's own personal representative of the devil. Hated Protestants, hated Jews, hated all persons of color and most especially hated Blacks, hated Italians, hated Roosevelt, hated Eisenhower, and hated Truman. Also wore no underwear. Or wore it only once a year, when she attended Easter Mass at Saint Patrick's Old Cathedral.

Sonny shakes his head. Grandma Baumen and Father Ricard made him what he is today, a man sitting in a child's chair in a room as alien to him as a spaceship. A man shaking his head to clear it, even as he knows these voices and demons are with him for the long haul.

●

The boy's name is James-William. He's ten years old. His mother is Janelle Vallieres, of the old and infamous North End Vallieres family. A Vallieres has served as the Mayor of Winooski, and for the past fifty years or so, at least one Vallieres or another has been serving time in the Chittenden Correctional Center. From the light-coffee shade of James-William's skin, Sonny concludes that James-William's father must be a man of color. But his father's name isn't on record in the files of the King Street Center. "You want to know about his father?" asks Mrs. Cole in the office. "Ask his mother. She's got plenty to say and won't be shy about telling you."

Sonny is afraid of Janelle Vallieres, whose face tells him she despises him and everybody in his tax bracket. And anyway, Sonny doesn't really want to know about the father. He'd like to know why James-William won't talk to him. The boy talks to other children and to a few of the regular King

Street staffers. The boy seems perfectly willing to sit beside Sonny in the computer room. He's happy to show Sonny the games he plays, the web sites he visits. He's okay about Sonny's sitting beside him at snack time, and he doesn't mind when Sonny reads to him, though he does prefer to pick out the book himself. Sonny is sure the boy can read, because when he reads to him, James-William runs his index finger just beneath each word as Sonny sounds it — if Sonny pauses, so does the boy's finger. Sonny even suspects James-William of being a genius because of his lively face, the speed with which he operates the computer, and a level of alertness that occasionally shocks Sonny when he catches a glimpse of it.

James-William's hair is maintained at the hair equivalent of a golf green. By King Street standards, James-William is exceptionally clean and well enough dressed that Sonny considers him a kind of child dandy. Somebody really thinks about colors and what shirt goes with what pants and so on. Sonny has to believe it's Janelle. Whether or not she hates people like him, Janelle looks after James-William with super-mom passion. It's just, as Mrs. Cole explains to Sonny, that Janelle needs for James-William to be able to come to the center when he gets out of school and to stay there until she gets out of work up at UVM and can walk down the hill and pick him up.

One night Sonny wakes with a start. James-William is asleep beside him. The boy's breathing — of which Sonny is always intensely aware when the boy sits with him at the center — has waked him. Slowly he realizes that, of course, it's Louise's breathing he's heard. Sonny is relieved that he hasn't disturbed her. He doesn't want to have to explain to her why he might dream of James-William. While he's trying to ease himself back down into sleep again, Sonny understands that it wasn't fear or anxiety that woke him. He thinks it might have been happiness.

•

As a boy, Sonny read William Lindsay Graham's *Houdini: The Man Who Walked Through Walls*. Though he never saw a professional performance, he took an intense interest in magic and magicians. When he was James-William's age, an acceptable — even if somewhat feeble — form of magic was the church. Sonny's first sight of Father Richard Hirschfield was when the young priest came to Sonny's Sunday school class to explain the miracle of the Eucharist. Father Richard actually brought a chunk of brown bread with him into the church basement and walked in front of each child showing the bread cupped in his hands. "It doesn't stop looking like this," he said. "Even after it's consecrated, it still looks exactly like this," he said.

Because Sonny was at the end of the front row, he was the last child to be offered a close-up view of the bread in Father Richard's hands. Father Richard stopped directly in front of him. He stood in silence so long that Sonny thought something was wrong. He stopped studying the bread and looked up into the priest's face. Sonny had never seen such an expression. Even now, as a man growing into his senior years, he thinks of that as a face transformed by some powerful force. Fanaticism, Sonny would say, but what he thought in Sunday school that morning was that Father Richard was clearly under the influence God.

"What's your name, son?" the priest murmured.

Sonny told him all four of his names.

"God bless you, Hans Michael Patrick Carson," Father Richard lightly brushed the top of Sonny's head and moved away.

·

The difference between what he knows now and what he knew then generates some disturbance in Sonny that he hopes he'll be able to resolve before he dies. Grandma Baumen, for instance, held enormous sway over him by what seemed then her mighty force of love, a fabulous eccentricity of personality, and something that was accidentally sexual —though sexual wasn't a word that he could have used with any precision in those days. What he knew then was that when he was around her, she often did things that excited his penis.

Two questions have troubled Sonny for years: Did she harm him? Did she know what she was doing?

Sonny is pretty sure he's always been inordinately interested in sex. Has sex on his mind too much. Has let sex determine his behavior in too many ways. Sonny thinks he has been too intensely drawn toward others because of it; at the same time he has been separated from others because of it. Sex has had its way with him more than it should have. But can he blame that on poor ignorant old Grandma Baumen?

Of course not.

But maybe so.

She wore dresses that allowed him to peek at her sagging breasts. She sometimes sat in such a way that he saw up her dress. Several times she let him see her stark naked, and she acted as if it was nothing out of the ordinary. She wasn't sneaky about what she did. Maybe clever. But it just seemed to be the way she was — reckless in how she presented herself to other people.

He's thought about it enough over the years to have settled in his mind that she was a flasher — a woman who took pleasure from exposing herself. Knowingly or unknowingly. Sonny supposes she did it with the opposite sex in mind, though maybe she didn't care whether those who saw her were male or female. He thinks maybe she never even admitted to herself what she was doing, never consciously acknowledged the thrill it must have brought her to show herself. Those were sexually oppressive times, the 1950s.

But why did she think anyone wanted to see her old body?

It disturbed him then, it even disturbs him these years later trying to think it through. He didn't move away from her, didn't turn his head. He did indeed look. Looking both horrified and thrilled him. But in not looking away, didn't he collaborate in the wrongness of it? Didn't his little boy dick get hard? Didn't that mean he wanted to fuck his grandmother? What kind of boy wants that? To think deeply about old Grandma Baumen makes Sonny shake his head, as if to do so will clear it all out of his mind. So many head-shakes over the years, and his mind still isn't clear.

Did she mean to arouse her grandson? To damage a child? Of course not.

Though not out of the question.

•

Sonny sits down beside James-William in the computer room and finds him typing — not with two or three fingers the way Sonny does but with all five fingers of each hand the way real typists do. He's not fast, but he definitely knows the right way to do this.

The boy doesn't want Sonny to see what he's typed, and so as Sonny settles into his chair, James-William closes the program, loses whatever he was working on, and immediately opens the web site for Armada, a video game he often plays by himself for Sonny's benefit. In the past, whenever Sonny has asked if he can play, too, James-William hasn't responded, has simply continued to move aircraft carriers, submarines, and destroyers around the board on the screen. Sonny is frustrated with the way James-William has disabled him by not talking with him, sometimes ignoring him even as he allows Sonny to sit in his presence. Now Sonny says, "May I try something?" He hears how his voice is different, not so much polite as serious.

James-William removes his hands from the keyboard. Which Sonny interprets as "Okay." Sonny scoots his chair to allow his hands to reach the keyboard though he still must re-align it more than an inch or so. The screen is not at a good angle for him to see it, but he'll make do. He minimizes Armada, finds the icon for Word, and opens the program. Then he types — with his old three-finger method — a question onto the white screen of a new document:

Do you have a computer at home?

He thwacks the enter key twice, then pushes the keyboard back to where James-William had it before. James-William doesn't hesitate. He sits forward and types — at least as fast as Sonny typed the question — his answer.

my mom does she lets me use it

The boy sits back, sets his hands in his lap, stares at the screen. Sonny feels his heart muscling around in his chest, feels a tight smile stretch his lips. Thirty years of teaching, and he's never had a breakthrough like this. He shifts the keyboard back to where he needs it.

How did you learn to type?

The boy's already leaning forward when Sonny pushes the keyboard back his way.

my mom got a program for her job she got me to help her learn

James-William starts to sit back, but then he leans forward and types more words.

she has to be in the room or i can't use it

Sonny is ready.

When I was a boy your age we didn't have computers.

James-William is ready, too.

i know that stupid ☺

·

Father Richard was the magician, Sonny the acolyte. Even today, when he thinks of Father Richard, he gets a little jolt of boyhood excitement. Doing good. Being admired and appreciated. Receiving beatific smiles from many people. The whole congregation of Saint Teresa's was infatuated with

Richard Hirschfield; men and woman smiled at him as if he were a young man who'd grown up as part of their families. And now he'd become the priest who made them proud of themselves. Some of their admiration fell collaterally on Sonny who tried to stand near Father Richard whenever possible.

When the Eucharist has been served to all the people, the priest partakes of it himself. The congregation silently sits and witnesses it. When Father Richard did this, Sonny stood beside him to assist. Father Richard broke out in a sweat as he sipped from the cup. Sonny was near enough to see how Father Richard very nearly fainted as he sipped and swallowed. For an eleven-year-old boy to be a foot away from such a man in such a moment was almost as profound as to see a man die or to witness the birth of a baby. The sight of Father Richard, sweating with the cup at his lips, his eyelids fluttering, shook the evil out of Sonny like salt from a shaker. Sonny knows that it was the one time in his life when he didn't just pretend to be a good person, he actually was a good person.

There was, of course, the fact that Sonny loved his own goodness, wallowed in it. But maybe he had to, because his friends fell away from him, didn't want to be around him, didn't want to hear what he had to say about anything. He was, Sonny knows, pretty much an insufferable little boy. He forgives himself now — or forgives the boy that he was — for self-righteousness. He doesn't see how he could have been any other way.

Father Richard's hand often passed over Sonny's head in blessing, his murmured words a comfort to Sonny whenever it happened.

Sonny knew that he was a good boy, but he also knew

that Father Richard's kind of faith wasn't anything that he possessed. As a boy, he thought his inability to believe in heaven or hell or a god who cared what he did or didn't do was because he was still a kid — and what kind of kid can understand salvation and Christ's dying for the sins of all mankind? Sonny knew he was a long, long way from such an understanding. All he could do was stay on the track that would eventually transport him to faith. Father Richard was the engine, he was the caboose.

Customarily Sonny found Father Richard in the changing room where they put on their vestments before the service and took them off when the service was finished. In that room was a sturdy old table and two large wooden chairs against a wall. Sonny would enter and find Father Richard sitting in one of those chairs. Sonny had the sense that Father Richard had been sitting there for a long while and that he'd remained almost completely still until Sonny's arrival. Sometimes his head would be bowed, his eyes closed. Sonny thought Father Richard was just thinking then, not praying. Or sometimes Father Richard would be leaning back in the chair, the back his head of his head against the wall. But then — after the slightest pause, just when Sonny had stepped fully into the room — Father Richard stood up and smiled, very obviously pleased to see Sonny. He extended his hand to Sonny for a handshake that both charmed and amused Sonny with its warmth.

This was when they talked — maybe a ten-minute interval of time when Father Richard's voice became not exactly a whisper but a very quiet instrument that Sonny believed he used just for talking to him. *You mustn't forget that your sister needs you, Hans Michael. She's little now, but as she grows older, she will need you to help her at school — to protect her, to make certain the other boys and girls treat her with respect. You should practice looking after her now, so that when the time comes, you will be prepared.*

"Yes, Father," Sonny would answer. "I understand." He tried to match Father Richard's tone in his answers, but his voice didn't have a man's strength and depth, and so he never spoke a great deal in these minutes before the service. And Father Richard required very little of him. He seemed to have saved up many things he wanted to tell Sonny, almost all of it practical advice for how to behave at school and on the way to and from school. He counseled Sonny about boys who would speak disrespectfully of girls and teachers. He advised Sonny not to spend time around girls whose behavior wasn't modest. He instructed Sonny in what he termed the ways a decent boy can defend himself from evil. While he talked with Sonny, he stood close to him with his hands clasped behind his back. Sonny thought Father Richard looked like someone had handcuffed his hands behind his back. Father Richard was a large man — not fat but well over six feet tall with a very solid frame. When he stood that way, it reminded Sonny of pictures he'd seen of Houdini, who allowed himself to be handcuffed and chained to demonstrate his ability to escape from all manner of imprisonment.

At five minutes before the hour, Father Richard touched a finger to his lips to signal the end of talking, and they turned to the row of hooks on the wall that held their vestments. Father Richard practiced a private ritual of preparing himself to step out into the church and present himself to the congregation. When they slipped on their vestments, each helped the other in silence, though Sonny's duties were more demanding since a priest's robes were elaborate and ornate. Sonny loved Father Richard's robes and the stoles that varied according to the seasons of the church. He even liked his own simple white robe and couldn't help looking at himself in the mirror a little more than he needed to. He could do this, because Father Richard seemed almost to have forgotten him altogether in the minutes before they entered the church.

•

If her flasher behavior had been all there was to Grandma Baumen, Sonny would have had little or nothing to do with her. But the summer he was nine, when he was in her company almost every weekday morning, she began conversing with him as if he were a grown-up, and almost no one else did that. At the time, he didn't think about why she might have done it. Now he understands that she was just lonely. She and his grandfather lived entirely separate lives, coming together only to drink whiskey before supper, to eat that meal at opposite ends of the dining room table, and to pick up quarrels that had been ongoing for most of their married lives. Because she was so extremely opinionated, Grandma Baumen had little contact with anyone, including family members. But such an interest the old woman had in him! She was a gifted questioner, asking him about teachers and the subjects they taught, about his classmates and their parents and their families. Asking him about girls, too, and she had a memory for what he told her.

The 1950s was the last era of children being seen and not heard. Sonny thinks the principle favored children more than it did adults. He's glad his parents didn't interrogate him as his grandmother did, or they'd have found out lots they didn't want to know. They were sweet and hard-working people, his mother and father, careful to let him know they loved him, happy that he was such a good boy, and so respectful of his privacy they rarely asked him anything. They were very pleased that he took so much responsibility for Katie, his sister.

Though he wasn't aware of it, Sonny had a lot on his mind, and Grandma Baumen could start him talking. She'd ask him about a teacher, ask him how she talked, what kind of clothes she wore, how she moved or didn't move around the classroom, and then — Sonny thinks her timing for the ultimate question was perfect, coming as it did after she'd gotten him started, gotten him speaking sentence after sentence—she'd ask, "What do you think of her?"

What did he think of Mrs. Gillespie? Until Grandma Baumen asked him, Sonny'd never considered that he had any particular thoughts about Mrs. Gillespie. Now that the question came to him when he was in the unnatural state of hearing his own voice go on at some length, he realized that he had quite a number of thoughts about Mrs. G. She wasn't a good teacher, but she was fierce enough to control her class, and so she got good results. Kids learned about Geography even though it was boring, and Mrs. G. plainly didn't care a fig about it. Sonny was a star pupil in that class because he actually did enjoy memorizing such useless facts as how much rain fell in Portugal, which southern state was the first to become industrialized, and what explained the monsoon season in southern Asia. It pleased him mightily to discover that he had opinions and that they spilled out of him this way while the two of them sat in his grandmother's kitchen. Sonny held forth while Grandma Baumen finished her breakfast, sipped her third cup of coffee, and studied Sonny's face as if it were a puzzle she was very close to solving.

·

Do you like school?

its ok

What's your favorite subject?

my mom says i can be in band next year

What do you want to play?

drums but she wont let me

So?

she says flute or clarinet not too much noise

What are you going to do when you grow up?

rob jewelry stores

Seriously.

how am i supposed to know

What do you want to do?

computers

You'll have to go to college for that.

ok jewelry stores can you help me get a gun

Maybe I can help you learn to play drums on the computer.

ha ha

No, I'm serious. I'll help you research it. We can write a program. Get some headphones. No noise.

im ten

You're smart.

how would you know

.

The day he got his school pictures, Sonny cut out one of the medium-size ones, put it in an envelope, and that Sunday, when he entered the changing room, when they'd finished shaking hands, presented it to Father Richard. The priest extracted it from the envelope and stood staring it, not saying anything. Sonny couldn't read his face and felt awkward in the silence that customarily Father Richard would fill with his quiet voice.

"My grandmother says it's flattering." Grandma Baumen had expressed surprise that Sonny'd gotten his hair combed and that the photographer had persuaded him to smile so naturally for the picture. In the family Sonny was known to be solemn-faced most of the time and whenever a smile did ambush him, he was quick to fight it off.

"No, no, I think it's a truthful picture," murmured Father Richard. "That's why I'm marveling at it." He set it on the table and stood over it, studying it from a distance. "You're a handsome young man, Hans Michael," he said slowly.

Sonny felt himself blushing, and he expected Father Richard's eyes to turn to him. The priest, however, turned to the hook where his robes waited for him. It was only a few minutes early to begin the quiet ritual of putting on their vestments, but Sonny felt a small disturbance in Father Richard's timing. It now occurred to him that he'd thought giving the priest his school picture would move them to another level of discussion. He'd thought that instead of filling his ears with advice, Father Richard might begin to question him as his grandmother did. He'd thought that he might have the opportunity to open himself up by talking to Father Richard as he was able to talk with Grandma Baumen. He wanted to see what he might say if he could speak freely to the priest. Instead, the picture seemed to have shut down Father Richard's interest in him altogether. Sonny didn't move to help him with the vestments, and Father Richard kept his distance from the boy. Neither of them looked into the mirror. When it was time to leave the room and enter the church, Sonny's picture was still on the table where Father Richard had put it.

·

Grandma Baumen could stand on her head. She was seventy-two years old. As a boy Sonny couldn't understand why she wanted to do such a thing or why she was so proud of herself for being able to do it. Fortunately she didn't think of the stunt all that often, but when she did, she'd challenge Sonny to see which of them could stay up the longest. It'd been a while since they'd had one of those contests, because he didn't like them, but this morning his sister was with him at their grandparents' house, their grandfather was away from the house as usual, and their grandmother had them at her mercy. When Grandma Baumen issued the challenge, Katie was excited by the idea — having never before gone through such a competition with her grandmother, and so Sonny had no choice but to go along with the old woman.

Grandma Baumen led the way up the steps to the guest room, which she used for her daily exercises. Among her several quirks — most of them dietary — the old woman did sit-ups, knee-bends, and push-ups every morning. She also had a set of two-pound lead-balled barbells that she lifted. This routine she carried out before dawn and before she took up her elaborate bathroom rituals. Sonny hoped his grandmother planned to fix her dress around her legs so that she wouldn't expose her private parts when she turned herself upside down. He'd seen the trick both ways, when she covered herself and when she didn't. He thought he wouldn't be able to bear it if he had to witness his grandmother showing herself to his sister. Grandma Baumen also had a great interest in bowel movements and enemas, and they'd already had a discussion of those matters before she thought to challenge the children to the head-standing contest. Sonny'd taken a vow to himself to avoid at all costs visiting his grandmother again in the presence of his sister. He was deeply embarrassed by the old woman interrogating Katie as to when she'd had her last bowel movement and what it had looked like. Katie was only seven, and her grandmother's questions just sent her into a fit of giggling. Sonny had wished he was far, far away.

Now the old woman positioned herself facing a wall and with her back to the children and began to tuck her skirts around her legs in the way Sonny understood to mean she would be modest this morning. He was greatly relieved and thought the contest might not be as awful as he'd imagined it would be. Grandma Baumen had to prop her feet back against the wall to help her keep her balance. Katie took up a position similar to Grandma Baumen — Sonny was fairly certain his sister hadn't ever tried to stand on her head before. At least she had on blue jeans, and so there wouldn't be the issue of her showing her underwear, a thought that also made him uncomfortable. Momentarily he thought of slipping out of the room.

"Ready, set, go!" Grandma Baumen called out as she put her head on the cushion she arranged on the floor and turned her legs and butt up.

Sonny caught a glimpse of Katie turning herself in imitation of Grandma Baumen, just before he put his head down and maneuvered his lower half up. He'd fixed himself so as to face away from his grandmother and his sister, and though it had been a while since he'd tried to stand on his head, he found it surprisingly easy to push his legs up and straighten them with his heels together up there where his head would ordinarily be. With his blood moving down into his head and face, Sonny realized that as long as he stayed like this he wouldn't have to see his grandmother and his sister. He'd never before cared very much whether he won or lost these contests with Grandma Baumen, but now he was determined to stay balanced upside down until he was certain she had righted herself. Even if she did have the advantage of propping herself up against the wall.

Sonny quickly lost his resolve and was trying to decide whether to let his feet come back to the floor or to let himself pass out from the exertion when he heard Katie wail, "Grandma!…"

"Oh, shush, child," his grandmother said. "Nobody's hurting you."

Katie kept sobbing, and even dizzy as he was, Sonny got to her pretty quickly. His sister wasn't a crybaby.

Sonny didn't look at Grandma Baumen. He knew she'd shown herself to Katie. After a moment the old woman left the room.

·

This afternoon James-William is waiting for him when Sonny enters the center. His face gleeful, he takes Sonny's hand, pulls him to the computer room, and hops up and down while Sonny sits and faces the machine. Because this is the first time James-William has touched him, Sonny is happily distracted. It's the most animated Sonny has ever seen him. When he has his glasses on, Sonny peers at the screen, trying to make out what he's seeing. It takes him a moment. He doesn't know why he's so dense right now, because the diagram he faces isn't complicated.

James-William can't contain himself any longer. "Don't need a program. Got it right here. Make my own drum set out of cardboard boxes." He points at the screen. "Get a trashcan lid for cymbal. This guy will teach me."

Though Sonny has seen him three days a week for several months, and the two of them have had extensive typed conversations sitting together in front of this very machine, these are the first words James-William has spoken aloud to him. Sitting with the boy standing beside him now, Sonny turns to find James-William's face less than a foot away from his own. The boy's expression is beyond exuberance. His eyes seek Sonny's eyes. Something is being asked. Suddenly an Old Testament saint, Sonny's whole body resonates with a call directly from Yahweh.

"Don't need your program," James-William says.

Spoken quietly, these words hurt; nevertheless, they are an intimacy. Simultaneously pierced and healed, Sonny waits.

"You have a credit card, don't you?" the boy asked.

.

In another ten years or so, he'd have the word for it — despair — to name what he felt that afternoon when he and Katie had walked the two blocks home from Grandma Baumen's house. At the time, it was just a pulsing, generalized pain — but what hurt him seemed to be all around his body rather than inside any particular part of it. Katie'd stopped crying, but she held onto his hand, and her face was grim. Though Sonny couldn't think of what he ought to say to her, he thought he ought to try again. "She doesn't know any better," he began.

Katie shook her head, which made her hair fly out in an alarming way. With her lips pressed together, she gave him a furious look. She couldn't have said it any clearer: *Shut up!*

"I should have stopped her," Sonny said.

Katie let go of his hand and ran several steps ahead of him. Then she resumed walking, but fast enough that Sonny knew she didn't want him beside her. He let the distance stay between them; he didn't want to upset her again. They made their way back home like that, Sonny following five or six steps behind his sister, keeping an eye out for anything that might hurt her, even though his own level of pain was so severe that all he really wanted to do was curl up on the sidewalk and wait for someone to kneel down and comfort him.

·

"Mr. Carson." Janelle's face tells Sonny he's going to regret this conversation. He hasn't wanted it anyway, but when Mrs. Cole informed that Janelle wanted to talk to him, he knew he couldn't say no.

"Yes, ma'am," he says. He hopes it's okay to call her ma'am. He wants her to take it as a sign of his respect for her, but he knows she might think he's making fun of her. Her face registers neither flattery nor insult. It occurs to him that Janelle is maybe ten years younger than he thought she was.

"Mr. Carson, my boy has to come here after school. I can't afford for him to be anywhere else." Janelle makes a face at Sonny that at first he thinks is a grimace but then quickly understands to be her effort to smile, to be polite.

"Yes, ma'am."

"I don't want you to think I don't appreciate your good intentions," she says.

Sonny nods.

"He probably told you I've asked him not to make noise in the apartment. What he didn't tell you — because he doesn't know it — was that before he was born, there was a lot of noise in that apartment, and my landlord gave me written notice."

Janelle sighs, and Sonny waits.

"He's not a kind man, my landlord. I used up all his patience years ago."

It's all Sonny can do not to turn his eyes away from hers.

"If James-William taps on those boxes just loud enough to make the people downstairs call my landlord, he and I will be out on the street."

Sonny knows he has to say something now. "I'm very sorry," he says. "I can tell the center I won't be coming back." He pauses before adding, "If that will help."

Janelle gives him her mannerly grimace. He can almost imagine what a real smile from her would look like. She shakes her head. "No man has ever paid attention to him before," she says. And now she turns her eyes toward her knees. "It would break his heart if you stopped coming down here."

Sonny waits for her to say more. When she doesn't, he asks, "What would you like me to do?"

Her lips move slightly before she raises her eyes and gives him her answer. "Make him understand he can't learn to play the drums."

.

Sonny called Father Richard to ask if he could speak to him that Saturday afternoon. As they worked out the time for Sonny to come to the church office, the priest's voice sounded strange, but Sonny was sure that was because they'd never spoken to each other on the phone. In the two days since he and Katie had walked home from Grandma Baumen's, he'd been able to think of little beyond how he would tell the story to Father Richard. The conversation had taken place so many times in Sonny's mind that he'd stopped dreading it and had actually started to anticipate it as a sure way to stop the pain that had come over him. Katie was back to her old self, but Sonny felt like someone had strapped him up in barbed wire.

He considered making a detour into the church to try to pray before he went to see Father Richard, but he thought he couldn't really pray against his grandmother. That would be like tattling on her to God. So he took the parish hall entrance and tried to keep his footsteps quiet as he walked down the hall.

Father Richard's door was open, but Sonny knocked anyway.

"Come in, come in!" sang out a voice it took Sonny a moment to understand was Father Richard's. When he stepped into the office it took him another moment to understand that the young man wearing jeans and a T-shirt was his priest. Books and papers were strewn around the room; boxes were on the floor. Father Richard came to him, embraced him hard —even lifted him an inch or so off the floor—then released him, stood beaming down and said, "I'm go glad you came to me, my friend. I have news I can't wait to tell you."

Sonny realized he'd never seen Father Richard acting happy. It was the last thing he needed to see today. He needed to tell his priest about Grandma Baumen. Even so, he was a polite boy. Though he knew he was in danger of breaking into tears, Sonny felt obliged to try to smile.

"Oh, my young friend, nothing can be all that bad." The new Father Richard chuckled and patted Sonny on the shoulder. "Come, sit down, let me tell you my news. I'll cheer you up."

Sonny sat in the chair Father Richard cleared for him, but the priest himself wasn't able to stay seated in his own chair behind his desk. Almost immediately he stood up, started pacing, and began explaining to Sonny how he'd realized he had no business trying to be a parish priest. He needed to be out in the world, helping people with the issues they faced in everyday life — food, health, safety, money. "I'm going to apply to Columbia — the oldest social work program in the country!" The brightness of his voice convinced Sonny that Father Richard had become another person. The priest who had cared about him had disappeared. Sonny knew he was supposed to respond, but he was too miserable even to nod.

"Do you know when the idea came to me?" The man stepped forward and knelt beside Sonny's chair, moved his face up close. "It was when you gave me your school picture." His voice was low and intense.

Sonny tried to meet the man's eyes during the silence. He was concentrating very hard on not releasing the sob that was building in his throat.

"Oh, I know I can't explain it to you." Waving his hand as if a fly had entered the space between them, the man stood up and began to pace again. "I'm not sure I understand it myself. I just knew I had to get out of that little room. It felt like the two of us were in a prison cell. Also, I knew I couldn't stand to hear another piece of advice coming out of my mouth about how you had to look after your sister. Do you realize I'm never going to put on those robes again?" He chuckled again, stopped pacing, clasped his hands behind his back, and stood beaming down at Sonny.

"The bishop is angry with me," he said quietly. "He told

me to clear out my things before the end of the week. He doesn't know how those words were music to my ears."

Sonny did his best to meet the man's eyes.

"Please don't be so sad, my friend. Don't you realize, you won't have to listen any more of my ridiculous advice? We're both free now."

Sonny stood up. Now he knew he was sure to cry.

The man knelt in front of him, put his hands on Sonny's shoulders, and tried with his eyes to make Sonny look at him. "We're free," he murmured, as if that were a comfort.

Sonny bolted for the door.

•

"Are you a queer, Mr. Carson?"

"I don't think so," Sonny tells Janelle. He keeps it to himself that he wouldn't tell her if he was. She knows that perfectly well.

"Maybe you have a thing for little boys?"

"Nope," he says. Then he says, "My wife asked me the same thing. Different words, but that's what it came down to."

"What's your wife's name?"

"Louise. Happy to introduce you to her if you like."

Janelle shakes her head and studies his face for a long while.

Then she nods. "Okay," she says.

Sonny releases the half a breath he's been holding. He nods, too.

•

Generating thunder, James-William executes a roll on the high tom, strikes six enormous blows to the floor tom, then delivers rim shots to the snare, the middle tom, and back to the snare, all the while his left foot crunches the hi hat to keep the pulse. Now he mounts fast attacks on the middle tom, the snare, then again the middle tom before settling into a steady frenzy between the ride and crash cymbals: On the throne at the center of his mighty storm, James-William writhes like a boy transmitting jolts of electricity. His relatively small torso goes rubbery with dispatching arms and hands all around the galaxy of drums. His sticks are blurs, his knees jump, he's four-armed Nataraja, dark-faced, light-faced, demon and angel. He adds two droll dings on the cowbell before flinging himself into a stream of strobing paradiddles on the floor tom.

Sonny feels that baritone throbbing take hold of him as if the chair he sits in is directly wired to the drums. When he watches and listens like this, Sonny's thoughts float up toward the high ceiling of this studio he's leased. From up here, mindless as a rafter, he looks down on the gleaming wooden floors, the great windows that look out on the lake, and the glistening black pearl shells of the drum set he's bought for James-William. That not-quite-shaved head is the black pearl at the center of Sonny's vision. Sonny's a man-size balloon James-William holds aloft, nudges this way and that way with the booms and rattles, whams, dings and crashes he launches like fireworks festooning up and out and around the enormous room.

Time, of course, must eventually be reckoned with — Janelle will call Sonny on the cell phone he holds in his hand so that he will feel its vibration. Then Sonny will raise his hand with the phone in it, and, no matter what he's working on, James-William will immediately cease his drumming. They'll sit there getting used to the silence. Sonny marvels at this single power he exercises over the boy — with that raising of the hand, he can switch him off. Neither of them quarrels with the arrangement they've worked out with Janelle. Their first hour in the studio, James-William works with Caleb, his teacher. Then Caleb leaves the studio, James-William listens to recordings or works on Caleb's assignments with the practice pad and the metronome or even reads something Caleb has left for him. Around four, he ascends the throne at the middle of the drum set, waits a moment, then begins with just a tap here, a soft boom of the bass, maybe a delicate roll with his tympani sticks on the floor tom.

At the opposite end of the studio Sonny sits in the middle of three chairs. The two on either side of him have been designated as Janelle's chair and Louise's chair. Both women have keys to the studio, and each came here several times when James-William first began his drumming lessons and his practice sessions. Once, without meaning to, they were here together. That afternoon, while James-William labored at making lightning and thunder, Sonny sat between the two women wondering what they made of each other. Neither obliged him with any signal about that. They hardly spoke to each other. Now it's been months since either of them showed up. Though of course either one could arrive at any time — that is the tacit understanding among all four of them.

In the first weeks of James-William's drumming, a thought about the empty chairs came to Sonny. Father Richard occupied one of them, Grandma Baumen the other. Soon after that thought came the piercing insight that those two had been hovering around Sonny for the past half a century, invisibly mucking around with his life, making him feel bad, pointing him in wrong directions. Their presence here in the studio is their most benign form of keeping him company.

His grandmother and his priest keep quiet while James-William carries out his work. The boy is drumming his way through puberty. Music requires just so much effort and attention, and James-William doesn't question that. He gives it everything he's got.

Around four-thirty — when the boy has gradually escalated into the middle section of his improvisation, when every one of the maybe hundred and ten pounds of his body is committed to the conversion of noise into pattern and variation — Sonny feels himself start to levitate. Sitting perfectly still, he rises up toward the ceiling. James-William pays him no mind. From deep down in the vortex of his drumming, he sends up billowing waves of sound. Held aloft, Sonny's all by himself. Grandma Baumen and Father Richard may cast up their forlorn eyes in his direction, but they can't touch him.

Invisible Horse

THIS IS BEFORE THE CANCER. Horace is turning himself into a horse. Every day he wills himself toward creaturedom. It's been going on for a while — he believes that if you do something every day, you get somewhere. He believes that if he wanted to, he could will himself toward becoming a rock or a tree. In a year or so he'd undergo notable changes. He says that long-term effort will surprise you with what it can accomplish. For instance, nowadays, he says he's developed this refreshing method of shaking himself. Says he's learned how to give his whole torso over to the shaking. You and I probably wouldn't notice, he says, but he feels his shoulders and hips imitating that twitchy shuddering you see horses doing when they're out in the rain or when it's hot and flies are bothering them. He says that shaking is more of a pure body act than most humans are capable of. Even if it isn't yet visible to the world, he knows he's made some progress.

How this began was when he read this Raymond Carver story called "Elephant" where a man does everything imaginable for his family, both immediate and extended. Paying for his kids to do this and do that, taking his wife on trips, lending money to his nephew, helping his brother-in-law build a tool shed, and so on. The man in the story enables others to victimize him, which is funny and horrible all at the same time. That's good in a story, but it disturbed Horace. He didn't want to be an elephant and have his whole family riding on his back and dragging him down. But he could feel it happening. Probably a lot of husbands with kids have moments when they feel like the whole freaking apparatus of their family is balanced up on their backs and they have no choice but to keep working harder, paying the bills and generating the cash flow. Nobody has to self-impose that kind of pressure, Horace knows that. He knows, too — though he didn't for a long time — that family life is what he lives for. He's ready to keep paying whatever it costs. He realizes that his own situation with the people he loves and his natural inclination to keep everybody happy is likely to turn him into an enormous, subservient work beast that will in the end just collapse. He'll kneel down, then roll over onto his side. They'll have to shoot him and hire a bulldozer to drag him away, push him into a hole or whatever they do with dead or dying elephants. Turning himself into a horse is how he's going to prevent his life from turning him into an elephant — he can't change his basic nature, but he can steer himself in a certain direction. He can still make a choice or two.

He's not sure he sees this in a true light, but for a while his age numbers were there for him to see, and he wasn't feeling them. Swear to God, he actually thought it wasn't going to happen to him. On up into his late fifties and even into sixty and sixty-one, Horace was chugging right along deep in the fog of his delusion—*Gonna be a young man till the day I die*. Then right around sixty-two, sixty-three, he started to feel some shortness of breath. At night he couldn't get to sleep because his right knee throbbed. His brain had been slipping him clues all along, but he'd been ignoring them. Finally the hints got through. He was forgetting things that young people just don't forget. He'd looked straight at his niece on Christmas morning when the whole family was opening presents, and the dear girl's name just wouldn't make its way onto his tongue. In the class he was teaching as an emeritus, Horace had blanked on the name of a student he'd come to know and admire, a young man he'd have been happy to have as his son. Horace was talking straight to this student, wanting to use his name in the sentence he was making up as he spoke, and the name wasn't there. Yes, of course, this happens to people of all ages, but Horace's brain was making it evident to him that *old* was the name of what he was, and he'd better take hold of the concept. He figures the word most often associated with *old* is *fool*. It's probably inevitable, but for as long as he possibly can, he wants to put off becoming an *old fool*. Horse is the way. Horse is the method.

Horace lost some weight, which seemed to correct the respiratory problem, most of the knee pain, also the stiffness in his spine. He got back a little strut in his walk and even took to sprinting up the steps of his office building. Six flights that he could power up two at a time without gasping when he reached the top. This was when *Horse* first entered his thoughts. The basic fact of a horse is that it's just enough bigger than a man that you can relate to it physically—instead of weighing, say 200 pounds, a horse comes in at something like

1,000 or 1,500. As a horse you're five or six times bigger than you are in your human self. You've got this enormous head, like a 75-pound head. Even so, you don't have to be smart. Intelligence isn't required the way it is with a human being. You're just *Horse*, neither smart nor stupid. Your function is transportation; your virtue is effort.

You'd be right to ask Horace what he knows about horses. He's got some answers. His grandfather fooled around with farming and owned horses — work horses, really, but they were animals that didn't have a lot of work to do, and so the old man would let his grandchildren ride them. The work horses, bored maybe, allowed themselves to be ridden. So even as a little boy, Horace knew what it felt like to be on a horse's back. Very strange up there — especially for a child — to be moving through space by way of a horse. You experience the movement as a living act, as opposed to the way a car, airplane, or train glides through space. Horse travel is not smooth — it's got a swaying, undulating, sort of choppy quality. The rider is directly involved. When you're riding, each little move the horse makes requires some corresponding movement of your own body — it sways, you sway. You and the horse are intensely together. Fact is, the points of contact are the rider's crotch and the horse's back — which makes for a singular relationship. Delicacy and intensity are givens. Maybe the horse doesn't think it's peculiar, but Horace never quite got his mind around the straddling requirement. As a boy, he liked saddles as objects — he wanted to own one, wanted to keep it in his room — but when he was up there on the animal, he never thought *saddle*, he always thought *horse's back*. Also, there was a smell component to the experience — when you were on top of a horse, you breathed in a lot of horse scent. But Horace never relaxed into the mode of horse riding.

After he got big enough to be up on a horse's back by himself, one of them threw him off. This was his grandfather's oldest work horse, they called it *Jim*, and Jim was tired of Horace and his brothers and their friends, their antics, their yips and shouts and incidental cruelty. Horace doesn't blame the animal for pitching him. Jim sensed that Horace didn't know what he was doing. So Horace learned that it's a pretty fair distance from the back of a horse down to the old terra firma. Knocked the breath out of him and bruised up his rib cage. Made the boy less than eager to get back up on a horse's back.

Horace thinks a major sadness of childhood is that you're constantly undergoing disillusionment. As a kid you don't know a darn thing, so you get cuffed around. Life knocks the ignorance out of kids. Horace's positive feelings about saddles came from a couple of sources, the first of which was the movies. Roy Rogers, the Lone Ranger, and Gene Autry owned highly desirable saddles. As a boy Horace nearly swooned over those scenes where the hero puts a foot in the stirrup, takes hold of the saddle horn, and swings himself up onto the horse. When there were outlaws to be pursued, Roy Rogers sometimes took a running leap at Trigger's rear end and propelled himself into the saddle like a cowboy gymnast. Even now, the memory of those saddle-related scenes holds a semi-pornographic thrill for Horace. His other source for information and vision was the mail-order catalogues of his childhood — Sears & Roebuck and Montgomery Ward. They offered enticing photographs of real saddles that could actually be ordered and that would come in the mail. The pictures and the catalogue descriptions encouraged Horace to think that the distance between his life and that of Roy Rogers could be closed with relative ease. All he had to do was persuade his parents to order him a saddle. For Christmas or his birthday. He almost didn't need a horse to put it on. Well, eventually he found out that the wonderful gift wasn't going to come to him, he was never going to get a saddle or a horse to put it on. Horace thinks he's probably lucky that he got thrown by Jim the horse and that he wasn't seriously injured because at least then he could stop lusting for silver-trimmed saddles and deluding himself that he was destined to be a cowboy hero.

Also, he saw a horse die. They called it *Joker*, and it was an old one. Horace was watching it, because its skin was really shuddering, and it was kind of staggering. Then he saw it fall down. Like ka-whump! When Joker hit the ground, Horace felt it in his feet. Joker just lay there, very still it seemed to him. This was when Horace was about eight years old. He ran down to the house and told his grandfather, who was upstairs in the bathroom, drinking whiskey with Horace's grandmother. Don't ask him why they did their drinking in the bathroom, because Horace never thought to ask them until after they were both dead. That day, when he blurted out his news, his grandfather said, "Aw shit, sonny, I don't think that horse died, he just probably lay down to get some rest." Horace was familiar with the way grown-ups like to brush away what an excited kid has to tell them. And he was starting to get acquainted the basic fact of childhood, which is ongoing disillusionment. His grandmother just looked at him over the top of her glasses and said *hrumph* in that way of hers that suggested she wondered what was going to become of him. Horace doesn't remember what came next. The story in his mind just stops right there. He doesn't even know if Joker actually died, or if the horse was just sick and maybe got better. He saw the animal fall, he was pretty certain it had died, he ran to tell his grandfather, his grandfather spoke, his grandmother looked at him, and that's the end. Like one of those old home movies where the film just breaks, and you don't get to see the rest.

Then they break the news to him about the cancer, and in Horace's adult mind, that horse's death is absolutely real. It's part of why he's taken up the project of trying to turn himself into a horse. On a sunny late afternoon he saw the big animal fall up there in the pasture out beside his grandfather's barn. It just toppled over on the grass and lay still. The whole landscape went silent. Maybe out of respect. The horse didn't die in its sleep, which he guesses is the best way for any creature to make its final exit. But Horace thinks the next best way has to be falling over onto the grass, hitting hard, and having your last moments of life infused with the smell of grass and dirt. Not the same thing as the elephant getting dragged down by human beings.

Around that time in his life, third grade, Horace had these schoolmates — Joe and Charles Dunford, who drowned in New River. Horace witnessed both boys pulled up out of the brown water by grappling hooks, saw them hauled into the boats the rescue squad men were using that hot day. Their legs and arms flopped loosely, their heads rolled on their limp necks. They were boys he'd wrestled with — he knew their bodies in that rough and intimate way. At the time, there in the gathered crowd of people, Horace didn't know how to think or feel about what he was seeing. What he mostly knew, while the minutes were ticking by, was how the water moved and how the river bank smelled. But as a grown-up he has decided the experience nailed him into the certainty that he didn't want to die down at the muddy bottom of a river to be hauled up to the water's surface with grappling hooks gouged into his skin. Please God, give him a sweet hard fall down on the grassy ground.

His thinking is that when the time comes, he wants his animal death, not his human one. This is, he realizes, not an idea to be taken seriously by anyone other than himself. Horace indulges himself in a whole collection of irresponsible thoughts, one of which has to do with an odd congruence between him and horses. But this particular crackpot notion has taken on substance and force in his life. If he were anyone else, he'd laugh at it. As himself, though, he sort of likes it that he's the single human being walking the planet who believes that before he dies, he can get pretty close to being a horse. And who cares if anybody else knows what's going on with him?

When Horace and Clara visited Vancouver a few years ago, they went sightseeing in Stanley Park, where of course they took the tour in a horse-drawn carriage. His wife was the one to suggest it out loud, which suited Horace just fine, because he'd already been thinking how he wanted to get close to those big-haunched Clydesdales. When he caught his first glimpse of them in the park, he was simultaneously afraid and filled with desire. This was a wanting similar to how as a boy he had wanted a silver-tooled saddle and a matching set of holsters and pistols. Those animals were huge even by horse standards. The sight of them set him off, but he didn't even have to say anything. His wife spoke the words — *Let's do the horse tour* — and he just nodded. That's mostly how it was when they traveled: his wife made the suggestion, and Horace nodded.

The tour itself was okay, but the really exciting part was set up by the carriage-driver, who also served as the tour guide. The carriage was a small, light-framed bus with open windows that carried about a dozen passengers. When they were trotting through a shady and boring section of the park, the driver explained to the group that they were approaching a hill where the horses would try to speed up, and he'd have to hold them back. "These guys really like to pull a heavy load uphill," the man said. Horace felt a mild thrill when the man called them *guys*. The man said that if he didn't hold them back, they'd be going way too fast by the time they reached the top of the hill. Horace didn't know why, but he just savored that fact, that the Clydesdales took their naughty fun by pulling a heavy carriage filled with people up a hill. "What a concept!" Horace said to his wife, and she gave him a look. She was so used to him that she usually didn't question his mystifying comments. And the driver wasn't lying, because the horses really did step up the cadence of their iron clad hooves as they started up the little hill in the park. The driver really did have to hold them back, Horace and his wife were witness to it. For him that was a moment of intense private excitement. He noticed that his wife's face was flushed by it as well. At the top of the hill, she turned and gave him a smile. The Clydesdales on that hill was his favorite part of the whole four days they spent in Vancouver.

Horace's theory is that everybody lives about ninety percent of his or her life in the privacy of the mind. For old husbands, he thinks it goes up to about ninety-five percent.

Pretty damn strange if you think about it, which he does way too much nowadays. For example, he recently had an eye examination after not having one for about ten years. Turns out his eyes were fine, but the technician used liquid drops to dilate his pupils, warning him that it would last a couple of hours. About half an hour later, when the exam was over, the doctor sent him out into the bright sunlight to make his way across the campus. Horace knew what was happening, but the world seemed to be trying to blast its way into his brain through his eye-sockets.

He felt like he was being turned into some creature whose identity he couldn't even name, a feeble spidery thing that would have to seek out shadowy places to survive. When Horace entered the library where they'd given him an office after he'd retired, the floor had changed into a sheet of fluorescent purple and pink that nauseated him. The shelves of books glowed like slabs of radium. The assault on his eyes drove into him an understanding of what a fragile and precarious thing his consciousness was. Four drops of a liquid could turn him into something so helpless it couldn't survive. He went into his little office, pulled down the window blind, sat in his familiar chair, steepled his hands at his chin, and closed his eyes. *Horse,* he thought. *Not a spider, please God. Not a slug, an aphid, or a moth. Horse. A strong thing. Something that wants to pull heavy loads up a hill. Something that when it falls will make a heavy thud on the ground. Horse,* he thought. *Horse.*

This was about a month before they told him what was coming. Horace sat in the dark room a long time. He was old — all through his body he could really feel it that day. But he still had a little time left. When he finally stood up, left his office, and stepped outside, the world through which he walked felt more hospitable. He was sturdy again, strong. Walking toward home, he picked up his pace.

Two Lives: A Story About Death

HE WAS JOSEPH, NOT JOE. He let people know that right away. He took it as conventional, superficial American friendliness that within a minute or two of meeting someone, he was likely to be turned into Joe. On such occasions, he made a point of not being friendly in making the correction. When he behaved like that — which was often — I always wanted to chime in and say, "He's not your average Joe!"

Unfortunately he had a small and mutated sense of humor.

By the lights of my grandparents and my mother, he was just the man they'd wished I'd marry. If anyone saw the truth of him, it was my father, but Bill was intimidated by what he called "the man's *operandus superfulous*." Plus, Bill always gave me credit for knowing what I was doing. For a couple of years, I didn't realize what Joseph was doing to me. Then for another year, I was willing to overlook it.

I did, finally, have to admit this: He meant to harm me.

Joseph Battelle — Pronounced Ba-TELL — was an entrapment specialist. He was like some highly evolved human version of a spider, though not a poisonous one — his method

234

was subtle and slow-working. It left him blameless for the damage he inflicted.

Joseph Battelle's talent was for using invisible strands of ideas, images, and phrases to lightly snare a tiny part of a person's spirit. He'd dispatch a verbal apparatus into your consciousness that stayed there and worked on you. He'd let you gnaw at yourself to try to get free from something you could neither see nor understand.

For example, he understood something about my mother that probably only my father and I knew about. Hannah was skittish about caring for people. She couldn't close the distance between herself and me or between herself and Bill. In a way, it was very dear of her. When what she really intended was a hug, a touch on the shoulder, or even a kiss, she'd turn away. Both Bill and I were so used to her that we covered for her when we saw her treating someone rudely. But we also found her maddening. There were times when I just wanted to shout at her that I needed her to put her arms around me and tell me that she loved me and that I was a good person. Let's say such a time might have been in middle school, when I'd been hurt by a boy, and she'd know I was in pain — so she'd listen to me and maybe shake her head. I'd wait for her to tell me something or touch my shoulder. A grim smile was the best I got from her. I thought it probably wasn't her fault that she didn't have it in her to give me what I needed. I pitied her for her affliction, but I also felt plenty of anger. I was thirteen, wounded, and out there in the world feeling worthless and unloved.

Within hours of knowing Hannah, Joseph understood her problem and mine. Maybe within hours of the understanding he began to use it against me.

After a long silence, I'd look up and find him studying me from the other side of the room. Often enough, he wouldn't say anything — because silence, too, was part of his method. Silence highlighted whatever words he did have to offer. But then he'd murmur, light as a feather, "I'm just thinking about how much like your mother you are."

Anyone hearing those words in that tone of voice would think he'd complimented me. I took it that way the first few times I heard it. My mother is, after all, a lovely and charming person. But over hours and days and weeks, the thought that I, too, possessed my mother's emotional cowardice would nag at me. I'd look up and see Joseph looking at me with his pretty face clean of evidence of malice. I'd have this little paper cut stinging the edge of my consciousness, but where it came from or who was to blame for it, I wouldn't know.

He was a Southerner. In my darkest moments, I suspect him of having married me as an act of revenge for the war his ancestors lost.

Two years, five months, and eighteen days since I last talked with or saw the man, I am still hobbled by Joseph Battelle.

•

When I did finally fight my way free of being Joseph's wife, I came home. At the time, the thought of going elsewhere didn't occur to me. But of course now I've come to understand just how problematic that move was.

For one thing, your family doesn't know what to do with you when you've shed your husband and you arrive back on the doorstep with that look in your eye: *Treat me like a person who matters. Give me what I need so that I can function in the world.*

Your family's gotten along without you long enough that they're used to living that way. You don't quite fit into the new pattern of household life — the pattern that evolved while you were away.

I had my dog with me when I came back, and Hannah and Bill hadn't had a dog in the house since we had to put down Midnight Junior.

Okay, I was a little self-obsessed. Show me anybody going through a divorce who isn't warped that way — it's just how you have to be in order to survive. And okay, I wasn't looking to help them out with their problems because my one problem was so huge I couldn't see around it enough to catch even a glimpse of somebody else's struggle.

They might not have realized how bad things were between them, but Hannah and Bill were on the verge of separating. Horace was getting ready to die, Clara was scared out of her wits — and on the surface of it, neither of them really understood what was going on with them.

In walks Eve with her luggage, and there's a U-Haul trailer hitched to her car out in the driveway. Instead of the husband that everybody's worked hard to accept into the family, she's brought her dog with her.

Welcome home, beloved child, adored granddaughter.

•

Joseph Battelle was physically beautiful. I say this as I might confess that at one time in my life I ate half a pound of chocolate every day. I'm ashamed of it, but my shame is diluted by some involuntary pride. Even now I count it among my points of self-esteem that I had a beautiful husband.

Joseph had one of those flat-bellied boy-waists, broad shoulders and what I privately think of as a "sensitive" chest, the kind that makes a tall man seem non-threatening to a woman. His body would have looked fine in just about anything he put on, but he had an eye for colors and textures and didn't mind spending the money on expensive men's clothing. Standing near him, you'd want to put your hands on his shoulder to see what his shirt or his sport coat would feel like to your fingertips.

His coloring was light—his hair wasn't quite blonde, but it was that reddish shade of brown that catches the sunlight. His features were so refined they made him look slightly feminine; his face gave the appearance of several generations before him having mated with each other in order to produce exceptional intelligence. And that was the truth of him, I have to give him that. I sometimes wished he'd run into somebody smart enough to put him in his place, but if it happened, I never witnessed it. He tried — with limited success — not to be smug.

In my view, Joseph *managed* just about everything about himself, including how he stood or sat and exactly how he modulated his voice. When he read his poetry—though few people claimed to understand it — he made it sound like chamber music. His most devastating quality was that out in the world he gave the appearance of modesty. Most people are vulnerable to that combination — intelligence, beauty, and modesty.

All right, finished with him as I am, I nevertheless haven't quite given up on my original idea of the man. Maybe falling in love with somebody does that, permanently installs one's adolescent response to the person. You could want to assassinate the person you discovered in your relationship but be unable to stop caring about the one who won your heart in the first place.

Joseph would never admit this, and I'm willing to believe that he wasn't conscious of his deepest desire. But I sometimes believe that he picked me out as someone whose spirit he wanted to crush.

•

Here's the Eve Collins theory of twenty-first-century evolution: You can't deeply understand anybody unless they'll tell you about their high school love life. I can say this because I never wanted to dismiss or disown mine, but many people do. Joseph Battelle never told me more than a few random details about the girls he knew when he was at Exeter. He said going back over what you did in high school was childish and prurient. One name is all I ever got out of him — Judy Durant. One weekend of their senior year, Joseph Battelle and Judy Durant lost their virginity with each other. They planned it out, took the train to New York, checked into the Algonquin Hotel — they were both English majors — and had sex five times before they went back to New Hampshire on Sunday evening. In the city, they went to the Blue Note to hear jazz on Friday night, the Guggenheim on Saturday afternoon, and the New York City Ballet on Saturday night. I believe they scheduled their five sex events into their cultural itinerary. Joseph told me they weren't in love, and that was the point. He said they spoke of the trip to New York as their "real graduation." He said he didn't enjoy the actual sex, and he was pretty certain Judy didn't either. But he said he thought their way of having sex was exactly what they should have done, he'd recommend it to anybody, and he and Judy have kept in touch for years. "I still admire her," he said. "I can still talk to her," he said.

"If I'd loved her," he said, "the whole experience would have been appalling."

I should have taken that information as a warning—that I'd hitched myself up to a man who believed in premeditation as a way of life. But he was also sending out another of his verbal entrapment devices: Since he was barely talking to me, I couldn't stop wondering why he was still talking to Judy Durant. What was wrong with me that was right about her? Even now that little stealth weapon gnaws away at my brain.

Here's the Eve Collins theory of human integrity: Intuition tells you the only worthwhile truth. Notice that I don't say reliable. It's anything but reliable. Following your intuition can get you slammed into a brick wall. The failure of my marriage would be Exhibit Number One. The limited success of my divorce would be Exhibit Number Two — the settlement came through last year, but I'm still going through it. Nevertheless, I say follow the old interior voice. Anything else is just a surrender.

Which leads me to what I have to tell you about Sylvester Dusablon. My high school accomplice, companion, lover-in-spirit-though-not-in-fact. Complication of my life.

All right, my high school love life was world-class peculiar. The love part was never spoken, it involved little physical contact, and I often had to navigate through experience for which I had no training or background. Also, I could never know for sure if Sylvester cared about me. After we finally started talking, he paid a great deal of attention to me and not much to anyone else. Isn't that testimony of a kind? On the other hand, whenever I tried to touch him, either he evaded me altogether, or if he allowed the touch, I could feel him willing himself not to pull away. Kiss the roadrunner or kiss a statue, either way frustration is your reward.

That spring I asked Sylvester to go to the prom with me. It wasn't easy making that decision — I had to prepare myself for the no I was likely to receive. When he surprised me by saying, "Of course," then I had to prepare myself for what it would be like for us to officially present ourselves to the whole school as a couple. A tux, a prom dress, a corsage. Strange costumes for both of us. I started imagining everything that could go wrong.

What I'd learned in the months I was close to him was that Sylvester could be blunt in what he said to me, that he didn't try to explain himself or what he did, and that he was evidently incapable of saying aloud the words "I'm sorry." But he was rock-solid about doing what he said he would do. Or in a more general sense, I could depend on him to be what he presented himself to me as being — whether or not that appearance was the truth of him. And I sometimes doubted that it was.

In this single way Sylvester was like my father and my grandfather.

So after I worked that out — Sylvester was like family — I knew that we'd be fine at the prom. If there was going to be embarrassment or humiliation that night, we'd share it together. He would commit no treachery toward me. When I came to that conclusion in the weeks before prom night, I found myself involuntarily lifted into a state of near-cheerleader giddiness. I'd never had a good time in the normal sense, the sense promised by the idea of prom night. A night of dancing among friends in a romantic setting. My thoughts about prom night led me to realize that what Sylvester and I customarily wanted was not the company of other people — but to go off by ourselves. And for there to be some element of danger or the forbidden in what we did. A good time for us was driving my old truck up into the mountain above East Middlebury and getting lost or following a logging trail as far we could and then figuring out how to get back out of the forest.

In the truck one afternoon after school, I blurted out my thought to Sylvester — that I had it in me to want what everybody wanted — music, dancing, romance. "I know it's stupid," I said, "but there it is."

He struck a classic Sylvester pose — leaned back in his seat, knees against the dashboard, his head resting on the seat-back, eyes almost closed, something like a smile on his lips. "I'm not sure," he said, "but maybe that's what I want, too."

My pulse picked up the tempo. "I must not know you as well as I thought I did," I said.

His eyes turned my way, though his look was still a little sleepy. "Must be," he said. But then he opened his eyes and seemed to take me in completely. "Here's the thing," he said. "Here's what I've been thinking," he said. "I sort of put myself together, and for a while that worked just fine. But now I'm not sure." He snorted and said that when his parents sent

him from Canada down here to the States to finish growing up, he was like this half-assembled boy kit, and now he
wasn't sure he had all the parts he was supposed to have or
if the ones he did have had been put together the way they
should be. "Eve, you had two perfectly good parents to help
you get yourself put together," he said, "but my grandparents
pretty much left the whole project to me."

"You seem fine to me." I knew it was a vapid thing say. "I
mean, you're the most confident person my age that I know."

"Got the confidence component working," he said. "It's
the desire part that I can't seem to get hooked up right."

So okay, this was a good moment, he and I were really
going to talk, and I was thrilled. I put the truck keys in the
ignition, started it up, and eased it out of the school parking lot. It wasn't the first time Sylvester and I had skipped
our afternoon classes. He acted like we'd talked it over
and it was no surprise to him that we were "getting out of
that hellhole," as we liked to put it when we left the school
grounds.

"Nobody told me I was supposed to be a kid," he said. "So
I had a grown-up mind. It's like there are some steps that I
missed. I mean I don't know if I can even go to a prom and
have a decent time. But right now I think I really need to
give it a try."

Oh I knew it was dumb, but it made me happy to know
that he felt the same way I did. It was like we'd gone in together on a scheme to take back what we'd been denied,
some piece of our childhood. Who'd kept it from us or who'd
taken it away, we couldn't have said. But that afternoon,
cruising out of town in my truck, windows down with the
breeze blowing his hair and mine, it felt like Sylvester and I

were going to right a wrong that had been done to us. I felt exultant and righteous.

Then he mumbled something.

I didn't exactly slam the brakes on, because when Bill gave me the truck, he said he expected me to be a careful driver, and so that's what I was. But I did pull over and stop quickly enough to startle both of us. We were still on North Avenue, heading into town, and it wasn't a great place to stop, but we sat there and stared at each other. "What did you say?" I asked him.

"Do you want to have sex?" Even that second time he said it — and I'd probably heard him right the first time — he said it just barely loud enough for me to hear him.

I kept looking at him for a while, trying to decide what I felt about the idea, but then I knew it was time to speak up. I sighed and looked out the window, away from him. "When did you have in mind to do this, Sylvester? Where would we go?" I could hardly believe that I was asking him practical questions and that my voice sounded calm and reasonable.

◆

Joseph Battelle despised William Carlos Williams and Robert Frost. He liked Hart Crane and Wallace Stevens. His senior thesis at Dartmouth was on "Sunday Morning," a 120-line poem about which Joseph wrote a 250-page line-by-line reading, using techniques of both the New Critics and the New Historicism. His advisor thought the essay was publishable, but Joseph said he didn't want his first book to be something academic. He'd had in mind writing poetry since middle school, and he'd known about the Yale Younger Poets

Prize for almost as long. He set out to win it, and win it he did. Before he was thirty.

However.

And this is awful to say, but if I'm to go on with this story, I can't leave it unsaid: Joseph won the prize because his first book was about his father's death in Vietnam. Robert Battelle had been an infantry lieutenant who was shot by a sniper near the village of Cu Chi during the Tay Ninh offensive. A reporter for the *San Francisco Chronicle* witnessed Lieutenant Battelle's death and happened to glance at his watch a moment after Joseph's father fell to the ground. The reporter also witnessed the death of the sniper — a boy fifteen years old — about five minutes after Joseph's father fell. The Vietnamese boy had carried letters from his family, members of whom the reporter later sought out and interviewed, and so a great deal of information was available about both soldiers. The reporter wrote a book *Two Lives: A Story About Death*.

Joseph was ten when the book was published and the reporter sent a copy to his mother. Joseph said the book was what he had instead of a father. He knew the story of his father's death in extravagant detail.

This is not to say that Joseph's book of poems deliberately exploited the event or that Joseph's poetry lacked literary merit. It is to say that without that subject matter, and the information the book made available to him — and Joseph himself would admit this — the odds against his winning the Yale prize would have been much higher.

I sometimes think *Two Lives: A Story About Death* killed our marriage.

If our marriage had had a title, it could have been *Two Lives: A Story About Death*.

●

"Want to turn off the truck?" he asked.

My mood had turned pissy, and blocking a lane of North Avenue just wasn't something I wanted to do right then. Sylvester and I had this peculiar history that hadn't been so easy for me to accept as it was happening, but I'd come around not only to acceptance but to thinking of it with reverence. We weren't like any other couple in our school or on TV or that I'd ever read or heard about. We'd taken pictures of each other naked, but the intimacy was all in our heads. It felt like we had a book full of secrets. When I was still a child, I'd felt his fingertips brushing my nipples, and I'd slugged him for that — which, a year later, he'd told me was exactly the right thing to do. We'd made road trips to museums in Montreal and Boston and Albany and even half a dozen weird little museums around Vermont and New Hampshire. We'd even slept in the same bed. But that he was now proposing sex struck me as just plain wrong — like a desecration of our story. Wrong, too, was trying to hold a serious conversation sitting in my truck cab with horns honking at us and people giving us the finger as they swerved around us. I put the truck in gear, drove five blocks to Battery Park, parked, got out and walked around to the passenger side, opened the door for him, and said, "Okay, now we can talk."

He said nothing, didn't meet my eyes, just climbed down out of the truck, put his hands in his pockets, stood there with his head kind of bowed and his hair curtaining off his face from me.

So he was going to pout.

It was raining but not in any straightforward way, just

one of those Vermont mud-season semi-showers that liquefy the air and turn it into a chilly mist that can soak your clothes but that aren't worth putting on a raincoat for or carrying an umbrella. So it was dunderheaded — a Bill word — of me to want to walk around in Battery Park to have our conversation. But that was fine, too. The kind of mad I was needed some space and fresh air and probably some walking around. Room to pace and breathe. I turned away from Sylvester and headed along the sidewalk toward the low stone wall where you can look out over the lake toward New York and the Adirondack Mountains.

"You don't have to be such a little bitch," he muttered.

That made me laugh and turn around, but I kept walking backward.

"You're the one who said let's fuck," I said. "How else am I supposed to act when my best pal in the world says that?"

"I don't think we have a choice," he said. He stopped walking and stood where he was, with his hands out on each side of him, palms open.

I studied him and took another couple of steps backward. He went back to his hands-in-his-pockets pose, which made him look even skinnier than he was, like he was stretching upward and sucking in his stomach. It was just about the least comfortable-looking way to stand that I've ever seen, but Sylvester stood that way pretty often. I stopped taking steps backward. "Ordinarily you're not a stupid person," I said. "It's *after* you have sex that your choices are limited. And even then — "

This is what he did. He had on this little jacket that he always wore with the collar turned up. He reached in it to an inside breast pocket, pulled out sunglasses I'd never seen before, and put them on. Then he looked at me through those — or I assume he looked at me because the green-black lenses were aimed in my direction. But for all I knew he could have had his eyes closed. If I'd been nearer to him, I'd have knocked those things right off his face.

This is what I did instead. Turned away from him and started walking toward Lake Champlain and the Adirondacks.

"Eve, I'm leaving," I heard him say.

I stopped in my tracks but kept my back to him.

"Say what?" I said.

"Sunday. Right after graduation. I'm going back to Montreal. My dad sent for me."

I turned to face him. He still had his hands in his pockets, still had those sunglasses on. I looked on the grass around me for something to throw at him. There wasn't anything. "Today's Tuesday," I said. I realized this wasn't logical, but that's what came out.

He shook his head.

"It's not like Montreal is California," I said. "It's two hours from here."

He shook his head.

"We've been there," I said. "We've been to the museum up there."

He didn't bother to shake his head, just stood still.

"I don't see what that has to do with sex," I said.

I thought he was just going to keep standing there, the skinny kid with nothing to say. But then he did speak up. Not exactly in his natural voice either. "Once I start working for my dad, I can't see you any more."

I had sort of figured his dad for some kind of Montreal

underworld boss. Or who knows, a spy or an undercover cop, a Mafioso or I don't know what. Instead of talking about him, Sylvester had always more or less talked around his father. I knew there was something weird about what he did for a job, knew his dad's work was part of why his parents sent Sylvester down here to Burlington to go to school. And I knew in this engraved-in-stone way that it wouldn't do me any good to ask Sylvester any questions about his dad or about why he couldn't see me any more after he started working for his dad. I understood what Sylvester was telling me. Or asking me. *Do you want to have sex with me before I disappear from your life forever?*

I didn't know the answer to that question, but I did understand that pain was what had moved him to ask me the question. So I went to him and put my arms around him. That was new for both of us. It was the first time I ever felt like Sylvester really wanted me to touch him.

•

Two questions with the same answer are 1) Where did I meet Joseph Battelle and 2) Why did I marry him. The single answer is that I attended his poetry reading at the Bread Loaf Writer's Conference in 2005. Because of that first book of poems of his, he had won a fellowship and had been invited to Bread Loaf. I was there as what they call a "contributor," which is actually a paying customer.

It was an August afternoon, warm but moving toward a cool evening and filled with light the color of an old white wine. On both sides, the doors of the Little Theater were open; air on its way from the valley up toward the mountaintop passed through the building in a current too soft to be called a breeze. If I say that seeing Joseph in a French blue shirt and a yellow tie and hearing him read from that podium brought up in me a feeling of huge intensity, I would be telling what maybe a hundred or more people could also say. For almost all of us who sat in that hushed place, hearing that voice, seeing that face, feeling the cadence of those sentences, was a transcendent experience. The words we heard did not process out into the sense one expects from the spoken language, and so the sound of Joseph's voice liberated us into a dimension where we could engage with words and images in an almost pre-verbal way. The poems clearly spoke to the violent death of a man and the poet's powerful yearning toward his lost father. And though we couldn't be sure, the poems also seemed to speak to the death of the other man, the soldier who had killed his father. But they did this in a way that was beyond grammar, beyond the mind's ability to send and receive rational observations and declarations.

In another setting or even in the same theater on another day, Joseph's poems might not have had the force we felt from them that afternoon. He might not have appeared so extraordinary to us. He read very softly, but the microphone caught every nuance of tone and register and irony. He gave such an effortless performance, it was as if we were hearing his rehearsal earlier in his room alone. Every element of those minutes was exactly right. I could say that I fell in love, but that would be nothing special to confess because so many of us in his audience felt the same — each of us perhaps shaking his or her head in wonder of it. So what happened to me was actually something common enough that seventy-five or a hundred others also experienced it.

But it washed away from them, while it brought about the marriage that very nearly did me in.

When his reading was finished, I walked up to the crowd of people around Joseph and waited my turn. When his eyes finally rested on me, and it was time for me to speak, I had no words to offer him. His face was kind, and his expression invited me to say something remarkable to him. I felt my eyes trying to convey what my tongue evidently couldn't manage. But I knew he'd felt similar eyes flickering at him before, probably only minutes before he'd turned his attention to me.

"Maybe you and I can talk a little later?" he asked. Out of mere politeness I was fairly certain. At the same time, I knew he'd spoken that sentence for me and for me alone.

So of course I nodded eagerly, the smitten schoolgirl.

Of that performance I am not ashamed.

·

Sylvester didn't know what I didn't know — whether or not he was gay. He must have decided that he'd better find out just how heterosexual he was before he took up his new life in Montreal. He must have surmised that I was the person in his life who could help him with his inquiry. But I hadn't thought he'd worked it out so coldly and clearly. I wasn't sure exactly what the nature of our connection was, but I knew that he took me seriously, treated me with respect, enjoyed my companionship, and told me more about himself than he told anyone else. And he was right to trust me.

"Prom night's like a free pass," he said. We were out of the damp weather and back in the truck cab. "We'd have to sneak to do it any other time." He wasn't looking directly at me, but I could feel his invisible sensors extending, turned up high, trying to read my slightest thought and feeling.

I studied him, maybe a little more freely than I ordinarily would have. I deliberately remembered how he looked without his clothes to see if that image would help me tap into whatever truth was available. I was trying to read him, but I was also trying to read myself. And I guess that's what he was doing, too. I couldn't find anything that I recognized as desire in either of us.

But there was plenty of curiosity emanating from my interior. *If I agree to do this, where will it take me?* Maybe that's what I felt coming toward me from him, too, but it carried with it an edge of fear. I knew him well enough to be pretty sure he was afraid of the life of a gay man. I couldn't blame him for that. And I'd have probably been better off if I'd been more afraid than I was. I actually had a better idea of what Sylvester was afraid of than of what I was.

"How do regular kids get through things like this?" I asked him.

He snorted.

.

I wasn't a virgin; neither was Joseph. But neither of us had actually lived with a sexual partner.

I'd known he wouldn't be selfish. I hadn't imagined how patient and attentive he would be to what pleased me. One Saturday afternoon a couple of months into our marriage, after we'd both achieved notably intense orgasms, Joseph's coming only seconds after mine, he told me, "You're like a puzzle that has to be solved a slightly different way every time." He was still breathing hard, and we were both sweating.

I was a little put off by being considered a puzzle, though I was also in too languorous a state to be really irked with him. "What are you?" I asked him.

"Men are simple," he said. "Combination lock. Same numbers work every time." I think he expected me to be amused, but I suspected him of having thought the whole thing up well before he told me.

"Not true," I said very softly. Somehow I knew he was wrong, but I didn't really know how I knew it. My experience with men wasn't extensive. His with women probably was, though he'd never said so.

He propped himself up on one elbow so he could look at my face. His smile was sociable. We'd already discovered that after-sex conversation had a kind of low-simmering excitement — we were both capable of surprising ourselves and each other with what we'd say. "So tell me how you think it is with men," he said.

"I can't do that," I said. "I don't know about men. I know a little about you. We've had sex, what, maybe seventy-five times? A hundred? But here's what I can tell you. If I do this" — I turned on my side to face him, touched my index finger to my tongue, then moved it to his nipple and began slowly circling — "this always turns you on at least a little bit. And usually your nipple tells my finger to *keep doing that, keep doing that.* But every now and then it says *enough of that, do something else.*"

"So?" he said. "But don't stop doing that."

"So maybe it's the same basic numbers — " I stopped the

circling and used my thumb and the curled side of my index finger to put the slightest pressure on his nipple, which became ever so slightly aroused and defined. I felt something go quiet in him. I pressed and released several more times before I went on. "But every time's got to be a little different."

He was quiet. If I'd looked down at his penis, I was pretty sure I'd see it showing signs of resurrection. After a moment he said, "It's more like that with women than it is with men."

"Okay," I said. "All right," I said. I was certain I knew where we were at that moment. I heard his breathing. I knew what it meant. I heard the sweet calmness inside him, and I knew what that meant.

Then he turned away and stood up. That was startling. His face gave me this blink of a look that said *You have no business thinking you know me like you think you do.* Without saying a word, he padded out into the hallway on his way to the shower.

Right there. Exactly right there, I knew I might have been living with Joseph Battelle, but I was also living with another man. The one who'd just gotten up to take a shower when I was dead certain we were about to make love. If he hadn't been my husband, I'd have taken it as a clear and slightly cruel message that he was through with me. Since we were married, I understood the cruelty, but since he couldn't be through with me without going to a lot of trouble and expense, it meant something else. *I think I'm going to play a mean game with you? Don't take me for granted or I'll hurt you? Every now and then I'm going to give your self-esteem a punch in the mouth?*

•

I admit there was some pleasure. Sylvester probably would, too. Somber as our mission was, he and I became zealous in our roles of a couple of prom-struck high schoolers. If the night had nothing else positive, I'd still be grateful to him for joining me in that silly and necessary spirit. We'd been cast in a movie for parts for which we were exactly right. "So this is what it's like to be in high school," he said when we went to pick up his tuxedo.

Our classmates moved through that night in packs, but we kept to ourselves. Sylvester's grandmother dropped him off at our house for the corsage pinning and the photo opportunities. Bill and Hannah dutifully played their roles — Bill acting like Sylvester was his own high school classmate rather than mine, but for some reason calling him Doctor Dusablon. Which, for some reason I couldn't fathom, amused Sylvester. Hannah looked him up and down, even made the excuse of adjusting his bow tie for him, I'm pretty sure, just so she could step close enough to examine his face. I've had time to think about that gesture — Hannah, who had a lot of trouble with emotional intimacy, stepping near enough to Sylvester to kiss him if she'd wanted to — and I've decided it was because his looks surprised her. The boy was anything but handsome. He'd shazamed himself into a proper black tuxedo that made his skinniness look elegant, and he wore the formal dress shirt with studs and a cummerbund as if he were accustomed to putting it on every weekend. But his nose and his lips were too big, his eyes were too small, he didn't have much of a forehead, and that night he'd tried to shave so carefully that he had razor burn blotching his cheeks and his neck. And you know what? I just adored the look of that boy right then, with Hannah scrutinizing him

Two Lives: A Story About Death

255

like a plastic surgeon looking for improvement opportunities. He had the face of a hoodlum trying to make good. He stood straight, he kept his best version of a pleasant expression, and he met her eyes as if to tell her that no matter what she thought of him, he knew he had something to offer.

Hannah had helped me find a dress. Truth is I couldn't have found anything close to the right one if she hadn't agreed to shop with me. When we'd looked in Ecco, Expressions, Ann Taylor, Filene's, and every other possible place, Hannah took me to Old Gold, where we found a black on black shot silk custom-made dress from around 1965. It had a high collar that gave it a Vietnamese look, and it was thrillingly short. Whoever had that dress made for her must have had a body that was identical to mine — not much of a bosom, narrow shoulders and hips, and long legs. When I tried it on, it made me feel like it must have been waiting for years for me to rescue it from oblivion. "I never realized you had such pretty legs," Hannah murmured while the two of us examined me in the triple mirrors. From the waist up, I was a Madonna; from the waist down, I was a whore — I was thrilled with the sight of myself.

When Hannah and I had discussed whether or not to wear pantyhose and if so what shade should they be, we'd reached the conclusion that the dress demanded my completely untanned legs, shocking though they were. Pale as the inside of a refrigerator. When I came downstairs and Bill saw Sylvester getting his first look at me in that dress, he said, "Doctor Dusablon, I do believe you're taking the whole history of womanhood to the prom tonight."

Sylvester gave me a fast grin and nodded like he knew just what Bill meant. I wasn't about to challenge either one of them. I was used to getting attention for what I said. I'd never gotten it for the way I looked.

·

For a long time, without realizing it, I treated Joseph's father's death as the key to everything I couldn't figure out about Joseph. I also treated it as a magical story, a legend, a myth. I was slow to understand that Joseph had created it that way in his mind and in his poetry — and so of course I received it in just that way. I still think of that snippet of time — the shot — the soldier falling, the second shot, the boy-sniper tumbling from a tree — as a vision. Something between a painting and a two-minute video clip — and all the more powerful for being absolutely local: It lived in my house. It lived in the man who slept beside me. When he woke up in the morning, the magical story lived in Joseph's every word and act.

Its effect on me wasn't so far away from religious craziness.

Scary to say so, but I still carry that piece of Joseph's history. And I do so with due regard. Even though I'm still deviled by the question of whether he should have used it as he did. The first year of our marriage was the year after the publication of *Conversations After KIA*; it was the year in which my husband — a Yale Younger Poet — began receiving invitations to read all over the country.

To Joseph's credit was that he accepted only a few of those invitations. Not so much to his credit was that he knew exactly which ones to accept, which ones to refuse.

To his credit was that he never encouraged fan worship.

But he did cultivate the respect of influential, older poets. In his defense, he would say that they were the poets he respected, and so of course he wanted them to care for his work.

•

Here is the Eve Collins theory of dancing. It can be done spontaneously and without training. As in alone in your living room. Or in exceptional circumstances, even before the not particularly friendly eyes of your high school classmates. Sylvester and I had planned to attend the actual prom for approximately an hour. Because of dancing, I forgive us for staying three times that long. The shadows around blue and red lights and the beam of pink light down onto the center of the dance floor tried to catch us in their spell, but Sylvester and I were way too ironic for that. We sneered at the Radisson ballroom as we walked in. But inside there were other elements to transport us into the spirit of prom night in America: A mist machine generated a cool stream. Couples we'd never noticed in school — country kids, Bosnian kids, Vietnamese kids, North Street kids, vocational ed kids, the zitted, overweight, hoody, halfie, Goth, outlaw, and held-back kids were out there on the dance floor fabulously dressed up for this one spring night of their lives. I watched Sylvester seeing what I saw, witnessed his old rocker sardonic grin — the look he had when our teacher Mr. Hazelton made a fool of himself over hallway behavior or when some idiotic announcement came over the intercom — and all of a sudden we both realized prom night was the great equalizer, the single occasion when the downtrodden children of the city's school system could claim some dignity. No wonder the college-bound snots turned up their noses at the prom. Sylvester grinned at me and said something that was completely drowned out by the Blue Condors breaking into "Gimme Some Light" at skull-shattering volume. "What?" I shouted at him, and he yelled back "Laissez les bon temps roulez!" and we were out there raising our fists and dancing like we'd been doing it since eighth grade. We made no decision to do it, we had no choice. And what it felt like to me was that maybe I'd missed out on most of my adolescence, but however much of it I'd been denied was given back to me right then, right there. My feet and legs, my butt, my belly, and shoulders received "Shine it bright, Shine it through the Dark, River of light, Wash me in the stars." I threw myself into that music and let my blood tell me what to do. And Sylvester? The boy's body looked like it had just found out about freedom. He didn't know the first thing about dancing, but the boy could have danced his way into paradise that night.

"What a dancer you are!" I shouted.

"Not me! You!" He pointed at me with both hands, and to answer, I raised my hands above my head, turned my back and shook my hips at him. We laughed as if we were making up for all the time we'd spent with each other without laughing. I hadn't realized what a somber twosome we'd been. And I wasn't sad we could leave that part of our lives behind us.

We were there until they closed the place down.

•

I woke to dim light, the sound of rain, and Joseph sitting in the chair where he sometimes liked to read aloud to me. He was fully dressed, and he must have come back into our bedroom after he'd showered. He must have done all that while I was sleeping, and then taken his place there in the chair while it was still dark. The rain would have muffled any noise he made. This was mid-May, and we'd finally been able to sleep with our windows open an inch or two for the spring air.

What a strange morning — later than it seemed, because the rain had darkened away the light that ordinarily would have brought me up out of sleeping. I didn't think I'd moved, I was pretty sure I'd just opened my eyes. But there Joseph was looking at me — as if I'd transported him out of my sleep into my actual life — which probably explained why I'd waked as I had. His expression seemed sad. For some moments neither of us moved or spoke.

Finally he said, "I dreamed you were old." His voice was softer than usual, and it had that melodious quality that I was used to hearing whenever he read from his poems. "Your hair was white the way it is with people who live on into their nineties. But it looked grand — distinguished — like you were still proud of how thick it was and didn't want it cut. Your skin had gotten dark and very wrinkled, you had white eyebrows, and your eyes were pure black. I don't know how I knew, but I was certain your sight had somehow become sharper than it's ever been. You had on that dress your mother wears when she and Bill go out to dinner on Friday nights, and you were sitting right here in this chair. I was lying where you are now. And you wouldn't stop looking at me. You just kept staring. You wouldn't say anything to me, though I kept thinking of questions I wanted to ask you. It wasn't clear to me why I couldn't make myself say them aloud. They were mostly about why you'd changed yourself so much and whether or not you meant to look so old. That's what I couldn't understand — it was like you'd intended to get old, but you hadn't discussed it with me, hadn't given me any warning."

He stopped, but I felt like I'd been sinking deeper into my quietness while he talked.

"After a while, it came to me." He paused, then he said, "I was dead."

"I was dead," he said, "and it was very scary. But even though it was disturbing that you'd suddenly gotten so old, I wanted you to stay here with me. I thought if you went away, then there wouldn't be any escape from being dead. If you went away, death would come down on me like a boulder toppling off a cliff, and the pain that would come when it fell on me would go on and on. I wanted you to stay, and you didn't look like you wanted to go anywhere, but I couldn't make myself tell you. I just keep thinking of questions to ask you to keep you with me. *What will we have for breakfast this morning? Should I go grocery shopping today? Do we have enough milk?* I knew not to ask you anything abstract. Just those little things like we do."

•

Prom night notwithstanding, Sylvester and I had agreed that we wouldn't drink alcohol. It goes to show what outcasts we were that neither of us had any interest in drinking. When we left the prom, sweaty and exhilarated, and stepped out into the cool night, we were completely sober. Walking to my truck, we jostled shoulders and arms and hands, silly in a way we weren't used to being with each other.

But then we were in the truck, the doors shut against the voices of other prom-goers calling out to each other in the parking lot, the cab of the truck mildly shocking with its deeper chill and relative silence, not to mention its smell. "Look out, future, here we come," I said because I didn't want our high spirits to dissolve so quickly.

"Yeah," Sylvester murmured. He looked at me with a face that told me he was doing his best to help me hold onto the good times, but he was worried. The Eve Collins theory of unspoken and speculative communication is that pretty often people do understand each other at the deepest possible level but they usually don't trust that knowledge. I knew Sylvester was on the verge of finding out his sexual destiny, which would make anybody anxious. I was worried, too — I mean I might turn out to be sexually incompetent, but at least I didn't have to wonder if I was gay and if my whole life was going to go one way or the other after what we were about to do.

"Didn't we dance, when we'd never done that before?" I whispered to him. He nodded, though he looked no less anxious. And this was when I knew that I wanted to do the deed with Sylvester Dusablon. Wanted to fuck him. When it came to me, raw and crude as that, I felt such a relief! But I wasn't about to tell him so.

"No matter what," I said in my regular voice. Enough of whispering in my own truck with the person I was closest to in all of life! I put my face right beside his, touched the skin of my cheek to the skin of his. "No matter what, it'll be all right, and I'll love you." I could hardly pull those last three words up from my chest and out of my mouth, but I did speak them out loud.

Okay, so he cried. It wasn't much of a cry, but he didn't try to hide it from me. And I'll swear to God, Sylvester scooted over to the center of the seat and put his arm around me while I drove. Kept it there the whole way to where we were going.

·

Joseph wrote every morning. He was up by five every day, showered and sitting with his coffee beside him and his computer on his lap by quarter to six. Not to disturb him, I caught only glimpses during his writing hours. He was a man who shaved carefully and closely, who put on clean underwear and a clean shirt every day, brushed his hair and tucked in his shirt as precisely as if he had to stand for a military inspection. When he was writing, there was something exceptionally upright in his appearance — though of course at that time of day, he could have sat in his underwear and no one would have known the better. We never spoke then, and I'm fairly certain he wasn't even aware when I passed by the door of his study.

I honored him for his habit — this was the part of writing that I couldn't manage after I finished my graduate program at BU. I'd get up early for a week, sit with the computer for a couple of hours every day, and just when I thought I'd gotten the hang of a daily routine, along would come something to distract me — a catalogue with a skirt on the cover that had to be considered, a bird on the railing of the deck, a shelf of the refrigerator that I suddenly remembered needed to be cleaned. I didn't fool myself, I knew the distractions were completely inessential activities, but the fact that I let myself be taken away from what I knew was necessary if I really wanted to practice an art sent me a message: *You don't want to do what you thought you wanted to do.*

One of the distractions was an ad in the *Boston Globe* for the position of Managing Editor at the *Harvard Review*. Joseph was teaching at Bowdoin, and we were living in Brunswick then. I'd seen the ad and instantly known that I wanted to apply — the office was in the Lamont Library, a place I'd loved from the first moment I'd stepped into it — but I didn't have to submit my application first thing the next morning. I didn't have to sacrifice my writing time to update my resume and write the letter. But that's what I did. Thus, in an hour or so of a single day, the course of my life was set: I would not become a fiction writer; instead, I would be a managing editor.

When I moved in with Joseph and witnessed him getting up every morning, sitting down with his computer and giving himself over to writing poems, I relished it. After a couple of months of living that way, I realized that the satisfaction I took from his routine was from the order it gave to both our days and, more subtly, from my sense that Joseph was fulfilling my own desire to have a writing life. And since I didn't have to be in Cambridge until late morning, I protected him from distraction. That I stayed quiet and out of his way, that I took any phone calls that came in at that time of day (there were very few of those), that I brought him his second cup of coffee, that I cleaned up his breakfast dishes, emptied the trash, took out the recycling, straightened up the apartment, took care of all the little daily details of a single day — each of those acts of mine made it all the more possible for him to accomplish what he did. Yes, I know my marital politics are retarded, I know he hardly noticed all my little deeds, but for the years that we lived that way, I actually enjoyed serving him as I did.

Never mind that he nearly spiritually suffocated me.

·

Horace and Clara, my grandparents, were in California. I'd had a key to their house since I was in eighth grade. When she'd handed it to me, Clara had said, "I don't care when or why you need to use this — I want you to know you can come into this house at any time of the day or night."

I knew she didn't give me the key so that Sylvester and I could have sex in their house. I didn't think she'd necessarily be horrified by the idea. Wishful thinking, maybe, but I wondered if her "when or why" might not have meant *If you can't find anywhere else to do it, do it here.*

I didn't look anywhere else — a hotel or motel seemed all wrong to me. Definitely I didn't want to go to a friend's house. Sylvester didn't even have to tell me his grandparents' place wasn't an option — though I'd have been fine with that if it had been. He and I had used their living room for Sylvester's Odalisque project, and so I'd have probably been comfortable there.

We parked the truck on Summit Street and took our time walking up to where it turned into Overlake Park and ended in the cul-de-sac where Horace and Clara had lived for at least thirty years. This was just before midnight of a sweet early May evening in Burlington, the weather generally turning warmer but still chilly enough at that hour that I accepted Sylvester's offer of his tux jacket. I liked his courtliness and liked the feel and smell of the jacket around me.

We didn't exactly sneak up to the house, but not to wake Horace and Clara's neighbors we kept quiet and took care with our footsteps. Like visitors, we walked right up to the front door, then after I'd opened it and stepped in, Sylvester followed me, and we stood in the relative dark.

We weren't touching, but I could feel Sylvester's fear. I was pretty certain he didn't want me to ask if he was okay or try to distract him with small talk, which was fine with me — I wasn't ready to speak yet. Since he'd never been in this house, I didn't blame him for being uneasy, but I knew it wasn't just that he was in a strange place. And here's a very odd thing: Even as much as I'd thought through this evening in detail, I wasn't certain where in the house I wanted to go. A definite no was Horace and Clara's room. A maybe was the guest room where I'd always slept whenever I'd stayed here. But something about all the little girl memories I had of that bed and the table and the white-curtained window made me hesitate to choose it. Also I wasn't sure I wanted to lose my virginity in any room where I knew Horace and Clara spent lots of time together. Which ruled out the living room and what they called the den, which was their TV room.

The Eve Collins theory of self-discovery is that you sometimes just unintentionally break through to what you need to know. The decision of where we'd go came to me in the dark foyer, and with it came a little piece of strange knowledge: There was a room in this house where I'd experienced some intimacy. I reached across about three inches of space to take Sylvester's hand. I still said nothing, but I led him into the hallway up the steps to the door of Horace's study.

I knew it was right when we stepped through the door. I'd never been in there at night, but I wasn't really surprised at how the windows of the room let in moonlight and light from the street. Horace always kept his shades completely raised in his study, and so this was a night version of how that space was during the day. Horace's high-backed leather chair faced his gleaming desk and the "guest chair" across from his desk. To me, this was a comforting sight. My experience of this room in the several conversations I'd had in here with Horace, the two of us seated across from each other with the desk between us, had been times when I'd felt understood. And when I'd felt I understood Horace. But I'd never even talked with Sylvester about my grandfather.

I closed the door behind us and felt for the knob — there was a lock that clicked when I turned it.

I stepped to Sylvester and put my arms around him. "This is a good place." I tried to make the tone of my voice put him at ease. "You'll see," I half crooned. "We'll be all right in here."

.

Joseph Battelle is a trochee followed by an iamb. He taught me that. *Joseph Battelle's special version of Hell / was to have a wife he'd never know well.* The first time he recited those words was after we'd been married about a year and a half. He wanted to mean the little ditty as a joke, and I tried to take it that way. But we both knew that his couplet was probably the truth of us. And its meaning shifted as we moved deeper into our marriage.

Joseph was surprised when he came upon things about me that he didn't understand. Maybe it's unfair for me to say this, but I think he thought having a wife meant having someone about whom he would have absolute knowledge. Maybe that was my assumption, too — that it was okay for your husband to know everything about you. At any rate, we sort of took this on as our project, for Joseph to know Eve. I had in mind to tell him everything. Eventually. And maybe the eventually was the hitch, because there were some things — maybe a fair number of things — that I kept saving to tell him when I was ready for him to know them. My grandfather's pornography, for instance. My collaboration with Sylvester on his Odalisque project, for instance. Or even things Joseph figured out for himself. He once said, "Your mother's keeping some kind of secret, don't you think? and I answered, "Oh, I don't know." Of course he probably had it right about Hannah — I'd often suspected she had something that Bill and I weren't seeing. But when Joseph brought it up, I must have thought to myself something like *After we've been married for twenty years, I'll talk to you about that but not right now.*

Selective revelation must have been my operating principle: I'd let him know everything but not everything all at once. I hadn't consciously worked it out, but that seemed to be how it was working.

"It's cute," he told me once over dinner, the two of us eating a risotto he'd fixed. "The way you practice evasion." He'd asked me something about my father's cooking, and I'd answered him vaguely. But only because I didn't feel like getting into Bill and Hannah's domestic life.

"I'm glad you think so," I said. I wanted him to note my tone of voice — I was burned by his accusation. Or maybe by his using the word *cute*, which he knew I detested. We both knew we'd entered a place where neither of us really wanted to be. He hadn't wanted to rile me up quite that much, and I hadn't meant to be quite as angry as I evidently was. We let a little silence into the conversation. A ninety-second truce, by unspoken mutual agreement.

"Very nice risotto," I said softly.

"Thank you," he said.

"I'm pretty sure Bill was ashamed that he liked to cook." I used the same soft tone. "Though he never said so. I'm pretty sure Hannah didn't really like his cooking. Though she never said so. I'm pretty sure that neither of them understood exactly how they felt about our family dinners. And I'm pretty sure that I collaborated with both of them in the mission of cheerfully carrying on in spite of the treacherous little feelings that worked on them both. You've heard the term 'family dynamic'? That's what we had. We all three used that term while I was growing up — for trips together, for school activities that required one or both of them to help or be there with me, or putting something on the calendar, or even when I went to the grocery store with Bill, or down to Hannah's office with her. Or dinner at home. 'Family dynamic,' Hannah would say, and I'd nod, and Bill would make a face."

I paused and looked across the table at Joseph Battelle, the trochee followed by an iamb. I made my face look as neutral as possible.

He stared at me. "That's a lot of information," he finally said.

"Don't say I never told you anything," I said.

•

We stood in Horace's study, bound together as if we'd reached the end of a slow dance back at the prom. I felt no impulse in Sylvester or in myself to do anything more than stand still and breathe. And wait.

We were both ready to bail out of our plan at the slightest sign that the stars weren't right for us. When I realized that we were breathing together, I understood that we must have been doing our best to stop time. To go neither forward nor backward.

I was the one who made the first move, a slow and unobtrusive ever-so-slight shifting that hardly counts as an act of will. I now understand that a dark room with light coming in can arouse me.

My chest shifted against his chest. Then it shifted back. Maybe a centimeter. The body doesn't have to ask the mind's permission. My breasts suddenly had my attention. And evidently Sylvester's, as well.

Primitive as such chest-rubbing was, we each must have realized in the silence that we'd passed a test: We could awaken desire in each other.

Eve, if you're going to do this, then go ahead. Exactly whose voice sounded in my brain at that moment I couldn't have said — Bill's, Hannah's, Clara's or Horace's. Maybe the four of them speaking in unison.

I led Sylvester around the desk to Horace's chair. "Sit here, please," I told him, and he did as I said. I turned my back to him, flexed my knees, and asked him to undo the hook at the neck and unzip the dress. He did that, too.

I stepped away from him only a pace and a half. I wanted to see his face — to *study* his face. I pushed the dress down my hips, off one foot and the other, then dropped it to the floor.

This was not a tease. Sylvester had already seen me and taken pictures of me. Now I wanted him to see me straight on. See how I was when he didn't have a camera. How I was in this light, this room. I knew I was neither pretty nor homely. I thought I was lucky to be in that neutral territory. Physically, your basic girl. He knew that, but I wanted him to know it better. I took my time. Maybe a minute and a half passed before I had every piece of my clothing on the floor around me. I meant my nakedness in front of him to be a correction of the ways he'd seen me or thought of me until this moment. *I am just this*, I meant to tell him. *Only this.*

I stood in the light of that room for what seemed a long time.

Then he nodded.

So Sylvester and I had our sex on the old daybed in Horace's study—an ugly old antique that had come down to him from his great grandmother. I put down a hand-towel from Horace's little half bath, because I thought I'd bleed, and I did but only a very little. When Sylvester took off his pants, his erection surprised us both with its eagerness—it sprang straight out from his body and nodded in my direction. "Well now!" Sylvester said. I heard in his voice how happy he was. I hoped my own body would be as ready for our mission as his was.

The act itself was difficult and awkward but acceptable. I think it just has to be the way it is. The word *fuck* suggests something that's idiot-simple, but for me it's never that way, and that first time now seems so deeply complicated that I don't know how Sylvester and I ever got through it. To tell the truth, I was glad for the embarrassment — and even a little glad for the sharp pain. I wanted it to happen, but I didn't want it to be easy. Such pleasure as there was came from my body's finally being able to move in that urgent way with Sylvester's body. That part, which didn't happen immediately, seemed to fulfill the desire I'd felt those years ago in the first minute of seeing him at the Burlington Country Club dance.

And I liked how his back felt to the palms of my hands. To be crude, I really liked how Sylvester's butt felt in my hands when he was moving in me.

I didn't come, but before we were finished, I knew I'd gotten on the right track. I was pretty sure that in the future I could figure out how to have sex that would give me orgasms, and I didn't mind waiting for them. Sylvester, however, came like a bolt of lightning and a clap of thunder. That boy came so hard that we both just froze and stared into each other's faces.

"Great God!" he whispered. Sweat shone on his face like silver. I pulled him into me as far as he could go and held him like that until I couldn't feel him any more. Even though we used a condom, I felt like I'd taken his body into mine. We'd separate, of course, but he'd be in me for the rest of my life.

·

At the beginning of our marriage, Joseph Battelle was one of two or three of the most promising young poets of his generation. Two years later, the critic William Logan in *Parnassus* suggested that perhaps Battelle was merely a one-book poet. Two years after that, our marriage was finished, and Joseph was still struggling to put together a second book manuscript. Though he never said so, I think he'd come to suspect that he might be just a one-book poet.

Which is not to excuse him for not being a better husband to me.

I believed in Joseph much longer than I should have. I still believe that in his writing he struggled with all his might.

I could say that the effort he gave to his poetry would have been better spent in addressing the problems of his marriage. I'd probably be wrong. I came to love him as a poet. I think he had no choice about what he was. "Even a failed poet is still a poet," he told me in the third year of our marriage, when he was still occasionally telling me what mattered to him. I thought it was a smart thing to say, but at that time I couldn't imagine he'd ever become a "failed poet."

At this writing—ten years this August from the first time I saw him, nearly three years after our divorce—that's what he is. There've been a few enigmatic verses in journals nobody reads, one or two of which I've known to be addressed specifically to me in his old way of putting a piece of language — *love that can't stay brave* — in my brain that would function like a splinter. But no second book. No twelve-page spread in *American Poetry Review,* nothing in the *New Yorker,* the *Atlantic,* or *Poetry,* all of which had published the poems that went into *Conversations After KIA.*

The first time I saw Joseph Battelle, he was the young man in the French blue shirt and a yellow tie, about to step into the Little Theater at Bread Loaf to read from his *Conversations After KIA.* He stood with new friends he'd made among the other fellows at Bread Loaf, his bearing was modest, his smile warm and confident. The afternoon sun lit his copper-gold hair as if the gods had taken an interest in him. Within the hour I'd heard his voice and his words, and I was in the spell of him.

The last time I saw Joseph Battelle was in the district courtroom where our uncontested divorce was finalized. I'd been depressed but determined not to appear damaged in the courtroom, and I think I managed it fairly well. I'd chosen good clothes and paid attention to my makeup. Joseph had dressed casually, as if he'd come to the courtroom from gardening or tidying up the garage. I'm sure he intended to convey his indifference, but he hadn't carried it off. When it came time for him to say the few words required of him, his voice had trembled. And as he left the courtroom, the man was actually weeping. I think he'd been shocked to discover that his emotions could get the better of him. I don't think he wanted to make such a show in front of me. I wanted to feel vindicated by it — to think that he'd finally realized the mistake he'd made in alienating me. But that wasn't possible. What I felt was sadness, for him for being such a mess of a man and for myself for having loved a man who could come to look so weak and shabby in public.

•

I had no choice but to accept Sylvester's leaving. But I couldn't make myself take it seriously. I had another year at BHS, and since he was graduating, it made sense that he'd leave Burlington. Nevertheless, the fact that Montreal was a two-hour drive stayed in my head. If he wanted to see me, he could. I liked the drama he made of his leaving — I took it as testimony to how much he felt for me. But I couldn't pretend to be in a state of upheaval when I wasn't. "Rent a car," I told him in our last phone conversation. "Hitchhike. Ask a friend to drive you down. Ride a bike. Put on a backpack and walk."

I attended his graduation mostly so that I could give him the present I'd bought him. When I saw him accept his diploma and shake the principal's hand, I clapped and cheered loudly enough that people around me smiled. I got a look at a vigorously applauding man and a woman some seats across from me that I'm certain were his parents. The man wore a dark suit, had a bony, deeply tanned face and silvering hair; the woman's white-blonde hair was swept up in back in a way that meant she'd been to a hair dresser that morning. As the last graduates were crossing the stage, those two rose from their seats and left the auditorium.

When I finally made my way through the crowd and out into the hallway, then out to the parking lot, I caught no sight of Sylvester or of the couple who must have been his parents. I stood out there for a while, holding the gift I had for him, hoping he'd suddenly appear. He didn't, of course, and so without speaking to anyone, I walked straight to my truck and drove it out of the BHS parking lot and down a hundred yards to the Rock Point School grounds near the lake. I could park there and sit as long as I wanted to and no one would bother me.

Down there, with not a person or a vehicle in sight, I shut the truck off and sat staring at his present for a while, turning it one way and then another. I was in a peculiar state of mind, needing to think but having no sense of purpose about it. Not seeing Sylvester as I'd planned to do that afternoon had stunned me. After a minute or two, I started picking at the bow of the ribbon, then found myself unwrapping the gift. It was a digital recording device, a little smaller than a wallet and capable of holding nearly two hundred hours of whatever he wanted to put on it. I'd chosen this because I was certain he'd appreciate how small, clever, and powerful it was. He loved cameras, but I don't think he'd ever seen anything like this. I took the little machine out of its box, read the instructions, put the batteries in, pressed the Start and Record buttons, and began talking, not so much to it as to the windshield in front of me. What made it feel especially strange was how dressed up I was — I'd wanted him to be proud of me when he introduced me to his parents.

This is wrong, what you've done, Sylvester. Maybe you had no choice, maybe your parents needed to get back to Montreal very quickly. Or maybe you just didn't want me to turn this into a sentimental occasion. I wouldn't have, and you should have trusted me on that. I've never embarrassed you. And you should have introduced me to your parents. You've met Hannah and Bill, and it's only fair. I don't even know your parents' names.

Okay, okay, I know fair isn't in the picture here. You've been trying to explain that to me all along. I haven't ever argued with you about Montreal and all your special circumstances. I haven't questioned you, and so maybe that's why you think it's okay to do this. Leave without a word. If you were here right now, I wouldn't have to say this, and since you're not here, I can't say it to your face. But I need to say it anyway. What you've done is wrong. Not because you owe me anything, and not because I don't understand. I do. But it's a violation of the contract we lived out this past year and a half. We had each other to face the world with. Now I have to face it by myself. I knew this was coming, but we could have said the words that would have made me feel okay about it.

Whatever you said, I'd have those words.

I want to think you meant this as a kindness. The Sylvester Dusablon special form of kindness.

But whether you meant it or not, I can't stop thinking that the way you disappeared was a performance.

"Now she sees me."

"Now she doesn't."

From where I was parked, I found the path that led down to Lake Champlain. I had in mind to throw the little recorder as far as I could out into the water. When I reached the water's edge, I began walking to find the right place from which to fling it. I must have walked half a mile along the shore in my good shoes, turning the recorder over and over in my hand, before I realized I couldn't throw it away.

I wanted to keep talking to it.

•

A marriage is very difficult to kill. Terrible discoveries can be made. Awful events can transpire. Violence and treachery can enter the picture. Cruelty, I've come think, in lots of marriages is so ordinary the husband and the wife hardly notice it. Usually the marriage survives all that, absorbs it like some sturdy vehicle that can navigate straight over mountains and deserts without being harmed. Or a turtle that just hunkers down beside the road until the threat has passed. But then some little incident can come along. An act as insignificant as seeing your wife pick her nose or knowing that your husband just came from the men's room in the restaurant without washing his hands and sat down to eat with you.

Or maybe it's a sequence of events and non-events. Say, that moment when you notice your husband ogling a girl at the Champlain Valley Fair, there's the fragrance of cotton candy in the air, and the combination of what you see and what you smell just pulls the trigger for you. "We have to talk," you say. "I can't go on like this," you hiss at him as the two of you walk back to the car in the twilight. His face tells you he can't imagine what led you to this conclusion.

This is a story about a dog. Or it's a story about the lack of a dog. When I met Joseph, there'd been no dog in my life for several years. In my childhood, we'd had Midnight, the black cocker spaniel, and after Midnight "graduated," as Bill put it, then we had Midnight Junior, a black pound dog of uncertain lineage — Lab, Great Dane, and something else, a rowdy, badly behaved dog that finally got hit by a car. Midnight Junior was more Bill's dog than he was mine. At any rate, I'd always planned to have a dog in my adult life. I think my whole family planned for me to have a dog in my adult life.

When I told Joseph about my dog destiny — not very long after we met — he was amused, but it was an affectionate kind of amusement. Though he didn't exactly say so, I felt positive that he was okay with dogs. When we moved in together, I raised the dog issue with him again, and he gave me to understand that when the time was right, we'd get a dog. I doubted him only slightly.

Then I brought home a puppy. Saw the ad in the paper, went to the owners' house, picked it out of the litter, and brought it into the house — all in a single day. Carried it into Joseph's study where he was working. This was early afternoon, a time when I knew he was doing what he called his busy work — tending to his correspondence, paying bills. I'd have never brought in the dog to him when he was trying to write poems.

This was in the spring of our third year of marriage.

When he turned around from his desk and saw the puppy in my arms, he didn't say a word, but his face told me I'd made a mistake. I thought he'd change his mind pretty quickly. As far as I'm concerned, a puppy makes its own case. And this one was especially charming — handsome, sociable, smart, curious about human beings, already well behaved.

Joseph quickly brought his face back to a neutral expression. I sat down in the chair beside his desk. The puppy stayed in my lap, didn't squirm or try to get down to the floor. He seemed to understand that this was an audition.

The two of them stared at each other. I watched Joseph.

"What is it?" he finally asked.

It took me a moment to understand his question. "A chocolate lab," I said. "I haven't named it yet," I said.

"You should have told me," he said.

"We've talked about this before," I said. I reminded him that we'd talked about a dog in the first weeks we'd known each other.

He nodded and was quiet. Joseph was never one to argue. He sat staring at the puppy.

"What should we name him?" I asked him softly.

And that was when the dog barked at him. One sharp yap that I felt certain was friendly. Or he might have meant something like *Why don't you touch me, you big galoot?*

Joseph jumped a little from the bark. He turned his eyes to me. "It's yours," he said. "I can't help you name it." Then he turned back to his computer. Just like that, the puppy and I were dismissed.

"All right," I said. I got up and carried the dog outside and set him down on the grass of our tiny back yard. He immediately took a gigantic poop.

"Good boy," I said. I was angry. The puppy's response to Joseph was brilliant.

Our landlord had put a half-size picnic table out there for his tenants, and I sat down and watched the puppy explore our limited territory for a long while. That was the first time I tested the idea of a life for myself that didn't include Joseph. I confess that in my mood that afternoon, I took a good deal of pleasure from imagining the dog and me having a place to ourselves.

I named him Apollo.

•

If I keep talking, maybe I'll say the words that will undo the spell that turned you into this metal box I can hold in the palm of my hand. Hannah's not much help for me right now, but then I wouldn't have expected her to be. But Bill exceeds my expectations almost every day. Communicating with him is like talking with somebody from another planet who knows your language but wants you to learn his. "Where does the dubious doctor reside this morning?" he will ask me. By which he means, have I heard from you and how am I feeling about your absence? And of course I really don't have anything I can say to him. I give him a shrug. "Busyology," he'll say. "Got a day full of what you need."

So we'll ride around in his new truck for most of the morning and visit with his workmen, or with his favorite guy in the world. He finds reasons to stop and visit with

John Engels at Aubuchon hardware — and will end up buying some little item I know he doesn't need. No matter, those two guys will fire up a conversation about how you keep bats from coming down an old chimney, what to do about dried-up putty falling out of window frames, what size fuses to use for fluorescent lights. Meanwhile, I'll walk the aisles of the store examining door handles, sump pumps, buckets of house paint, bags of bird food. Odd as this may sound to you, the merchandise on the shelves at Aubuchon hardware comforts me more than anything else nowadays. That stuff reminds me that the world is still here and it's just going to wait for me. I can take a break and come back to my life when I feel better. And maybe it's the combination of hearing Bill's chit-chat with John Engels that releases the medicinal effect of the merchandise. It's as if those two guys have been saving up their small-talk gems for these occasions when I'm with Bill and taking my walkabouts in the store. Aubuchon has a smell, too, some combination of paint, plastic, picnic tables, lawn-mowers, and potting soil — a fragrance that if you were still here, I'd probably find repulsive but that with you in outer space or wherever you are, is the exact aroma I want to be breathing into my lungs.

Okay, I confess that I see you all the time. Suddenly I want to shout at Bill to stop the truck, you're back there getting out of a parked car we just passed, or you're going into Pure Pop on South Winooski Avenue. This afternoon, on Battery Street by the cathedral, I was so certain that was you in your black windbreaker that I rolled down the window and stuck my whole head out the window to look back. But then you turned, and you were somebody else, and I pulled my head in, my face hot from my foolishness.

Bill didn't even ask me what my problem was. Just gave me his little quarter-smile. I think the man has ESP when it comes to my Sylvester syndrome.

•

Dogs come to you with a built-in heartbreak — they're going to die before you do. I'd had two of them, and now I had Apollo, a puppy so alive as to seem immortal. Who also, in ordinary moments of average days, just ripped the love out of my heart and instantly absorbed it into himself.

This was not an unpleasant sensation.

If you don't have a feeling for dogs — and I know many people don't — then a person like me seems a fool or a crackpot. But may I say that the integrity of almost any animal stands as criticism of us humans. Dogs understand us and commit to us so completely that they can't help showing us our slutty ways. Apollo was the most restrained critic I've known, but that made his presence all the more poignant. Almost any chocolate lab is unfairly winsome, and Apollo was way above average.

At a time when Joseph was gradually taking back the life I thought he had given me, Apollo gave me a new one. The long walks he needed took me all over Brunswick. At the edge of the old North End, there was a corner where Russell Street curved around into Charles Street and the residents of three houses in sequence had collaborated in gardening and crafting lawn décor to make a kind of outsider-art outdoor museum. All three places had these miniature homemade fountains — one had goldfish in it. There were arrangements of rocks and plants and driftwood. There was an arch, and there was a lovely set of wind chimes up in a tree that you had to really look for the first time you heard them. Apollo took me through this little grotto every morning if I didn't suggest that we choose an alternate route. He liked it mostly for the squirrel life that went on in the trees over our heads. Plus there were a couple of kitties that lived in the territory and that witnessed our passing without hostility. Apollo treated most kitties with fearful reverence.

A collateral benefit of our walks was that Apollo gave me an ongoing course in what I'd call the Secretly Civilizing Activities of Ordinary People. That corner of Charles and Russell Streets was inhabited by citizens committed to mildly artsy middle-class life. Their houses were modest, small by the standards of my upbringing, and in a state of ongoing repair and/or modification. Only occasionally did I encounter the residents — people who, as far as I could tell, were still working full-time jobs but whose children were grown and out of the house. My guess was that they were familiar with the academics who, like Joseph, taught at Bowdoin — they might even have been employees of the college — and they probably went to college themselves, at less pricey schools, but I supposed that they were not really sympathetic with the politics and culture of higher education. Apollo gave me no guidance about them personally, though he taught me to pay attention to their dwelling places.

Joseph did his best to ignore Apollo. He asked me not to let the dog up on the sofa, which seemed reasonable to me, and he didn't want the dog in the dining room when we ate in there. I balked at the dining room request, though I did train Apollo to lie down at the side my chair where he'd be out of Joseph's sight. I hoped Joseph would gradually soften his resistance to Apollo, but he didn't. To his credit, he wasn't mean to the dog, never shouted at him or expressed anger toward him. It was as if he'd taken an intellectual position against the dog, had deliberately chosen to oppose him. And that made his resistance all the more wrong in my eyes.

As for Apollo, it took the puppy a while to adjust to the man who wouldn't touch him or speak to him, who resisted all the charming little butt-shaking routines he had that were so effective with every other human he encountered. But when he was about ten months old, he seemed to understand. From that time on, he ignored Joseph every bit as successfully as Joseph ignored him.

"It's not so much dogs themselves that I don't like," Joseph explained to me a few days after I brought Apollo home. "It's the human need to have a pet. That's a form of illness. It's like needing the world to be a Walt Disney movie."

"What about when you were a kid?" I asked him.

He shook his head. "If I'd had a father," he said, "I'd be a different person."

I recognized those words as his explanation to himself for how he was. That was the sentence that gave him license to do or not do anything he wanted to.

•

I've started saving these files into my computer — "The Sylvester Monologues" is the name of the folder. I haven't gone back to listen to any of it — I'm not sure I could stand to do that. Plus I haven't said anything all that interesting anyway. But if you ever do come back to Vermont, I'm going to make you listen to every word I've put on this machine.

Punishment for leaving me this way. I'm the sailor's wife of Burlington. I go down to the waterfront every day now and sit on a bench — the same one each time unless somebody's already taken it — and I talk to you. By now I may have spoken as many words into this machine as I did to the real you when you were around. As you know, even when we were together, a lot of silence passed between us. Which I always thought was one of the great things about us — that we were okay with not talking.

It's impossible for me not to scheme about ways to see you. I guess that's a form of daydreaming, except that so much of the dreaming part of it would be easy enough for me to actually do. For instance, driving the truck up to Montreal, parking, and spending the day in your city trying to catch sight of you. Nothing to stop me from doing that. A few minutes of basic detective work. Okay, so I've already Googled "Dusablon Montreal." Dumb thing to do, and when the results came up, none of them seemed to apply to you and your family. Even so, it gave me a thrill to think that some little piece of information in all those entries that came up might be a key to — What? Finding you would just be a way to put more distance between us, wouldn't it? Because, let's say I found an address for you, found your apartment, walked up and knocked on the door, and you came to answer and saw me standing there looking at you with my pitiful abandoned-girl face, what would you do? I know it exactly — you'd close the door without saying a word. You wouldn't even slam it, and you wouldn't tell me not to come back. You'd just close the door. If it had a lock that would make a noise, then you'd turn the lock just so I could hear the click. So I do understand how absolutely impossible it is for me to reconnect with you. Nothing I can do will make any difference. We see each other again only if you decide to make it happen.

The power is all yours.

Please note that I don't say, "God damn you, Sylvester!" I think I should say it, and in my mind, I try those words out fairly often. So far I can't say them with any conviction.

But I'll tell you what I can do — and you'll laugh at me. "Freaking ridiculous," I can hear you say. But I want you to know anyway. I can make a little movie in my head. Or a scene in a book, however you want to think of it. Here's how it goes:

I drive across the border. I've studied the map of Montreal so I know how to get to the Museum of Fine Arts. I need maybe ten minutes to find a parking lot where I can leave the truck all day for ten dollars. I find a place to buy a coffee and a croissant, I take them to go, and I find a bench to sit more or less where I can watch people coming and going to the museum. You're vulnerable in just this way, God damn Sylvester — you need to see those paintings every once in a while. You might not need to see me, but you've got to have your art fix. I'd bet a lot of money that you go in that museum at least once every couple of weeks. So on this day, let's say I get lucky. I know, I know, the odds of this happening are about a thousand to one, but so what, maybe I drive up there more and more often, and I cut those odds down every trip I make. They get to know me at the border. There's a woman customs officer on the French side, a very happy person, evidently, who smiles at me in this dark way and asks me if I'm going to see my boyfriend — like maybe it's a crime if I am — and every time she does that, I grin back at her and say, *Yep, that's what it's all about, isn't it?* and she winks at me, and she and I understand each other very well. She knows I probably don't have a boyfriend, and of course she's right, and I know that if she's got one, he's mostly giving her a lot of trouble, and we're a couple of girls commiserating with each other over man trouble. Which must be just how we like it, huh? because I'm driving up to a strange city so often, it's like it's become my life, and I'm sitting on a bench for hours and eating cheap food, and all I'm asking for is just a glimpse of a boy who made himself dear to me months ago, and that glimpse of you is exactly what I don't get. Fool of a girl! I know.

But one day, I'm sitting on my bench, thinking I'm keeping my lookout but in fact I'm spacing out and not really being the sharp-eyed girl detective, not really examining every skinny young man who passes before me because I'm so used to never seeing you, but then this one afternoon, just after two or so, a cloudy day with a spring rain about to start, and I'm considering going back to the truck and driving back over the border, when all of a sudden you're standing in front of me. Out of nowhere!

In your black windbreaker.

Your hair's cut shorter than I've ever seen it, which surprises me, but I'm like somebody getting half-electrocuted, I've got jolts of shock shooting through my body, so I can't say anything, can't even really move for a minute, because I'm reading your face, I'm reading your face, God damn Sylvester, and it's telling me you're so glad to see me you can hardly stand it, you've got some jolts of shock shooting through you, too.

Then I'm standing up, and we're pulling each other against each other, body to body, all up and down our whole torsos, and we can't even really talk, all we can do is make these animal noises like gorillas or dogs or cattle, grunts and coughs. It's too bad we never really practiced kissing very much, because kissing's what's called for here, don't you think? Or maybe this is the exact time that we get started learning how to kiss really well. Like the angels do, if they kiss. Good time for it, God damn Sylvester, good time to learn how to be with each other the way we're supposed to be.

So you see the power I have. It's not like yours, which is real. You can show up on my doorstep and be pretty certain I'll be happy to see you and will go back to being your girl who's so crazy about you, she'll do whatever you ask. Tell me to take my clothes off so you can take pictures of me? I can't strip them off fast enough. So you're right, that's probably how it'll be when and if you show up.

But maybe not. I could even surprise myself and take a look at you, a good long look, long enough to see that you just came back into my life to find out if you could have another dance before you cut me off again.

So maybe this time it's me who shuts that door in your face.

It could go that way, God Damn. It could definitely go that way. Your absence is teaching me a lot of things, and anger is one of them.

But my power is to have that afternoon outside the museum go whatever way I want it to. My power is that I keep sitting on the bench. I don't even stand up when you're all of a sudden standing in front of me. My power is that I look you in the eyes and say, *Get down on your knees, young fellow. Get down right here on the concrete of your city and put your hands together and beg me to say hello to you.* And if you do that—get down on the sidewalk politely and say the words just right, maybe I'll go have a coffee with you before I have to drive back down to Les États-Unis. Beg me, God damn Sylvester, and I'll think about taking you back.

Okay, so it's not real. Nevertheless.

It's power I know you understand, my old friend.

•

When his friend Sonny Carson died, my grandfather called one evening to ask if I'd come back to Burlington to attend Sonny's funeral with him the next morning at eleven — Clara had a virus, and he didn't think she should go. Bill and Hannah were on a tour boat in Alaska.

I was moved by Horace's request — it meant I was right about what I'd always thought, that there was something really deep between my grandfather and me. I knew he was hurting much worse than he could let on — he loved Sonny better than most men love their brothers — and he didn't trust himself not to break down at the funeral.

Truth is, I loved that he called me. He'd never asked me to do anything like that before. Horace wasn't a man who asked favors of anyone if he could help it.

Brunswick to Burlington is five hours. The evening of the funeral I had planned to go with Joseph to a dinner party given by his chairman. We agreed I'd come straight back from the funeral. The one hitch was that Joseph would need to look after Apollo. Which required almost nothing of him. Let the dog out into the back yard maybe a couple of times during the day was all that was really necessary. "If you walk him around the block, he'll be your friend forever," I said, and Joseph smiled at me and said maybe he'd do that. His face and his voice told me he was fine about my leaving the dog in his charge.

I confess that I'd gotten so used to the way Joseph and Apollo lived in the house with me — absolutely separately — that I didn't imagine there'd be a problem. How much trouble can it be to open a door and let a dog out, then let him back in when he comes to the door and thumps it with his paw? Apollo did that if I wasn't waiting right there to let him back in immediately, but he was an exceptionally reasonable dog.

I left Brunswick at six the next morning. Since Joseph was working in his study, I didn't bother him. Apollo walked right by my side to the back door, hoping for another walk even though I'd just taken him around the block. I kissed the place between his eyes, which I know sounds gross to anybody who doesn't know what a sweet spot that is on the face of a chocolate lab. Apollo understands that kiss means that I'm serious about not taking him with me. "Goodbye, sweetheart," I whispered to him, then I was out the door and on the road.

Horace seemed sad but composed at the funeral, but after he'd finished reading his eulogy for Sonny and come back to his place in the pew with me, he took my hand and held onto it until the service was over. Then at the graveside, he took out his handkerchief and dabbed at his eyes. Because I knew he didn't really want me to see him like that, I avoided looking at his face. I moved close enough to him for my shoulder to press lightly against his. As we were leaving, he actually put his arm around me and leaned on me more than I expected he would. That was when some tears welled up into my eyes, but they were more because I suddenly had to think of my grandfather as probably not so far away from death himself. He was, after all, a few years older than Sonny Carson. But when I took him home — and I never entered that house without blushing with remembering the night I spent there with Sylvester — he wouldn't let me stay. He said my grandmother was resting, and he wanted me back home as soon as I could legally get there. He persuaded me that he and Clara were fine now. "We have each other, you know," he said.

Something about his face when he said that made me want to be back in my own house with Joseph. Maybe things weren't perfect between the two of us, but what occurred to me as I was driving back to Brunswick was that Joseph and I were gradually learning what it meant to "have each other." That's when I came up with the Eve Collins theory of couples: You can't realize it when you start out, but you have to *learn* to be one of a couple. It's like some very intricate and sensitive machine that is invisible and for which there isn't any instruction manual. No wonder people have trouble. I wasn't sure I could tell Joseph what I'd figured out — I didn't think he'd take me seriously. But I felt comforted by the feeling that at least I'd come to some kind of revelation that could help us survive whatever difficulties came our way. If I did my part of the learning, then maybe he'd do his part without even knowing what he was doing.

·

If there were even a breath of wind, today would be too cold for me to sit here. It feels like the thin layer of my skin is all that's keeping me from freezing to death. My face and ears tingle, but they don't really hurt. It's still December so the lake hasn't frozen over, but between the shore and the break-water, the ice is flat as glass and reflecting the chilly blue of the sky. The world is trying to tell me something, trying to show me that if I'm able to let go of you, it'll still be here. But it's speaking in this very reserved way — no flowers, no sweet breeze, nothing in the way of birdsong except for the forlorn squawking of the gulls. No spin, no pretty stuff, no timid little slice of hope anywhere I can see or hear. Maybe the world is saying that with or without you, it'll be a difficult place, and since you're not helping me live my life anyway, I might as well let you go.

I want to let you go. Can you tell?

Maybe I already have.

This morning I was sitting in the kitchen, my cereal bowl in front of me, the milk already poured, spoon in my hand, but evidently I'd forgotten I was supposed to be eating. Bill walked in and didn't say anything. That's not unusual — we're both short on words first thing in the morning — but this time we held our silence for the whole time we were to-gether. He made his coffee, then sat down with it and looked me in the eye. Then he sort of nodded at the bowl in front of me. When I looked down, I realized what he meant, so I waved the spoon at him and started in. I was glad he was there, but I really didn't want to have to say anything. And I didn't. We cleared the table together, he washed the dishes, I dried, and we went our separate ways.

"Peculiaritis" is what Bill would probably say is wrong with me. I've got a missing boyfriend that I talk to on a stupid little machine at least once a day, and I've got a present and completely understanding father that I go for long stretches without saying a word to.

·

The instant I saw our house a bad feeling came over me. I didn't feel any better when I stepped out of the car in the driveway. The house was quiet, everything looked normal, there was nothing to suggest that anything was wrong. I decided it was driving ten hours that had warped my thought process and made me feel like I'd go in and find my husband and my dog missing or murdered and lying bloody on the floor. But it was still daylight. I'd been away from home not even a complete day.

When I stepped inside, Apollo was crazy glad to see me, jumping and running into the kitchen and back and even jumping up on me. If it were possible for a dog to tell you that he'd thought you'd abandoned him, that's what Apollo was communicating. While I crooned to him and got him to sit still enough for me to hug him, I heard the shower running upstairs and understood that Joseph was getting ready for the party. It was six, and we were to be there at six-thirty. I'd need to change clothes, but I'd probably be ready to go before Joseph finished dressing.

He came downstairs still drying himself off. This was not unusual — he did it occasionally. Joseph was proud of his body, and to tell the truth, I liked seeing him that way. I liked it that he didn't mind my seeing him without his clothes. He was relaxed and in a good mood. "You made it back," he said, and he sounded glad to see me.

"Feels like I've been gone forever," I said, standing up

and moving to the bottom of the staircase to give him a kiss.

With his eyes on Joseph, Apollo moved away from us and walked quietly into kitchen. Looking back with his eyes on Joseph the whole way. It wasn't me he was looking at, it was Joseph.

"What's up with him?" Joseph asked me. Something in his voice sounded ever so slightly forced.

"I don't know," I said. I started to study Joseph's face, but then he raised the towel to dry his hair some more. He turned toward the steps down to the basement. "Gotta get some clean underwear out of the laundry basket," he said. "Be up in a second."

．

Enough time goes by without your seeing somebody, and no matter how much you care for that person or how clearly you remember every little thing about him, he just starts evaporating. And of course your imagination runs to the rescue, starts making up this little piece of his face that's gone missing, that little gesture with a hand, a mole on a wrist. The Sylvester I see in my mind right now has probably had all his parts replaced. He can't possibly be the person he was when he left, and he certainly can't be the person he's become while he's been away.

What I thought was my power — that I could make you do whatever I wanted you to — has turned out to be my illness. It won't stop bringing you back.

．

When Joseph went down to the basement, I stepped into the kitchen and found Apollo sitting at the door. Quiet and very evidently wanting to go out into the back yard. I opened the door, let him out, and stood watching him. He walked over to the old picnic table out there and lay down beside it. He kept his head up, nose pointed in my direction.

I turned around when Joseph came into the kitchen. In his underwear now.

"How was it?" he asked.

Ordinarily I'd have asked him if he meant the drive or the funeral, but I wasn't about to make small talk with him. I studied his face. "Did you let Apollo out?" I asked him very quietly.

"Of course I did," he said. "Twice. And I let him back in both times." He met my look with a pleasant smile.

I gave him a grim little smile of my own and kept my eyes on him. Rage was coming up in me, and I knew if I kept looking at him, I might start screaming at him. I thought about it — I imagined flame blazing out of my mouth and blistering my husband into a cinder right were he stood. Before this moment Joseph and I had had our disagreements and misunderstandings, but we hadn't even raised our voices at each other. I actually calculated it out: Was I willing to risk my marriage by accusing him of having done something horrible to my dog? Accuse him of lying to me?

I think I was. I opened my mouth to let it out. The blaze of accusations and curses.

"Joseph," I said, my voice as eerily quiet as a stranger's. "I think I despise you."

And there it was. No scream, no curse, no accusation.

Just a truth ripped up from some deep part of me that I hadn't realized was in there.

He blinked as if I'd splashed water in his face.

"Well," he said.

That kitchen had never been so silent.

He shook his head. "I've got to get dressed," he said. "Do you still want to go to this party?"

I didn't. "Yes," I said.

When Joseph left the kitchen, I called Apollo in, fed him, and told him what a fine dog he was and promised not to leave him like that again. Then I went up to our bedroom, where without exchanging another word, Joseph and I dodged and do-si-doed around each other, getting dressed to go to the Gildersleeves' dinner party. That dance ought to have made me laugh, but it just kept feeding my anger.

I took about five minutes to get out of my funeral clothes and into my dinner party dress. In the bathroom, while I was brushing my hair, I got this idea for a movie I wanted someone to make. When I began to see the scenes, I knew I wasn't the only one who needed such a movie to be made. It begins with a couple in love and gradually builds to a final scene in which the man and the woman, who are of equal size, strength, and skill, fight so viciously that one of them knocks the other unconscious. Fists and feet, elbows, knees, and teeth. I know I can live with the man killing the woman if that's how the fight comes out, though of course I'd rather it be the woman who wins. I just want this movie to tell a truth that's never been told before. I want it to feel like a documentary. I want the couple to be attractive and intelligent people. Educated. Innocent at first. I want the two of them to charm everybody in the whole theater, and I want their love scenes to be so sweet and exciting they take your breath away. I want the decline of their relationship to be slow and deeply compelling and so poignant that you keep thinking they've still got a chance to rescue the marriage and to keep caring for each other. I want you to hope for them so much you squirm in your seat and whisper, *Go back, please stop this and go back!* Then I want their lines to become more and more shocking as they start throwing harsh truths at each other. I want somebody in the audience to stand up and say, "Would you please just slug him in the teeth?!" That's when she slaps him. And he pushes her away. Which is when she really does slug him in the teeth. And he punches her in the gut. I want blood to fly and teeth to get knocked out, broken fingers on one, a broken nose on the other, him to yank her around by her hair and her to kick him in the crotch so hard he goes down like a sack of dirt.

"You ready?" Joseph calls up the stairs.

"Just a sec," I said, setting the hairbrush down beside the sink. Smiling into the mirror. Horrified. Pleased.

◆

The morning came when I woke up knowing what I needed to do. It was the Saturday before I'd graduate, and first daylight was just sneaking into my room. I couldn't remember what I'd dreamed, but it must have been good, because I got out of bed feeling like somebody had given me back my childhood.

Mount Holyoke had accepted my application for early admission, and I had a summer job working for Parks and Recreation in Burlington. Last night when I'd gone to be bed, I'd felt sad because of how programmed how my life was going to be for the next four years. But this morning my future looked so sweet I could hardly wait to get a taste of it.

In the kitchen, I had pink grapefruit juice and Cheerios over which I sprinkled raisins. One percent milk, and presto I had myself a miraculous breakfast. I took my Earl Gray tea back to my room with me, because as good as I felt, I didn't want to have to talk to either one of my parents.

I closed the door. Opened my laptop. Went into "My Computer," found and clicked on the "Sylvester Monologues" folder, deleted it and all its files. Then emptied the Recycle Bin. Invisible and complete destruction of almost all the words I'd spoken to Sylvester after his disappearance. Accomplished by my fingertips in less than three minutes. I plucked the digital recorder out of my desk drawer, and headed out of the house.

The morning was cool and fresh. I had it to myself.

Rode my bike down the hill and out North Avenue to Rock Point. Didn't have the slightest doubt. Rode the bike straight down to the lake shore, got off, and stood with the little black item in my hand for no more than about ten seconds before I tossed it out and watched the splash it made.

Pretty good throw, if I did say so myself.

•

From that evening on, Joseph and I played out our endgame with tact and precision. At the Gildersleeves' party, I was probably the only one who noticed his restraint and his sadness. I couldn't help thinking that this was a man who could be severely wounded by his wife telling him she despised him and still be kind and considerate at a social gathering. But I never doubted that he'd committed some sort of meanness to my dog. And that I couldn't love him again.

·

In William Faulkner's *The Bear*, the boy learns that he must leave his watch and compass behind before he will be allowed the sight of the bear. When he leaves those little devices hanging on a bush, he must walk only a little deeper into the wilderness before the bear reveals himself. And as Faulkner describes the revelation, it is the grandest experience of the boy's life.

We'd read that book in Mr. Bohn's English class back in the fall — hunting season, Mr. B. told us, was the only time anyone should be allowed to read *The Bear*. I'd liked the story, or at least I'd liked the parts about the boy and the bear, but I hadn't thought about it until I was riding my bike back out through the gate of Rock Point and up beside the familiar buildings of Burlington High School. Then those scenes came back to me just so vividly — the boy leaving his treasured objects on the bush, the bear showing itself to him.

So I believed I was going to see Sylvester again.

I'm embarrassed to tell you how long I thought I would see him.

How many times I thought I did see him. But didn't.

And never did again.

·

Two Deaths: A Story About Life.

◆

Other side of the river, babe. Bill's voice comes to me. *Calling you collect, will you please accept the charge?* I laugh and tell him of course I will. In these early morning hours, when I'm tossing and turning, Bill likes telling me about *the trillion trillion ghosts,* and how Hannah can't fit in with them. *She won't talk to anybody, and she keeps on looking for a place to be alone,* he tells me, because he knows I understand. Even in their spirit lives those two still have their affection. In my dark room, Bill's voice calms me and talks me back down into sleep. *Go ahead and let those old bed bugs bite you, Sweet Splendor,* he whispers just loud enough for me to hear. *Wake the mind, speed the blood, get you ready to meet the day.*

Acknowledgments

Chapters of this novel appeared in the following journals:

Conjunctions, Blackbird, The Georgia Review, A River & Sound Review, Fawlt Magazine, Michigan Quarterly Review, The American Scholar, Solstice, and *Green Mountains Review.*

Other books from Tupelo Press

See our complete backlist at www.tupelopress.org

CPSIA information can be obtained at www.ICGtesting.com
Printed in the USA
LVOW061628261211

261111LV00002B/6/P